ALSO BY KATHARINE WEBER

Objects in Mirror Are Closer Than They Appear

The Music Lesson

The Little Women

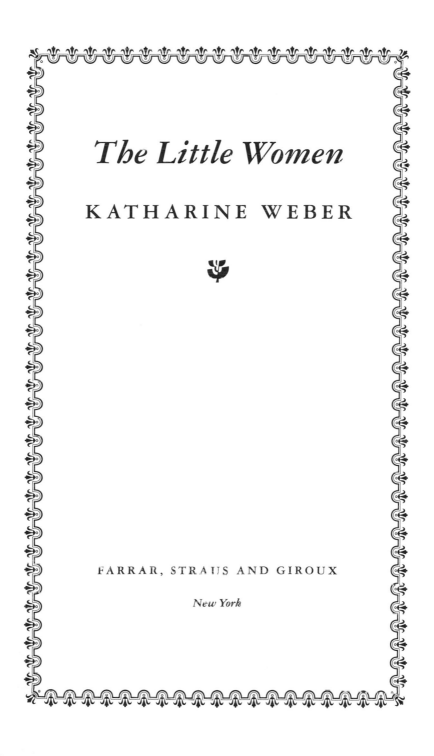

The Little Women

KATHARINE WEBER

FARRAR, STRAUS AND GIROUX

New York

Farrar, Straus and Giroux
19 Union Square West, New York 10003

Distributed in Canada by Douglas & McIntyre Ltd.
Printed in the United States of America
First edition, 2003

The epigraph is from Alice Munro's story "Open Secrets," published in the collection
Open Secrets (New York: Alfred A. Knopf, 1994).

Library of Congress Cataloging-in-Publication Data
Weber, Katharine, 1955–
    The little women / Katharine Weber.— 1st ed.
        p. cm.
    ISBN 0-374-18959-5 (hc : alk. paper)
    1. Autobiographical fiction—Authorship—Fiction. 2. Women
college students—Fiction. 3. New Haven (Conn.)—Fiction. 4. Parent
and child—Fiction. 5. Teenage girls—Fiction. 6. Adultery—Fiction.
7. Sisters—Fiction. I. Title.

PS3573.E2194L58 2003
813'.54—dc21

                                                    2003044062

Designed by Jonathan D. Lippincott

www.fsgbooks.com

1   3   5   7   9   10   8   6   4   2

For my little women, Lucy and Charlotte

I dare you to run away. Was it possible? There are times when girls are inspired, when they want the risks to go on and on. They want to be heroines, regardless. They want to take a joke beyond where anybody has ever taken it before. To be careless, dauntless, to create havoc—that was the lost hope of girls.

—from "Open Secrets" by Alice Munro

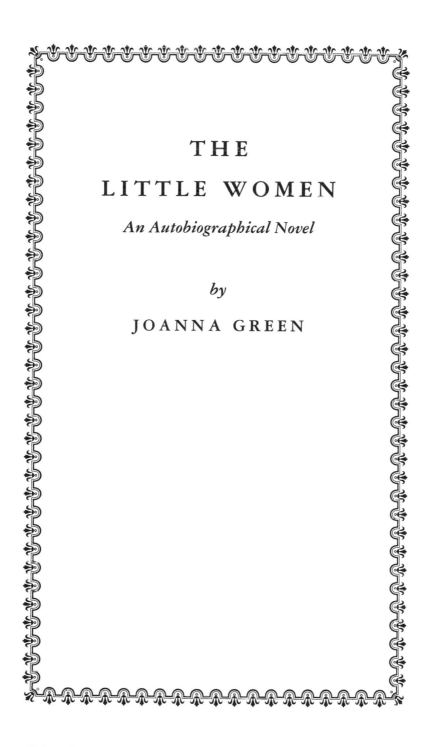

THE
LITTLE WOMEN

An Autobiographical Novel

by

JOANNA GREEN

Contents

Is It Autobiographical?

A Self-Interview by Joanna Green

This is the story of the year we left our mother and father in order to live on our own, away from their bad behavior and their infuriating pretense that they were the most splendid parents in all the world.

It was four years ago. Meg was twenty then, I was about to turn seventeen, and Amy was just fifteen. The three sisters. All my life, whenever we've walked down the street together, people have smiled at us. *Look, sisters.* When I walk down the street by myself, I never get those smiles. I have a theory, actually, that people have never noticed me on my own as they do Meg and Amy, though we are all technically pretty, because I'm only interesting to look at in the context of my sisters.

I'm neither the beginning nor the end of the series but the one in the middle, the bridge, the link from adorable little Amy—who is not exactly beautiful, with her pale blue eyes and too-small nose and too-wide mouth (she says), but instead, possesses a wonderful kind of grace and unconscious harmony—to Meg, the reliable competent one, the sweet-tempered romantic with her curly hair and carefully organized features and strikingly long and pale hands—looks that often remind people of John Singer Sargent portraits.

That leaves me as the let's-see-now-which-one-are-you sister, but unlike Amy or Meg, I am indifferent to clothing, I whistle on the street, sometimes I stare at people, my hair is cropped short and I never wear makeup, I'm not especially quiet and nice, and I have never minded being defined by what I do rather than how I look.

Which one am I? Through childhood, I was always the author, stage manager, director, and ticket seller for Amy and Meg's living room musical entertainments, though I happen to have something close to perfect pitch, like our mother, who sings like a lark, while neither of them can carry a tune in a bucket, which is their unfortunate musical heritage from our father.

I appear in very few family photos—which are arranged (by me) chronologically, on a shelf of photo albums in our mother's study, as no one else in the family is that organized—because I'm the snapshot taker at birthday dinners. It seems that I am the family narrator. My name is Joanna.

Okay, so now I might as well get the usual raised-eyebrow-reaction-to-our-names thing out of the way. Margaret, Joanna, and Amy. So, yes, we were more or less named for the Louisa May Alcott characters by our inventor father and English professor mother (whom we have never, ever addressed as Marmee, not even at the best of times, when her love and approval and goodness bathed our family in its golden light), and no, there are just the three of us, and yes, that's right, very good, Beth is the one who dies anyway, so you can see why they skipped her and went straight to Amy.

(For the record, we had a painted turtle named Beth for a couple of years, when we were in grade school, though we never knew for sure if it was a girl or a boy, and it turned out that Beth, true to his or her name, was doomed to a tragic and early death, though in his or her case it was a solitary shuffle off this mortal coil under the bathroom radiator.)

Some people can't resist calling me Jo, but unless they've known me all my life (Meg called me Jo-Jo when I was a newborn and so that was my nickname throughout my childhood) it bugs the hell out of me, because usually it's someone who is utterly convinced that to call me Jo is an incredibly clever, insightful, original, and highly literary act, second only to wondering why our last name isn't March instead of Green.

We left our mother and father because we were angry. We left our mother and father because they wouldn't leave each other. We left because our mother was sorry but refused to be guilty, and our father refused to be angry and chose instead to be sad. Neither was a sufficient response. The situation demanded more. We three sisters were part of the hateful situation, and we demanded more, much, much more.

We left our mother and father in the last week of August, four years ago, after a bitter summer of debate and negotiation that was all too cerebral and theoretical and without substance. Our parents had hedged us round with principles. They had made us who we were but they couldn't live up to the standards we were raised to admire—standards we demanded for others as we demanded them for ourselves. They only had weak words of insufficient explanation. We wanted good strong words that meant something. And then we wanted more than words. The Green sisters wanted action. The Green sisters wanted blood. Somebody's, anybody's. Everybody's.

What happened?

Our mother had an affair and we found out.

Her husband of twenty-three years could forgive her, but we, her three daughters who had known her all our lives, could not. We could not forgive her this trespass against us, against our family, this act that made everything into a lie. We just couldn't. I think Meg tried, but I know I didn't want to try. Why should I? And sweet little Amy, the baby sister, the tagalong kid, Amy who still liked to snuggle and sing softly with our mother sometimes before bed—her bitterness and rage were like an eclipse of the sun.

We couldn't forgive our mother for what she had done, and then we couldn't forgive our father for forgiving her, and so we left our mother and father and went to live on our own, the three of us, in order to form a more perfect union, to live by the values we had been raised to honor.

We wanted them to be strong so we didn't have to be strong, but they couldn't do it, not on our terms. Our mother and father refused to proceed down the path we believed they had laid out for themselves. These were horrifying circumstances which called for horrifying solutions. We wanted divorce proceedings with all the trimmings: cruel threats, vicious scenes, custody battles, rapacious lawyers, selfish declarations, divisions of property, petty accusations, Pyrrhic victories.

We could not imagine life going on otherwise from that moment in time, that motionless pause of the pendulum's swing between before and after, between not-knowing and knowing, between faith—oh, so much faith—and loss of faith.

They thought everything could be exactly the same and we thought nothing could ever be the same. We three sisters cherished our anger until it grew strong and took possession of us. What did they imagine? That the superior culture of our family, the counterentropy of the magnificent Green family, some essential wonderful Green family-ness, was sufficient to keep everything together? They didn't get it. Right up to the humid August afternoon Amy and I closed the door on the big, messy West Seventy-fifth Street apartment in which we had lived our whole previously happy lives, they didn't get it.

A moment: Amy and I are standing in the hallway with our bags, waiting for the elevator so we could walk from our corner of Amsterdam Avenue down the three familiar blocks to the Seventy-second Street Broadway IRT station, from which we would go downtown to Times Square, to the shuttle to Grand Central Station, to the 4:02 Metro North train to New Haven, and, finally, to an overpriced taxi ride to Meg's apartment—our apartment—on High Street. While Amy and I packed our things, they had just sat there on the big floppy green couch in the living room, not getting it, reading left-over sections of the Sunday *New York Times* in companionable silence, drinking their muddy Ethiopian coffee from their favorite Italian coffee mugs procured on a romantic trip to Italy before Meg was born, offering the Week in Review in exchange for Travel, so very civilized, husband and wife at home on the Monday after a languid weekend at the beginning of a new term.

So confidently evolved and original and in touch as parents that instead of Mom and Dad they had chosen to be called Janet and Lou by their daughters, they failed to notice that we were really moving out and not just being dramatic teenagers. They failed to say or do anything to stop us. They failed to take us seriously. Or perhaps that's wrong, perhaps they did take us seriously, but in doing so they failed to take us literally.

As I closed the door I made myself look at them sitting there with their newspapers and their certainties, and I made a promise to myself that I would always remember that moment. As I so clearly have. There they are: Lou and Janet on the couch, affecting no concern about the door closing on their two daughters who have announced their plan to leave, to go live with their older sister at college in New Haven.

Is there just a hint of desperation behind the smugness I think I see on their faces? Lou in his weekend yellow Lacoste shirt he's had since college, Janet with her kind "can-I-help-you" look that makes her so popular with her students—are they really so united in their certainty that we would be back in a few days, so complacent about their theory of indulging us correctly through this adolescent acting-out festival? At that moment I doubted that I would ever love them again in the way I always had.

They didn't get it that the poisons of her actions and his failure to take action had transformed the glorious landscape of our perfect little Green family existence totally and utterly into an unrecognizable lunar wasteland, a moonscape with no air to breathe and very little gravity to hold us in place. We didn't understand what held them in place, and we didn't want them in place, and we couldn't remain in that Potemkin village of a family for another moment, yet all that either of them did that day was lift a diffident hand to wave goodbye to Amy and me as if we were merely going out for a walk around the block. And so we left.

J.G.
September 2003

A NOTE TO THE READER

Owing to the nature of the actual events that inspired this novel, the author was obligated not only to alter first or last names and characteristics of some, though not all, of the principal characters, but also to invite members of her family to voice their concerns about the manuscript. By the terms of a binding agreement that was required to satisfy the wishes of two family members who have in return consented to the unchallenged publication of *The Little Women: An Autobiographical Novel*, their comments appear within the text at certain stipulated points as "reader's notes." Consequently, several "author's notes" in these pages respond to those remarks. In some cases a further response has been made, and, in some instances, answered. These notes and comments, therefore, form a dialogue of sorts in several unfortunately intrusive places in the narrative. The casual reader of this novel has no obligation to take notice of any of this marginalia and has the author's every encouragement to ignore it.

J.G.

ONE

The Dark Day

❦

Joanna and Amy left home in the fall of their older sister Meg's junior year at Yale. Meg had already gone ahead to New Haven three days earlier in her car—the family's old green Subaru wagon, which had been her Warren Prep graduation present (along with a trip to France). There would have been no room for Joanna and Amy had they wanted to drive up with her. The car was crammed to capacity with boxes and duffel bags and computers, Amy's music stand (she played the flute), and also her art supplies, including the drafting table, the base of which took up an annoying amount of cargo space. Their three bicycles had been awkwardly tied onto the roof rack with the assistance of Mike the doorman, whose helpful intentions were as genuine as his knot-making skills were poor.

Meg had gone ahead, she said, because she needed those days to get started organizing the apartment, and also because of some confusion with her class schedule that required a meeting with her dean. Meg had driven away in the loaded old Subaru with a certain belief that she could not have survived being with her family for even one more hour. She never liked analyzing and speculating about emotions, her own or anyone else's. A very reluctant passer of judgments, Meg did on occasion discover that she was deeply disappointed by some person or turn of events. At such times she grieved horribly and felt burdened by the gravity of her conclusions.

Although she had a reputation, both within the family and among her friends, as a good listener, Meg really had no idea of what compelled people to confide in her as they did. Too much information about other people's feelings bothered her tremendously. What often struck people as wonderfully receptive and sympathetic listening on Meg's part was, in actuality, inadequately conveyed distress, which she endured only until sufficient evasive chat could diffuse an overly intimate atmosphere.

Joanna and Amy, on the other hand, at almost seventeen and just fifteen, always loved a good dissection. They relished their rages. This had always been true, and was not merely a consequence of their being a bit younger. These differences in temperament had long created a bond between the two younger Green sisters just as it caused some distance between them and Meg. From the days of earliest school-yard controversies, Joanna and Amy had believed with all their hearts in rehashings, begrudgeries, tattletalings, and creative vengeance.

One particular Halloween, the school year had gotten off to a particularly rocky start for Amy and Joanna. Their parents, Janet and Lou, concerned about unattractively pugnacious inclinations, had hoped to make a point by creating a mock, and mocking, family crest for the two littlest Green sisters. Amy and Joanna, in third and fourth grade at the time, were then gripped by an extreme Arthurian legend obsession, and they were utterly thrilled with the fancy nature of the ironic emblem that adorned the cardboard shields they carried to accessorize their matching aluminum foil suits of armor.

Meg went that year as a Hershey's Kiss, a typically diplomatic solution that provided both a material link with her sisters' costumes—each of the three outfits required some six hundred feet of heavy-duty Reynolds aluminum foil—and a conceptual distance as an unassertive piece of chocolate.

The twin mock family crests—designed by Lou, executed by Janet with great care, and, regrettably, taken with happy oblivious literalness by Amy and Joanna—showed a multi-armed, sword-and-dagger-wielding griffin perched over a small green house, with the motto emblazoned in carefully lettered mock Olde English: "NEVER FORGIVE, NEVER FORGET." Joanna still had hers all these years later, tacked to her closet door.

It would not have been possible for Meg to nourish with her sisters' kind of devotion the terrible disappointment she now felt toward her parents. In the past few days, Amy and Joanna had become so savage that they could say anything and hurt anyone while seeming to enjoy it, while Meg had just become quieter and sadder.

Meg was not an indifferent person, and was in fact made sad very easily by many things. Certain heartwarming television commercials for office products made her cry. (Their mother, a woman given to characterizing pronouncements about matters large and small, always said Meg had a soft heart that melted like butter in the sun.) A glimpse of a beggar on the street could be Meg's undoing for the rest of the afternoon. She had been known to empty her wallet for a homeless—or allegedly homeless—person on numerous and not always well-timed occasions. "Meg went out with the grocery money and no blindfold" was Green family code for those nights when scrambled eggs or take-out food was on the menu as the consequence of a Meg encounter with some convincingly pathetic soul somewhere en route to shopping errands. One suspiciously robust and persistently present character, who sat perpetually on a stoop on their block with his dog beside a ragged cardboard sign claiming late-stage AIDS infection and homelessness, had been so successful in extracting grocery money from Meg over recent months that everyone in the family had come to think of him as "Meg's miracle bum."

Their mother had an affair and they found out.

By the time they found out—a careless matter of a single incriminating e-mail—it had already ended. Who was he? He was Philip Hart, a graduate student in his twenties for whose dissertation—concerning obsession in the late novels of Henry James—Janet had been the adviser. That it was Philip Hart was especially shocking to Meg, Joanna, and Amy, as he was one of Janet's cultivated collection of devoted, bright NYU graduate students, who, on countless nights, were invited to be part of the famously delicious and stimulating Green family dinners. Phil had struck them as so sweet and gentle and soft-spoken when he first came into their orbit the previous winter, so sensitive and funny, that the Green sisters had debated for weeks the question of his sexual orientation.

Henry Jamesish in his own ambiguities though he may have been (it was a small and bitter irony that the nature of his personal sexual desires should ever have been in doubt, let alone the object of now retrospectively mortifyingly detailed speculation on numerous occasions within earshot of their mother), he was a dear boy, the three sisters agreed, and Amy in particular had developed a small crush on him that had lasted many months. It was especially unfortunate that it was she who found the damning evidence on the computer in the study.

Home after an exhausting day of working as an arts and crafts counselor for six-year-olds in a summer program at the YMCA, she had merely been checking e-mail and then rummaging the family computer in an idle, mindless fashion. What she found was a beseeching message from Philip Hart begging their mother, his "little fuckbird"—yes, their own darling mother, a.k.a. Janet Green! Somebody's little fuckbird!—the very same woman who had nourished them in so many ways, soothing their fevered brows with those same cool, slender fingers which had, apparently "inflamed the very core of" Philip Hart every time she "caressed" his "John Thomas"—not to break off with him because they were, after all, "in ecstatic cahoots" as no other man and woman had ever been at any previous time in history. He could not stop thinking, he further declared, about certain mutually experienced "midnight implosions"; to hell with everything and everyone else, they were meant to be together.

When Meg and Joanna arrived home from their summer jobs a short while later, they were stunned by the irrefutable meaning of what Amy showed them.

"It's got to be part of something he's writing," Joanna said unconvincingly even to herself, grasping at this flimsiest of explanatory straws, after her first reading over Amy's shoulder. "Aren't these mostly some kind of literary references?"

"I don't think you're right, Jo-Jo," Meg whispered sadly, from Amy's other side. Her hand rested soothingly on the back of Amy's neck. "This is addressed to her. It's an e-mail. It's not a big quotation from something, and there's nothing here that sounds like Henry James, either. Except for the long sentences. There might be some literary references we don't get, sure, but this is something personal to Janet from Phil Hart."

"How can this be happening to us?" Amy wailed. "Are Janet and Lou getting divorced? I can't stand it! I hate Philip Hart! I hate him! I want him to die! Him and his fucking bow ties. What if he has AIDS? What if Janet dies? Then if Lou dies we would be orphans! This is like something on television! I don't want to be part of an after-school special."

"Philip Hart was the one getting the after-school specials, apparently," Joanna said bitterly, now having reread the damning message three times. There really was no other explanation she could imagine. "Did she answer this? Is there a reply here?" She reached over Amy's shoulder and jabbed at the computer mouse,

searching for sent messages or others from "phart@nyu.edu."
(Philip Hart's unfortunate elision would have provoked much
mirth under other circumstances.)

"Nothing. No sent messages from her at all. Just all of yours,
Amy. Here's one of mine. Meg, Meg, mine, Amy again. No, nothing else of hers. Nothing else in the inbox. She either used her office computer or she's deleted anything else on this one that was to
or from him, I guess, except for this one message, and it's dated,
what, three days ago. Tuesday. What were we doing on Tuesday?
So, wait, where did it go? It's not in the inbox. Where did you find
it, Ames?"

"In the trash," Amy said sadly. "There were three things in the
trash, and they were all Janet's, but the other two were just regular NYU things." Joanna relinquished the mouse and Amy clicked
open the trash folder. "See, here they are. Blah blah the meeting,
blah blah the committee."

"Oh, honey, you were so bored you were reading Janet's old
NYU e-mails in the trash?" Joanna said. "We have to get you
more good books. Did you finish those Maugham short stories?"

"Yeah, whatever," Amy agreed. "It *is* totally pathetic. I had
started to practice my flute piece, but it was just too hot and my
fingers felt like sausages. I don't really know why I did it, I wasn't
thinking about anything, you know? Don't you ever just click
around for no reason? Sort of zoning out, you know? Like reading
a homework assignment from fifth grade when you find it in an old
backpack, or like really, really reading all the insane personal ads
in the back of Janet's *New York Review of Books?* Anyway, the trash
doesn't automatically empty every time you shut down the way it
used to. Daddy told us at dinner, remember, last week, the night
you burned the couscous, Meg, you know, when Janet's nonverbal
Swedish student—with the braids, you know, the one in the beautiful blue striped shirt—the night she was here?"

"The D. H. Lawrence girl, yes, so, whatever, and I wasn't the one who turned the heat up, someone else did, but what's your point?" Meg replied impatiently.

"Yes, so, that was the night Lou talked about the article he had read in some journal. Whosis, Astrid, Estrid, Pippi Longstocking, what was her name? Anyway, she had accidentally trashed a chapter of her thesis? Remember she was talking with Janet about that? And that was when Lou said he had changed the settings on both computers in the apartment plus all of our notebooks so the trash isn't automatically deleted anymore, because he read about some scientific laboratory where they save every day's actual trash in different wastebaskets for a week in case someone throws away an important equation on a scrap of paper or something. So I deleted the trash like maybe four days ago, because it was full of junk spam like all those 'Enlarge your penis now!' e-mails, and now we have to do it manually—"

"Whatever, and I think her name was Astrid, but who the fuck cares?" Meg interrupted, having studied every word of the horrible message all the way through once again while Amy was rambling. "The trashed yet not-trashed message is here and we're reading it. We get the picture." She gave a small shudder and took a little step back from the desk, closing her eyes for a moment, needing physical distance from what she couldn't help but read over and over.

"What are we going to do?" Joanna said. There was silence. "You guys? Hello? We have a major crisis here? We need a plan? Like, what the hell are we going to do?" They stared at one another for a long moment.

"Meg, you first," Amy whispered, sucking on one of her knuckles.

"Nothing, maybe?" Meg suggested tentatively. She mentally calculated how many days remained of her summer internship at the literary agency, which she loved. Almost three weeks to go before she could escape back to New Haven.

"PhilHartPhilHartPhil, heart-fill, hurtful," Amy murmured in the way she had of playing with words, often without even realizing she was doing it aloud. "FuckPhil. KillPhil."

"You mean just act like we don't know?" Joanna said dubiously. She couldn't imagine this strategy working for an hour. How would they face their mother at dinner in a little while? And every day after that?

"Don't you think that's an option at least, Jo-Jo?" Meg, the voice of reason.

"We have to tell Lou," Amy interrupted. "Oh my God." She turned to each of her sisters. Tears streaked her cheeks. She thumped her hands against the sides of her own head in anguish. "Oh my God. God. God. God. He'll want to kill himself. We can't tell him."

"Do you think maybe he already knows?" Joanna wondered, leaning forward to take Amy's hands in her own and gently pull them down. She perched on the corner of the desk and swung a foot against Amy's chair, rocking Amy slightly with each movement. She felt oddly detached and rational, not like her usual firecracker self at all, more like a scientist in a laboratory gazing at a microscopic specimen in contemplation of an experiment gone awry. "Lou knows Janet a lot better than we do, after all. And anyway, he's not just going to do something crazy."

"How do you know?" Amy moaned. "She's been doing something crazy! Who would have thought Janet could do something like this? Maybe they're both having affairs, I don't know! And you don't know either, Jo-Jo, even though you think you're such an expert on everybody in this insane family."

"Look, maybe it really does have some other meaning," Meg said, attempting to start from scratch all over again. She hugged herself for a moment as if warding off a chill. "We don't really have any way to know what it means. We just can't be certain, no matter what it looks like."

"But I *do* think I know what it means," Amy said in a muffled voice, having put her head down on her arms as she began to weep in earnest, her eyes squeezed tight shut. "You're just saying that because you don't want to admit the truth. Neither of you do. Don't you get it? What else could it possibly mean? Nothing else."

"I don't know," Meg said in a sorrowful tone, starting to rub the back of Amy's neck in a familiar, Janet-like gesture, which Amy shrugged away. "I really just don't know. But you can't be certain."

"Well, there's one person who does know exactly what it means. So let's ask her," Joanna said grimly.

The dark day got worse. All three of them were further shocked, though they would not have known that could have been a possibility, when they confronted Janet moments after she came jauntily in the door from the gym, with groceries for their dinner. They launched their fusillade of accusations while she was still putting things away in the kitchen. They attacked her in the direct and forthright style in which they were accustomed to communicating with their mother. She did not falter or slow down even a little as they uttered their accusations and demands for explanation while she put the groceries away, folded the brown paper bags with her usual orderly efficiency, and stowed them in a cupboard.

The moment her daughters fell silent, she turned to face them with her arms folded, and, standing there in their formerly jolly kitchen, leaning against the marvelous big soapstone sink they had salvaged from the town dump while on a Vermont camping trip three summers before, she told them in a very quiet, matter-of-fact way, in a manner tinged with an unfamiliar and unconsoling coldness they had never experienced in her before, that it was a private matter, something that did not concern them, something personal that had now concluded, a matter of finished business with which she and Lou had already dealt. And then their mother, this perfect stranger who answered to the name Janet Green— among other names—folded the last grocery bag and went off to take a shower.

Reader's note: I don't think it's fair that you're not letting her speak for herself. Janet should have a voice in this novel, after all, given that the three sisters are reacting to her behavior. Why can't she explain herself here? MG

Reader's note: I think it's just fine the way it is. I like it that she isn't given any dialogue. Why do you always have to make sure everything is fair? AG

Author's note: Consequent to the transgression that set this story in motion, the character of the mother has been deliberately deprived of dialogue.

Hurt and angry, furious, really, that she had not, as they each wished, offered some marvelously reasonable explanation that would have undone the devastation, the three of them next stormed down the hallway to Lou in his workshop, where family law forbade afternoon interruption except in the event of dire emergency.

They found him at his computer, fiddling with the prototype software for what would, in a matter of months as it turned out, be another of his extraordinarily successful inventions, "The Cliqk."* His ingenious Couch Potato,† a hand-held, potato-shaped device that offered sage advice "for people too cheap and lazy to go to a shrink," had still not reached what would be its peak of success in

---

*"Connect Your Clique With a Cliqk," *The New York Times*, January 10, 2000; "Popular 'Couch Potato' Inventor's New 'Cliqk' Kicks Shares, Makes Noise for Fledgling Software Firm," *The Wall Street Journal,* January 22, 2000; "Your Friends Are in Your Pocket With the Cliqk," *Newsweek,* February 12, 2000; "People Are Talking About: Chicks With Cliqks," *Vogue,* February 2000.

†"Couch Potato Alternative to Therapy While Shrinks Vacation," *The New York Times*, August 18, 1999.

the following year. In its first few months it had already attracted
a great deal of attention and had earned Lou an astonishing sum of
money.

They were undivertable, though he tried at first to banter and
enlist them in brainstorming some of the applications for this new
electronic toy.

"Come on, girls, you're always so imaginative at this stage.
We're going to have some fun with this one. Click your clique?
Click to connect? Connect with a click? Get a kick from a click?
No, too Cole Porter. Come on, what do you think?"

But they weren't buying.

"Lou, we're here to talk about Janet and Philip Hart. Nothing
else," Amy told him coldly, her arms folded across her chest. "Stop
trying to distract us." Her sisters, who flanked her in matching
poses, agreed.

"Okay," Lou sighed. He squared his shoulders and tilted his
head from side to side in a habitual gesture he had of unkinking
his neck after long hours at his desk. Joanna thought she had never
seen him look so tired. He swiveled around to face them. "I am so
sorry we are having this conversation. You can't imagine. I feel
terrible about your being aware at all that this has happened. But
it's over and done with. I'm just not going to tell you whatever
it is you three could possibly want to hear. It's been resolved. I
assure you that nothing has changed. Why can't you just accept
that?"

His daughters scowled at him as one.

"How can you say nothing has changed?" Amy said angrily.

"How can you say it's resolved?" Joanna challenged. "That's
impossible."

"You just have to talk to us," Meg implored. "She won't give
us anything and we need to know more about this. You just have
to tell us."

Lou sighed again. "So who's going to speak for the tribunal?
Regan? Goneril? Or is it Cordelia?"

Reader's note: I think you should be consistent. Why does the father get to speak when the mother doesn't? MG

    Reader's note: Yes, I would prefer the consistency of keeping them both quiet. And who cares about the details of the Couch Potato or the Cliqk? And this is supposed to be a novel, not just the story of our screwed-up family. Why are you putting in so many real facts from our lives, or details that are so close to the reality that it makes almost no difference that you've changed it a little? You're just slowing the story down. AG

    Author's note: It is regrettable that these intrusions will serve to slow the story down far more than any discursive descriptions that have been deliberately crafted in order to illuminate elements of the characters' personalities and histories that pertain to the narrative.

    Reader's note: But these discursive descriptions are boring! AG

    Reader's note: She's doing this and you get to make your point even though she isn't going to change anything, no matter what she said about being responsive to our comments. You know she doesn't have to change things we don't like. A deal's a deal. MG

    Author's note: Indeed.

Harshly confronted, an immediate response having been demanded, Lou would only wearily confirm that yes, he knew about this business with Philip Hart, had known for a while, but would really prefer that they drop the matter, and no, he wasn't going to "do" anything about it. The important thing was that it was over. There was nothing more to discuss. He was sorry they knew about it. He was sorry about the whole thing, but it was now over.

    "Lou? Daddy?" Amy said tremulously. "How can you let her do this to us?"

    "This isn't about 'us,' girls, it's something private," their father began, "and I really don't think—"

Meg burst out, "How can you say there isn't an 'us'! What else is there but us! Doesn't our family mean anything to you?"

"Are you willing to let her just destroy everything? Don't you care about what she's done to our family?" shrieked Joanna. "Why aren't you angry at her?"

"How long was this going on?" Amy asked plaintively. "How do you even know it's really over? Why do you trust—"

"Stop. Stop it, you three. You must stop right now." Lou raised his hands as if to ward off blows, and Amy stopped in midsentence. He was definitely upset, Joanna thought with a mixture of satisfaction and guilt. He had seemed about to say something, but now he fell silent.

The silence lengthened, punctuated only by the squeak of their father's chair turning very slightly as he looked into their faces, first Amy's, then Joanna's, then Meg's. Amy glared at him. Then she turned away, and tilted her head in a clenched sort of determined way as if she were trying to read the titles on the spines of the books in the overstuffed bookcases that lined two sides of his workshop. Joanna looked away into the middle distance of Lou's bulletin board, on which she saw, haphazardly thumbtacked among his sketches and notes, several curling snapshots of all three sisters and their mother, photographs of family moments. Her eyes rested on a washed-out snapshot of the three sisters on the couch with their old Airedale, Soames, who had tried to look dignified in a Santa's helper hat. The wonderful Green family. Beside them were two funny examples of Amy's hilarious caricatures (Meg on the telephone, Janet cooking), and, not yet framed, the abstracted geometric watercolor of the view out their living room window that Amy had presented to Lou for Father's Day.

Meg couldn't look directly at her father at all. Instead of meeting his eye, she tried very hard to look at the corner of Lou's eyeglasses. She studied the tiny pattern of screws that held the frame together, making domino patterns and unmaking them, focusing on maintaining sufficient distance to suppress the bitter sob welling up like a thick bubble somewhere deep inside her chest.

Louis Green, inventor of what would soon be the country's most popular problem-solving device, just sat helplessly in his old swivel chair and gazed at each of his three daughters sadly, unable to provide sufficient comfort and reassurance.

"Are you okay, Lou?" Meg whispered. "I'm sorry for what I said. It's just that you—"

"Fuck it," Amy interrupted. "He is so completely whipped. This is just pathetic." She turned on her heel (truly, that is exactly what she did, with a little flounce that would have been comical had it not been such a serious moment) and she stamped away to her room.

Their father swiveled abruptly away from Meg and Joanna to face his desk. If they weren't going to help him brainstorm about the new device, he said over his shoulder in a falsely ordinary tone, then he really had no more time for conversation at the moment. He dismissed them then, clicking open a document on his computer before beginning to type rapidly on his keyboard, as if acting out a parody of a man engrossed in his work, the way he might perform precisely such an action for one of their Sunday night after-dinner family charades marathons.

"What are you doing?" Meg said in disbelief. "This is an incredibly important moment in our family!" Lou kept typing, his face averted from theirs. It was a desperate bluff, Joanna thought, furious at his retreat into his own woundedness which he thought he had to conceal from his daughters at all costs.

"I don't believe this," Joanna said with a flinty voice she had never heard herself use before, addressing the back of his head. "Mr. Ultra-Rational Computer Man doesn't have another moment to interface with his family today." How nasty could she be? It was horrifying yet strangely thrilling to hear herself speak to her father this way. It felt exactly like the dreams Joanna sometimes had about smashing windowpanes—a forbidden act she would resist until she just couldn't any longer, and then in her dream she would break one after another in a confusing flood of rage and ecstasy.

"Hey, Lou," she megaphoned unpleasantly to the back of his shirt collar, as if from a great distance, "Send me an e-mail sometime, okay? If your work isn't too intense, I mean. That's J Green at fuckedupfamily dot com. But don't bother if you're too busy. Come on, Meg." She turned away, feeling her viciousness expanding sharply, blossoming like a bleeding wound. She felt freakish, not knowing where she would stop.

"Lou? Daddy?" Meg, the last to give up, stood in his doorway for another moment. He gave a little, not-now shake of his head without looking up, and then she, too, fled.

TWO

The Wonderful Green Family: A History

The Greens were a wonderful family, and they knew it. Everybody knew it. Their nursery and kindergarten teachers were happy and proud to have the Green girls in their classes. When, in future years, their elementary school teachers would reflect back on the highlights of their careers (something elementary school teachers are especially compelled to do in order to reassure themselves that it has been a worthwhile life, particularly as they face retirement, given a teacher's grossly inadequate salary and social status), the golden era of the Green sisters would inevitably come to mind with special fondness, most definitely in the case of those dedicated souls who had been blessed to teach two or even all three of these rewarding children.

Before they produced their wonderful children, Janet and Lou had been a wonderful couple, the kind of obviously connected pair who made people smile fondly and daydream about their own youthful passions and first loves. Whether observed simply buying tickets to the movies or stocking up on coffee beans at a grocery store or kissing passionately and obliviously at a street corner, while the red light changed to green, and back to red again, they had a marvelous, unwitting effect on numerous passersby.

To notice Janet and Lou at those moments was to be reminded

of personal desires, whatever they might be. Perhaps someone observing them went home and began to play the piano again, while another was motivated to sign up for Italian lessons. To know them well—to be included in a group of their friends spending, say, an entire Sunday afternoon with them in their apartment, perhaps feasting on one of Janet's brilliant risottos with many glasses of wine, nibbling away at an entire wheel of Brie with grapes and walnuts while arguing enthusiastically about anything and everything—was to go home and bake a pie, make love, telephone a lost friend, polish all the silver, enlist in the Peace Corps. They had the effect of making people feel simultaneously content with all that life has to offer while feeling restless to participate more in all that life has to offer.

Reader's note: This doesn't really feel like a novel to me in the first place, but just when it seems, at least, really to capture actual events, you make things up. It's confusing. The characters in this novel have our same first names, and a lot about them is true, but certain things never happened at all, or are completely distorted. AG

Reader's note: If the truth is going to be so manipulated, I don't see why you didn't just change all the names and places completely and write a totally fictional account, instead of this weird blend of truth and fantasy. Since it's neither fiction nor memoir, the result seems like a compromise either way. It's like a fictionalized memoir, or a memoirized novel. What's the point of this? MG

Author's note: Certain readers of this manuscript who do not understand where fiction comes from, no matter how autobiographical it may be in its origins, have insisted that there is no way the author could possess sufficient insight about her characters to write certain observations and descriptions, and have, in fact, accused the author of indulging in some slightly icky personal fantasies. So be it. First it's not fiction enough, then it's too fictional. The general reader will not struggle with these issues. Certain other readers who have these issues should feel free to go write their own novels.

Reader's note: So just because you call this a novel you can say what-ever you want about the characters no matter what the truth? AG
Author's note: My only concern is the truth of the novel.
Reader's note: That's what they all say. MG

How did they meet? Their daughters would ask for this story over and over. Janet Templer met Louis Green in the checkout line on the second floor of the Eighth Street Bookshop; Janet was buying a collection of Somerset Maugham stories, and Lou, early for a movie at the Eighth Street Playhouse (which he never did see), was buying a Margaret Mead memoir out of curiosity because his installation work at the American Museum of Natural History occasionally brought him into traumatic contact with the wizened, tantrum-prone anthropologist.

Janet noticed him right away, she claimed, because he just wasn't like anyone else she had ever seen. He seemed somehow more observant, more engaged, more present. He was like an anthropologist taking notes on the curious social rituals of an interesting people.

When he stared at her it wasn't rude, it was inquisitive, his gaze clear and thoughtful, somewhat childlike. The line moved slowly. Janet, an intense and academic-looking woman with an amused smile and unflirtatious yet openly inviting way of looking back at him when he looked at her, intrigued Lou.

As if he had known her for a long time, because it seemed like the most natural thing in the world to speak to this woman, though in fact it was very unusual for Lou to initiate a casual conversation with a stranger, Lou began to talk to Janet. He described the bizarre incident that had occurred earlier in the week at the museum when a new assistant had obtained an erroneous sandwich from the local coffee shop for Dr. Mead's lunch.

Lou had been passing by the fifth-floor Anthropology office on his way to a meeting with a curator in vertebrates (to discuss a lighting problem in a bat exhibit vitrine on the main floor) when he heard shouting. He had stopped at the open office doorway to see if there was a problem he could help solve, and for his trouble he had been beaned in the head by a loosely-wrapped tuna fish sandwich. The sobbing new assistant had fled past him an instant later, and he had found himself reeling and off balance, festooned with gobs of soggy tuna fish and bread and pieces of iceberg lettuce, the sandwich having more or less exploded on impact.

Nevertheless, he tried to look properly sober under the gaze of the enraged eminent anthropologist, who brandished some sort of Pacific Island shillelagh in the direction of the fleeing assistant while she continued to shout imprecations about the essential differences between tuna fish and chicken salad—and the deficiencies of those who cannot tell them apart—into the dim, echoing hallway of the fifth floor.

"Are you an imbecile? Are you a cretin? Can you not distinguish tuna salad on rye from chicken salad on whole wheat? Have you no intelligence whatsoever?" thundered the small renowned expert on sexuality in primitive societies. Her words were absolutely destined, from that moment of Lou's hilariously precise imitation on the checkout line in the bookshop, to become a Green family catchphrase in future years for any commission of trivial error.

It was a cold afternoon in early December, and after an hour of leaning against the anthropology trade paperbacks in intense conversation about all sorts of things neither of them would ever be able to remember later, they both admitted to hunger, neither having eaten lunch, and so without a break in the flow of talk they went up the street to the coffee shop on the corner of Greene Street.

They were each only children, they discovered. They each had one living parent afflicted with an old-age infirmity, living in a nursing home. Janet's mother was aggressive and increasingly senile; Lou's father was mild-mannered and sweet but almost totally unable to communicate owing to a progressive neurological disease that had left him limp and mute.

They didn't notice as it grew darker, and then it was dark.

Janet had craved both chicken salad and tuna salad, inspired by the Margaret Mead story, but she ordered what Lou ordered, and they wolfed down club sandwiches and shared a heap of greasy french fries while they drank innumerable Cokes.

Janet would discover only later that part of Lou's intensity that day was a consequence of his being out of the habit of talking in a very personal way. Or for that matter, talking at all. He had a few very close friends, but he didn't see them often, and he was otherwise perfectly content to spend time alone. The friends he had knew him as a rather minimal conversationalist. Ask him a question and he would give you a precise, measured answer without a syllable to spare. He was the Calvin Coolidge of Museum Services. And yet here he was being witty, ironic, loquacious, delivering himself to Janet in a torrent of words.

Lou, on the other hand, would soon enough discover that one of the ineffable somethings about Janet which captivated him from the start, namely, her ability to be perhaps not so much a fascinating person as a *fascinated* one, was not a private characteristic reserved for his pleasure alone. This essential element in her nature would account for her tremendous ease in making huge numbers of friends and acquaintances wherever she went, whatever she did.

Lou would be confounded by this phenomenon when, a few years hence, he would find that at his tenth college reunion, Janet, by then hugely pregnant with Joanna, with toddler Meg in tow between them, nevertheless managed on that day to accumulate a dozen new friends, people Lou never knew during his four years at Columbia, some of whom would remain in touch for years, so that Janet ended up having more friends from the Columbia class of '71 than Lou did. She simply attracted people. Janet was marvelously popular with her colleagues and students as well.

Reader's note: So, wait, time out, is this narrative from the point of view of the middle sister or not? Otherwise, how can the reader be told this stuff? Whose voice is this? Are you using the literary device of the omniscient narrator? Does anyone still do that these days? Are you just trying to be as ultra-literary as possible by writing about all of our family history and our experiences in this narrative voice from above? And are you trying to sneak a little foreshadowing in here with the reference to popularity with students? AG

Reader's note: I think you go into way too much background here about the parent characters. What has it got to do with the rest of the novel? Isn't the novel supposed to be about our story? What happened to the three sisters? Are readers just supposed to wait for you to go back to the main story when you feel like it? MG

Author's note: The Little Women *is a narrative in the third person. If one wanted to call the voice omniscient, one could, though the perceptions and observations are, by necessity, not truly omniscient. The point of view of the middle sister will be emphasized, yes, but the narrative point of view is not exclusively hers. Foreshadowing? Janet's affair has already been revealed in the first pages. Aftershadowing, perhaps. The revelation of the affair isn't the heart of the story; the consequences of that revelation are. What has the background of the parents got to do with the three sisters? A great deal. Context. The past interacting with the present. The story of the parents as it exists in the minds of their daughters, the history of the romantic family myth, which is, after all, what is at stake, the element that drives the novel forward.*

Reader's note: So, tell us please, what exactly is at stake here? AG
Author's note: Family happiness.
Reader's note: Isn't that always at stake? MG

Janet, unlike Lou, had many people in her life and was very used to lots of casual conversation. But when she met Lou she felt that there was something new and unfamiliar about this encounter. She felt it in her bones—that this conversation with Lou was important and completely unlike anything in her experience. (Stopping to describe her recognition of this feeling at this juncture was always an essential element in Janet's ritual telling of the story of how they met. If she skipped it, one or the other of her daughters would be sure to remind her to describe how she *felt* having that very first conversation with Lou, and then she would have to reverse herself, get her bearings, and settle into the comfortable, well-worn grooves of the story, to say how new and unfamiliar yet important this conversation had seemed.)

Janet told Lou a troubling yet amusing tale of English Department politics at NYU, where she was in her final year of graduate school. (Lou had pegged her right, as he would remind his daughters when he was the one telling the story. "Your mother had that academic, everything-that-matters-occurred-in-the-nineteenth-century-and-I-can-find-the-reference-somewhere-in-the-library-stacks look about her," he would inevitably say.)

There was, she explained to Lou at that fateful lunch, a ruthlessly ambitious teaching assistant, a rival and a real nuisance from Janet's point of view, whose outrageously forged rave student evaluations had, it seemed, guaranteed her a particular, much coveted fellowship. Now the forgeries seemed likely to come to light, owing to a complex side story involving a disgruntled student's complaint about the class to the dean of undergraduate studies, and disciplinary actions could follow, which would mean a new chain of maneuverings and jockeyings for the desirable fellowship, which would be available all over again. It was a complicated story and Lou couldn't quite follow all of it and it made him glad he wasn't an academic.

Finally, when their coffee refills had begun to annoy the waiter and the dinner crowd was filling up the adjacent booths, they split the check, left a generous tip (something else they discovered they shared, a tendency to overtip), and exited the coffee shop, a bit dazed. With no particular plan or direction, they started to walk, enjoying big gulps of the cold night air after the oily humidity of the restaurant. They saw a man walking an Airedale and they talked with the man and his dog for a moment; they both loved Airedales.

Soon the damp air grew damper and then it started to sleet. Janet lived just around the corner on Waverly Place. Lou didn't get home to his apartment up by the museum, on West Eighty-third Street, for three days.

Reader's note: You're kidding! AG

    Reader's note: Are you sure about this? MG

    Author's note: This is a work of fiction.

    Reader's note: That's what you keep saying, but did it really happen this way? You can't just pull that "It's a novel" stuff whenever it's convenient for you to avoid accountability. AG

    Author's note: The reader who has been distracted by this marginal commentary is urged to return to the narrative without delay, having been reminded by these notes that this is a work of fiction which has been somewhat inspired, as is the case with many if not most novels, by actual events.

    Reader's note: So a novelist has no accountability? AG

    Author's note: See Author's note above.

Janet and Lou married four months after they met.

They were married in the courtyard of an Eighth Street apartment building that was part of the secret warren of West Village life that was as familiar and ordinary to Janet as it was mysterious and confusing to Lou. A graduate school friend of Janet's had an apartment in the back building and had agreed to let them use what she called her bonsai bathroom and kitchen for the twenty people they invited.

Neither Janet nor Lou had any family to speak of, beyond their respective parents, neither of whom attended the ceremony. They had in common that they had both been born to parents who had been almost too old to have children. Lou's father, Gilbert, was so feeble that he really couldn't manage the day, they decided, and Janet's mother, Lillian, was so unpleasant that she really shouldn't be allowed to attend, they decided also, after Janet took the optimistic Lou for an I-told-you-so audience at Serenity House, the inaptly named Bronxville nursing home where Lillian would spend her final and not especially serene days.

"How mean could your mother be?" Before Janet, Lou had never met anyone who spoke so matter-of-factly about disliking her own mother.

"Plenty mean. She's been banned from the Friendship Table at Serenity House."

"What did she do?"

"Something about telling someone to fuck off when he asked her to pass the salt substitute. And then there was the remark about someone's sausages resembling a plate of turds. And she's been ramming people deliberately with her walker, though she won't admit it."

"I don't believe you."

"Okay, fine. You'll see for yourself."

Lillian had responded to being introduced to Lou by telling him she thought his shirt was ugly. Then she asked Janet right in front of him why she was marrying someone who looked like Bugs Bunny and also did Janet know her hair looked like a fright wig and also why the hell did the dining room run out of peppermint stick ice cream on weekends? It was a brief encounter, as Lillian had rolled away on her motorized scooter abruptly, without saying goodbye, because it was a Bingo afternoon and she always liked to get there early to claim a place right up front, even though Bingo had become too challenging for her to follow without the assistance of an amazingly pleasant nurse's aide who found her every disinhibited and misanthropic remark sidesplittingly funny. (Regrettably, this nurse's aide was to be terminated several months later, when it was discovered that she had been regularly filching cash from several of her patients, including Lillian.)

Lou (who, needless to say, did not in any way resemble Bugs Bunny—he didn't have even the slightest overbite) was a good sport about this encounter and even thought to bring a quart of peppermint stick ice cream the next time they visited Lillian, but he did not argue with Janet after that about inviting her mother to their wedding or to anything else, either.

The tree-shrouded courtyard was entered through a door between two discount shoe stores that led to a grimy hallway (it was the sort of hallway in which one would buy heroin or have life-threatening sex with a transvestite prostitute, Lou was pretty sure, the first time he was taken by Janet for a drink with this friend, as he always added whenever he was the teller of the story of their wedding day). The grimy hallway led to another locked door that led to the surprising courtyard. It was small, but it was grass and trees.

What open space there was had been diminished by a tangled profusion of so many identical cheap black bicycles stacked along one wall that all through the marriage ceremony Lou half expected a gang of Chinese takeout delivery boys to appear at any moment. The courtyard was heavy with the curiously musky, animal scent of the ailanthus trees, which loomed with incongruous dignity, so close by the hurly-burly of Eighth Street.

It was a very simple and unornamented event on a Sunday afternoon in April. The photographs of this event—a mere dozen out-of-focus snapshots grabbed by a friend with an Instamatic camera—would be studied ritualistically over the years by the three Green sisters, as if the tattered photo album contained the key to understanding the meaning of everything, like some sort of family Rosetta stone.

It was 1976. All the men had bushy hair and sideburns and

some of them wore bell-bottomed pants. ("They look like terror-
ists!" Amy would usually exclaim.) Most of the women had long
hair, parted humorlessly down the middle, and they all seemed to
be wearing outfits that resembled costumes for some low-budget
musical about jolly milkmaids in the Ukraine. There was Lou's
friend from grade school, and here was Janet's thesis adviser, and
here were Janet's friends from college, and here was the friend who
lived in the building, and there was Lou's college roommate who
had just come out to everyone that day, with a sentimental toast to
his lover just before the ceremony, and there was the college roommate's lover, who would later become a famous shoe designer.
Years later Janet still owned a couple of pairs of his early, very sexy,
but almost completely unwearably chic sandals that the girls liked
to try on, but even they had to admit nobody with normal feet
could walk more than a block in them, and then, when the girls
were still in grade school, the shoe designer was the first person
any of them knew to die of AIDS, though he was not the last.

No one could identify the horsy woman in the aqua blouse
pouring wine from a jug into a paper cup in one shot, and holding
her cup aloft in a group toast to the couple in another. She had
come to look totally familiar to the girls, like family really, because she was in those two photographs. Perhaps, Meg would suggest each time they pondered her identity, the three sisters sitting
together on the green couch in the living room, turning the pages
reverently, reliving a moment they never lived, she came from one
of the adjacent buildings and had joined in the festivities to help
herself to some wine.

No, she was a CIA agent sent to infiltrate this group of sub-
versive antiwar protesters, Amy would declare next, though Lou
had explained to her quite thoroughly that it was a couple of years
too late for that to be likely, though some of their friends had been
involved in all sorts of antiwar protests and the SDS. (In fact,
though Lou didn't know it, one of their guests that day, a quiet
guy called David Aaronson who worked in Museum Services and

never seemed to have much to say about anything, had shared an apartment with Ted Gold, who had died in the accidental Weather Underground bomb explosion in the Wilkerson town house on Eleventh Street six years before.)

She was an old flame of Lou's, one of them would announce with grave assurance, studying the aqua blouse woman from a fresh angle. She was half-crazed with jealousy and had arrived in disguise in order to spy on him and had almost interrupted the ceremony but then at the last moment had decided to forever hold her peace. Occasionally they would all tease Lou, Janet included, about his secret romance with the obsessed woman in aqua who did not want to give him up but had, out of a sad and secret yet noble love.

A rabbi in a white Indian shirt embroidered with Jewish stars performed the ceremony. Lou, a half-Jewish atheist, had wanted a rabbi of some sort out of respect for his mother's background, even though he had no contact with her family (they had never approved of his father, an unambitious and nominally Episcopal civil engineer). Janet thought his loyalty to tradition was touching and it was she who located the rabbi, one willing to preside over a mixed and irreligious wedding ceremony, through a friend of a friend. Rabbi Matt had a beard and a ponytail and did not wear a yarmulke. He arrived so late, on a motorcycle, that they were afraid he wasn't going to show up at all. He insisted on wheeling the motorcycle through the narrow hallway to the courtyard where the wedding was to take place. It was visible at the edge of several of the photographs.

The rabbi (who had just been fired, they heard some time later, from his New Jersey "Rapping with Rabbi Matt" radio show for advocating the legalization of not only marijuana but also group marriage) rambled through a bizarrely groovy ceremony that was so not about Janet and Lou that presently everyone was stifling giggles, including the bride and groom, including the rabbi himself, but he was probably high.

He declared them husband and wife and then added, "Sprinkle, sparkle, do art!" before revving up his Harley to speed off to another hippie wedding ceremony on the Upper West Side. (Thus was born another Green family catchphrase—"Sprinkle! Sparkle! Do art!"—an all-purpose benediction for any creative endeavor large or small.)

Lou's minimal (his word), wretched (Janet's word) bachelor apartment had been two blocks from the museum. When they married it was but the work of one afternoon with a rented van to consolidate his few possessions with Janet's in her orderly, spacious Waverly Place apartment. Until he met Janet, Lou had never really cared where he lived and what he owned, and most of his possessions of any significance were books.

Janet had moved into the four sunny rooms with a fireplace and a view of the Washington Square Arch (if you stuck your head out the window) on Waverly Place in her senior year at NYU, because she was counting on staying for graduate school. She had a roommate, the now legendary Lola, a histrionic drama student who was the only person to answer Janet's bulletin board notice for an apartment share. (Lola later admitted to Janet that she had taken the notice down.)

Things had not gone well. Meg, Joanna, and Amy could never hear enough about their mother's months with Lola. Lola stories had even been known to soothe Amy when she was miserably sick with chicken pox the summer after second grade, when nothing else could distract her from her misery. Lola wore only black and red, and she smelled rather unoriginally of patchouli, and she drank green tea of a special type that came in silk tea bags which had to be steeped in just a certain way in a special little iron pot that could never be immersed in tap water but only rinsed lightly in toxin-free bottled water, though she also consumed copious bags of Chee-tos, and sometimes she left orangey handprints around the apartment.

Janet told her daughters that for the six months she shared her apartment with Lola, she could never figure out when Lola was in character for a part (she was in a different short play every other week at a cultlike repertory theater in the East Village) and when she was just trying to be a character herself. Lola often glued sequins on her not-unlarge breasts and buttocks before she went out on dates. She was the first person Janet ever knew who waxed her pubic hair, and she left horrific centipedes of wax and hair in the bathtub, which had really panicked Janet the first time she encountered them because she didn't know what the hell she was looking at.

Lola spent many hours smoking cigarettes through a long black cigarette holder while talking on the telephone and posing in front of the mirror, making faces at herself and doing leg lifts and gesturing with the cigarette holder while her nail polish dried.

"Daahhlink," she would say into her telephone. "Mon Dieu!" she would exclaim at other times. "'Allo, luv," Janet heard her say more than once. Lola's accent drifted from continent to continent, all the way from Cockney glottal stops worthy of an East End native to the occasional nasal locution from Bayside, Queens, whence she actually came.

Lola referred to Bayside as her childhood village and referred to her time there as having taken place when she was "a wee lass." She referred to her mother as "Mumsy," which did not at all bring to mind the dowdy, divorced, perpetually exasperated Barbara Horowitz, who commuted into the city every day from Queens to a law office in midtown where she worked as a paralegal and who once revealed inadvertently on the telephone to Janet that Lola's actual name was Cheryl.

Lola/Cheryl had the habit of writing her initial on half the eggs in every carton, and she counted cookies and pickles chronically, with a demented efficiency. She kept a little chart on the door of the refrigerator with all pertinent statistics, and she marked her shampoo and conditioner bottles in the shower with enormous initials, too. Daily, she marked levels on soda bottles, and on her huge squeeze bottle of Vermont Maid syrup, and on her ketchup, and on the sides of her Special K and Sugar Smacks cereal boxes. Whenever Janet got to this, her daughters would beg for more examples. There were the sardines, Janet would recall, which as it turned out were difficult to share because they tended to come in odd numbers in the tin. And the dental floss, which had to be measured periodically and then rewound into the dispenser. ("Did she really do that?" Joanna would invariably marvel at this point in the story. "Are you sure?" And then Amy would ask, "Why did you have to share dental floss? You couldn't have your own in your room or something? What was up with that?" The explanation, part of the ritual, was always something about how Lola's feelings were easily hurt whenever Janet tried to avoid sharing things with her.)

"Weren't you tempted to eat an egg that was marked with an 'L'?" Amy would always ask. "I would have been." Not really, her mother would reply, though there was once a mix-up involving an egg that Janet had marked "H" for hard-boiled. This had thrown Lola for a loop, her entire system threatened by the possible presence of a hitherto unidentified third roommate. ("And dividing in thirds is so hard to do!" Amy would add.)

"Did she really think she had to mark everything or otherwise you would steal her food?" Meg would wonder. Janet really didn't know. Clearly, Lola had many boundary issues.

"Why was she like that?" Joanna would demand. "Did she realize she was really neurotic? Did she know she was a pioneer in the field of eating disorders? Do you know where she is now?"

Lola was just one of life's mysteries, Janet would always answer. Who knows where she ended up?

Janet was able to persuade Lola to go away when she discovered that Lola had borrowed a quite original *Wuthering Heights* junior-year term paper of Janet's from her desk in order to copy it for a different class, credit for which she needed in order to graduate. Janet went to her and put it very simply: she could report this transgression to the dean's office, or not, depending on how quickly Lola signed off on the apartment lease and got out.

Lola moved to a shared macrobiotic loft in Chinatown in dignified haste, aided by everyone in the cast of her final play of the spring, a mimed production of *The Cherry Orchard* that was set in a pioneer colony on Mars a thousand years in the future. They all looked dramatic daggers at Janet as she passed them trundling boxes down the stairs.

"You should have reported her," Lou said, when he heard the saga of Lola for the first time, over omelets at the coffee shop where they had their first marathon lunch, and where they had taken to going for late breakfast on Saturdays. "She took your Brontë paper."

"I know," Janet had replied. "But I just wanted her out of the apartment more than anything. If I hadn't discovered the thing with the paper, I don't know what I would have done to get her out of my life. It might have been something really bad. You have no idea how much I wanted to keep the apartment. After all, I was the one who found it; most of the furniture was mine. Those months with Lola made me realize I am just not able to live comfortably with someone I don't love."

"Still," Lou persisted, while making a mental note about the increased significance of a conversation the previous night about the possibility of his moving in with Janet. "What she did was terrible. You should have reported her. You, of all people, in your field, should have minded the plagiarism the most."

"I'm not as moral a person as you think I am, I guess," Janet had replied with a shrug. "It was more useful for leverage to get her out. You should probably know this about me—sometimes I just do what I want to do in order to have things be the way I want them."

Reader's note: I always thought the "Lola" story was unfunny, but the way you tell it here is chilling. It calls into question Janet's whole moral outlook in ways I had never considered. Was that your intention? MG

Reader's note: I always thought our family scorn was "Lola's" punishment for being a cheater. I thought this story was told to us because it was one of those moral lessons by example. Now we have to reconsider all of our moral lessons by example, of course, because we were the innocent good children being instructed by our saintly mother who turns out to have been somebody's little fuckbird. AG

Author's note: In a work of fiction, details about a character's personal history help build the reader's sense of that character and what she brings to the present action. Details are the sensual spirit of a novel.

Reader's note: We weren't criticizing your inclusion of this story. You don't need to be so defensive, not to mention pretentious. You can say all you want about how details are the sensual spirit of a novel, but the details you are choosing to use in your so-called novel are the truths and lies of our family. And it's not up to you to decide what the truth is, even if you think you can organize everything to suit yourself because you've written a novel. AG

Throughout their childhoods, Janet would regale her daughters with stories about the condition in which she had found Lou, much the way one might describe a pathetic, stray dog who, before being taken in and properly nourished, had been living in the streets, foraging for his sustenance in trash cans, drinking out of puddles. She had been both touched and faintly alarmed by Lou's one dish, his one bowl, his single knife, fork, and spoon, his bare walls, his cupboards stocked with nothing but many cans of Progresso chicken noodle soup and StarKist chunk light tuna, and his lunatic habit of eating a big bowl of shredded wheat every night (he had boxes of that stockpiled as well) last thing before sleeping so as to save time eating breakfast in the morning.

Lou's job at the Museum of Natural History, when he met Janet, was behind the scenes, where he labored sometimes late at night when the galleries were closed, devising and installing the lighting and mechanical programs that animated the most popular displays. He had never worked anywhere else.

Lou had started at the museum, or "the Natch Hist," as Amy called it, with a summer internship when he was just a sophomore in high school. His had been a dirty job in invertebrate paleontology, down in the cavernous basement of the museum, sifting through many cubic yards of compacted mud brought in from a dig in Texarkana, searching for tiny pre-Cambrian fossils. Lou enjoyed the precision and mess of the work; it was like panning for gold. He worked all alone at his table and sink under the bright work lights in the otherwise dark, moist space filled with forgotten objects and curios and obsolete equipment stacked against the oozing brick walls.

Whenever he found an especially good specimen, he would set it aside for Eric Bowman, the paleontologist whose project this was. Eric stopped by to see how it was going twice a day, and he always congratulated Lou extravagantly on the fossils he had found, as if Lou himself had intuitively known just how and where to extract the hypothesis-confirming specimens from beneath the earth's crust.

The regular vibration of the passing subway trains made the overhead lights sway, and sometimes Lou felt as if he were down in the hold of some vast cargo ship. He never knew what the day-

time weather was like that whole summer. It was always cool in
the basement. There was a dirt-encrusted radio on the table, but
Lou had no idea if it worked, as he never turned it on. He liked
working against the rhythm of the reliable train rumble that came
every few minutes, then the vacuum of silence that followed,
which was gradually filled in by the constant clicking, dripping,
slithering basement sounds of the museum guts, then the growing
rumble of the next train.

All the staff liked him and various curators and assistants found
other projects for him after that. By the end of college he had held
part-time, weekend, or summer jobs in almost every department.
He cataloged hundreds of Indian artifacts, including a collection
of ancient, nearly petrified moccasins. He spent a long weekend
replacing wall texts that contained the word "Indian" with wall
texts that said "Native American"; the museum was ahead of its
time in political correctness. Dangling from precarious scaffold-
ing, he dusted dinosaur bones, late at night, while the museum
was closed and still. Dressed in a makeshift loincloth, he had once
participated in a discreet emergency extermination program target-
ing rats that had set up housekeeping in a World of Man diorama.

Lou cleaned the graffiti off the now politically unacceptable
Teddy Roosevelt statue on the front steps once a week for a year.
He sorted thousands of crumbling, nineteenth-century bird nests.
In ichthyology, he topped off the alcohol in the tank holding the
coelacanth caught off the east coast of Africa in 1938. One winter
he spent every weekend cataloging meteorite fragments, and then
seeds and nuts, and after that amber specimens with insects tens of
thousands of years old trapped inside each one. Lou made labels
for thousands of beetles one entire summer. In the museum's
twenty-five interconnected buildings, there were huge stacks of
drawers filled with the damndest things, he discovered, lining the
hallways almost everywhere he went. If you opened enough drawers you could sooner or later find everything that had ever been
made by people or that had ever existed in the natural world.

There was a permanent job waiting for Lou in the Museum Services craft shop after his graduation from Columbia with a degree in Earth Sciences, and he had worked there ever since. His responsibilities were varied, but the electronic and increasingly more complex technologies that he employed in creating lighting and mechanical solutions for the museum over the years led him to experiment with building some crackpot inventions that he had begun to sketch out and imagine during his off-hours, just around the time he met Janet.

Reader's note: Boring, boring, boring! This is totally dragging! How much family history will most readers be willing to tolerate? You've got our family displayed behind glass in a museum diorama. See them in their natural habitat! Where's the gift shop? I want to get a Wonderful Green Family T-shirt. MG

Reader's note: I don't think it's boring at all. I like it. But readers like you can always skip ahead to the next chapter. That's what I do when I'm reading a novel and I get to parts that don't interest me. AG

Reader's note: A good writer leaves out the parts that readers would skip. MG

Author's note: The informed reader should be willing to take it on faith that there is worthwhile information in these pages. This isn't simply family history so much as it is the history of the family as perceived by the three sisters, which in turn casts light on their response to their mother's breach of faith.

Reader's note: Surely I qualify as an "informed reader" and I say it's boring. What are you trying to prove here? MG

Reader's note: What you call boring, our sister calls the requirements of fiction. AG

Reader's note: I think she's lost her grip on what serves her novel and what serves her need to report on actual events for her own reasons. MG

Author's note: Nobody else will read this novel through the lens through which you both inevitably see.

Reader's note: Not true. I can name at least a dozen people who have a personal stake in what you're doing here. MG

Author's note: With any novel, there are inevitably a handful of individuals who cannot read it at face value. I am concerned with the experience of every other reader outside our circle.

Reader's note: So entertaining strangers means more to you than trampling on the feelings of your friends and relatives? MG

Reader's note: Our sister is not just entertaining strangers, she's enhancing their intellectual experience as readers while she advances her career. But I still like this part of the novel. AG

Author's note: Your opinions are duly noted for all the world to see.

Just weeks before Meg was born, when they had been married for a little more than three years and Lou had worked at the museum for eight years, Janet and Lou moved from Waverly Place to the big apartment on the Upper West Side in which their three daughters would grow up. They were suddenly able to afford the price of the rambling apartment on West Seventy-fifth Street because of a remarkable bequest from Lou's great-aunt Hodgson, a spinster psychoanalyst who had worked with Anna Freud in London for several years. Great-aunt Hodgson was his father's aunt. She had lived and practiced in New Haven after the War, and Lou had only met her occasionally throughout his life, at holidays mostly, and then she had discreetly stashed herself away in an "assisted living" facility for her final years. She had evidently approved of him, more than he ever knew from his rather awkward and formal chats with her from time to time. The bequest was shockingly, life-changingly generous.

At first Janet had missed the five-minute walk to work—she had found her niche as a Victorianist in the NYU English Department at a young age—but the commute was a small sacrifice for the wonderful space and light of their apartment. It was, in fact, such a perfect home for them that none of the Greens, until the time of the precipitating events of this story, could imagine ever living anywhere else.

The bequest allowed Lou to stop working at the museum and devote himself full-time to his inventions. He would never know if this was the sort of thing that Great-aunt Hodgson had in mind when she left him her money, but he hoped she would have approved of the decision.

Lou's workshop, where he designed the oddly appealing devices that were destined for so much success, one after another, was situated beside the big, airy living room, in a room that would ordinarily have been used for dining, but the apartment's front entrance hall was so spacious they had simply put a big dining room table there instead, and Lou had designed double-sided bookshelves that effectively walled off his work space from the clamor of family life. The dining room in the front hall was pleasantly welcoming. Whenever the Greens were gathered at the table eating a meal, Lou could reach out to open the apartment door from his place at the head of the table, simply by leaning back, in order to greet any late-arriving family member or guest.

Amy's room was across the hallway from the others, sharing a wall with Lou and Janet's bedroom, so it lacked the privacy in which her sisters luxuriated; Lou and Janet never heard them when they stayed up too late, while Amy was often instructed to get off the telephone and go to sleep. It wasn't really fair. On the other hand, as a croup sufferer in her toddlerhood, she had been closer to parental comforts in the night. Joanna had once been furious at her parents when they failed to hear her coughing and gagging miserably for hours while she had lain in bed expecting their ministrations. Finally she had vomited and even then Meg had been the one to soothe her before going to wake their parents. ("I'm sorry, I'm sorry, I'm sorry! Now stop torturing me with that! Save it to tell your analyst!" Janet had finally snapped at Joanna when she brought it up for perhaps the twentieth time a good three years after that bad night.)

There was a long, narrow playroom occupying the windowless space, really an oversized hallway, which connected Meg's room to Joanna's, which also could be reached through a shared bathroom. When they grew older, the shelves of toys and games that lined this space gave way to books and CDs, and their shared music system. (This was also the spot where both Meg and Amy first kissed a boy with any seriousness, during certain socially pivotal parties, though each thought it was a secret from the others.)

Reader's note: Hey! AG

Reader's note: What do you expect? Be glad for all the private moments and the little humiliations and traumas in your life that have not been described by the end of the novel. MG

Their parents' bedroom, a cozy place where the girls had always felt welcome for Sunday morning snuggles, was as bright as the playroom was dark, as it had light coming in from two sides. There was a floor-to-ceiling bookshelf lining a third wall, and in an alcove beside the bathroom Janet kept her old rolltop desk from her childhood, which she mostly used for paying bills and filing household paperwork, as she rarely worked at home unless she was grading student papers. The so-called den was actually a tiny room off the kitchen, not much larger than a generous walk-in closet, which was originally intended to be a maid's room. It was the perfect study carrel, with the shared computer, shelves, reference books, and room for very little else. (It was here that Amy would find the incriminating e-mail message.)

Their kitchen looked like something from the cover of a vintage Fannie Farmer cookbook, and it was a wonderful, inviting place in which to cook, with every implement or pot you might need somehow just where you would expect to find it when you opened a drawer or cupboard. Janet was a highly competent, intuitive, and inventive cook, in a slapdash sort of way, and there were always interesting things to eat in this kitchen.

When they moved in, the kitchen had seemed a miracle: a perfectly preserved museum of original kitchen furnishings, circa 1930, in nearly mint condition, the previous residents having very mysteriously inflicted no signs of wear. The Greens had made very few changes over the years, beyond the soapstone sink from Vermont and a granite countertop that replaced one of worn Formica. The red Bakelite knobs on the white enamel cupboard doors glowed like chiseled rubies. Each of the girls had secretly tasted them at some point.

Long before feng shui was something people in New York had ever heard of, the Greens' apartment had good feng shui. There was nothing immediately special about the furniture or the way the rooms were arranged. There was just some indescribable essence of rightness in those rooms—the way sunlight fell generously through the windows at all hours onto the geometrically patterned hooked rugs that were scattered over the plain wood floors all through the apartment; the way ordinary museum posters looked especially rich and meaningful when framed and hung in oddly low spots on the walls (they were low so the children could see them from the floor when they were small); the way the front hall door clicked shut, just so; the way any music sounded marvelous when played on their crazy mess of stereo equipment, which featured the old KLH speakers that Lou had in college.

The Green family apartment was one of those places that felt more right than any place you had ever been, except that couldn't be true or it wouldn't seem so perfectly familiar; it wouldn't make you feel as if it reminded you of some other wonderful place you

must have once visited long ago, a place you had forgotten until
now. Spending time with the Green family made people simultaneously content and filled with longing.

Reader's note: You said this already. What's the point? AG
   Author's note: There is a difference between repetition and reiteration
of a theme.
   Reader's note: It seems repetitious. MG
   Reader's note: I don't mind it here, though it makes me sad. AG
   Author's note: Regrettably and at the risk of true repetition, it must be
pointed out one more time that this is a work of fiction.
   Reader's note: I don't see how your repeated declarations that this is fic-
tion support your argument especially. MG

The piano in the living room was covered in framed family photographs, each of which seemed to document a lustrous family
event. The rack held tattered Rodgers and Hart scores. There was a
wonderful dog, too, the Airedale named Soames, who struck even
the people who had lived their whole lives convinced until this
moment that they didn't like dogs as one of the most graceful and
intelligent animals they had ever been privileged to encounter.
   When the three Green children were babies, they were so pro-
foundly cute that more than one purposefully single, career-
obsessed colleague of Janet's—truly, these were, in a couple of
cases, hard-core politically nonpropagative feminists who were
openly critical of Janet for abandoning her maiden name—after
simply stopping by for a drink in the adorably bourgeois Green
household, had left in a confused, ovulating state, anguished and
bereft in her childlessness. One dazzled poly, bi, nonpropagative
Marxist, famous for her *Queer Lear* studies, had even stopped at the
newsstand on the corner to buy an armload of magazines on her
way home, and had then been compelled to claim to her partners

that she had acquired *Good Housekeeping, Gourmet, Family Circle, Working Mother*, and *Child* for entirely ironic purposes, something about an essay she had in mind.

Ending an encounter with the Greens could feel like a personal tragedy, a terrible fate. People would get in the elevator after an evening with the five Greens that would have involved simple yet brilliantly inventive food, hilarious and deeply meaningful conversation about everything in the world, perhaps the singing of old half-forgotten show tunes with Janet or Meg at the piano, and it would just be devastating, the idea of having to leave. This was especially so if there had been a game of Blink, a complex and thrilling family card game played in teams which also involved dice, dominoes, checkers, and Monopoly money, the playing of which occupied three separate rooms and took a minimum of two hours for the short version.

Sometimes guests were treated to an "order," which was the name for a ritual in which the three girls, having got into their beds for the night, would call out the commands for a sequence of good-night visitations from parents and honored guests in a particular order, the meaning and significance of which was known only to the Green sisters themselves. After such a night, departing guests would feel that they had just missed total happiness by mere seconds, somehow.

Growing up, the three Green sisters loved everything about their building, a classic of Upper West Side prewar proportion and elegance grimed by the unkindness of time. The girls sentimentally cherished every feature: the clouded mirrors, the ornately carved and now heavily chipped stonework at the entrance, the yellowed marble and granite features in the lobby and hallways, the thickly varnished panels lining the elevator, the surprising stone gargoyles that loomed in the mailroom. They assumed that everyone who lived there felt the same way.

Certain of their neighbors doted upon the Green family. Very small stuffed animals appeared in their mailbox with some regularity for several years, gifts from Sol Rabinowitz from across the hall, a button wholesaler who had some sort of connection with a stuffed animal company which used his buttons for eyes.

Then there was Kromesky, as he called himself mononymously, a science fiction writer of indeterminate age who lived silently in the apartment right over them. He didn't exactly dote on the Greens—he was, unlike most people, simply indifferent to the girls—so much as crave the approval of Janet and Lou. Meg thought he smelled strangely of some citrus product, and it was in any case weird that he never seemed to have any visitors.

Joanna reported on the disturbing quantities of Jones Little Link sausage boxes that were always spilling out of the trash can beside his kitchen door on the back stairs (she liked the province of the service stairs, for the same reasons she liked play rehearsals and orchestra tune-ups), and Amy especially thought his lemony smiles, when they met in the elevator, were fake, like clown smiles. Kromesky frequently left offerings of his used copies of obscure and costly British literary periodicals on their doormat, along with the very occasional issues of the old-fashioned science fiction magazines in which his gothic stories appeared.

Some of their neighbors in the building seemed compelled to provide the Greens with a constant supply of baked goods. When the girls were very little, there had been sweet tiny Mrs. Wisniewski in 2B, no taller than Amy when she was seven, whose dense yet ethereal orange sponge cake recipe could never be duplicated, though Amy and Joanna tried for years and came close a couple of times, and whose funeral was the first the Green sisters ever attended. Then there were the spinster sisters O'Brien from the ninth floor, retired public school teachers from County Cork whose Christmas cookies were spackled with pink frosting which Lou diagnosed with terrible certainty as consisting entirely of lard, sugar, and food coloring.

In more recent times there were perfumey (in a good, though nonstandard way, owing to the cardamom and rose water) apple pies from Harris the Maid, as everyone called him, a compact gay man with a goatee and ponytail who was unabashed about identifying himself as someone who earned a living cleaning apartments in a latex maid's uniform (he had a loyal clientele and a waiting list, both top secret).

The Green sisters grew up with the confident expectation that many of the residents at 165 West Seventy-fifth Street were as close as family, which was absolutely true. Given that both of their parents were only children, which meant that they had no first cousins, and given that by the time they were in high school their two remaining grandparents, whom they had hardly known anyway, had died, it was especially nice that they could count on the fond attentions of their neighbors.

There was always a good supply of loving adults around to remember birthdays, attend school plays, and be really interested in and charmed by homemade Green family Halloween costumes. (Amy especially put a lot of effort into her costumes as she grew older and was frequently disappointed when they were simply too obscure for their meanings to be clear without explanation, as, for example, when she went trick-or-treating as a shooting star in a Garbo mask, wielding a six-shooter.) Janet and Lou were grateful for the attention to their children, but they certainly didn't engineer it—there were just always people around who wanted to do things for the girls.

There were invitations for chess lessons (for Meg, and sometimes Joanna, from ancient Mr. Anderson on the third floor, who had once played Bobby Fischer to a draw) and watercoloring afternoons (for Amy, with Irving Getz in the so-called penthouse, a drafty sun-filled studio littered with a half century of his illustrations for various magazine covers). There was even, on one occasion, a demonstration of optimum cleaning techniques. (This was for Joanna, in eighth grade, because she was really interested, and so she spent a long, fascinating afternoon learning from Harris the Maid about the sins of "blind vacuuming" under beds and also how to maintain a glisten on latex clothing with the judicious application of a product called Perv-O-Shine.)

Mike the doorman thought of them as his favorite family, and not because they gave him the biggest Christmas tip, which they didn't (that would be Harris, who rewarded him for all the usual doorman services plus a great deal of extra discretion), but because of the kind way they spoke to one another. Doormen hear a lot of very unpleasant things that people say to each other when they are going out or coming home and they don't realize anyone else is listening.

Picture for a moment all five of the Greens together, crammed in a coffee shop booth eating club sandwiches and french fries and arguing passionately about a movie. Amy has requested butter instead of mayonnaise for her sandwich, which always disgusts her sisters, and she is happily unwrapping the gold foil "butter presents" brought by the waiter. They're a genetic equation written out for all the world to see: one tall attractive man plus one tall attractive woman equals three tall attractive daughters. Mendel's pea plants were no more perfectly expressive than the harmony of the Green family features and coloring. There was something deeply satisfying about the sight of them. They made people feel the way you do when you have bought a terrific present for someone. The anticipation of giving the gift makes you feel especially generous and loving.

Reader's note: Really, really enough! This is getting obsessive and embarrassing. Surely even the most dull-witted reader who's been skipping around gets the point by now. It's a wonderful, terribly attractive family. It's time to move on. MG

Author's note: Nabokov said the good reader should notice and fondle details; I have taken that as a suggestion about what the good writer should provide. The last few pages of this chapter might have a more subtle cumulative narrative impact had they not been interrupted by this commentary, which has gone well beyond the boundaries of the original agreement at several points and has begun to verge on the most unintellectual and intrusively presumptuous sort of literary criticism.

Reader's note: Oh, come on. Who do you think you're fooling with that pompous literary tone? AG

Reader's note: If you're so sure of yourself as a practitioner of the high art literary tradition, why do you sound so defensive when we challenge your narrative strategy? MG

Reader's note: And anyway, a deal's a deal. AG

Growing up in the snugness of their family, Meg, Joanna, and Amy each felt a natural entitlement to approval, the way a person blessed with perfect facial features might look into a mirror in full expectation of seeing, every single morning, an exquisite, familiar face. The Green sisters were certainly always aware of the way people responded to them as a family. The approval they felt glowing around them no doubt influenced, for better or worse, their own way of responding to one another.

Because one of the first things anyone noticed was that they always had a terrific kind of intense engagement with one another, no matter where they were or what they were doing, the sisters could usually sense this, and always felt a little bit on display, a little bit as if in the middle of some sort of lifelong performance. After all, complete strangers noticed something dazzling about the Green family when they walked down the street.

"What a wonderful family!" Amy and Joanna and Meg once heard a woman actually exclaim to the man walking beside her as she passed them, giving voice to what so many people felt. The

girls were trailing behind their parents on a spring vacation afternoon on their way to the Park, illicitly picking pansies and petu-
nias for doll bouquets from the occasional tubs of flowers flanking
the stoops that lined the street.

Soames, the opinionated Airedale (in the future, each of the
five Greens would look upon his not unexpected death ten years
later, in the spring of Meg's sophomore year at Yale, as the beginning of the bad times that followed), had been swerving at their
father's side while their mother, who could read and walk at the
same time, read aloud from the draft of an article she was writing
for a literary journal. (The article would become the basis for her
first really significant publication three years later, a book about
Angria, Gondal, and Glass Town, the secret worlds of the Brontë
children. The book* would attract a great deal of attention and
advance her academic career significantly.)

The three sisters hopped adroitly over sidewalk cracks for purposes of an ongoing competition with complex rules about which
nobody agreed. Amy, a fiercely independent five-year-old, claimed
to be ahead by ten thousand points at least. The sisters exchanged
thrilled looks at the woman's remark. *What a wonderful family!*
Each in her own way traversed the remaining blocks to the Park
with a little more grace, a little more consciousness of her place in
the world.

Meg stopped playing the game and simply walked in her most
ladylike manner, placing one foot with great deliberation in front
of the other, heel to toe, heel to toe.

Joanna landed on sidewalk squares with graceful leaps the way
she had seen ballerinas leaping in *Swan Lake* (which she had been
taken to see at Lincoln Center not long before), immediately
springing to the next, and the next, feeling as if she could hover
above the sidewalk with the same floating ease she possessed in so

---

*Janet Green, *Secret Places: The Imaginative Worlds of Angria, Gondal, and Glass Town* (New
Haven: Yale University Press, 1992).

many dreams. *I will always remember this moment,* she told herself, as she often did at times when a feeling of completeness and perfection was so unbearably exquisite that she could tolerate it only as an anticipated memory to be savored. She thought of such occasions as "moments." (Looking back on her childhood from her twenties, she could conjure up a series of these moments like a collection of perfectly preserved butterflies, each pinned to memory by this declaration.)

Amy skipped daintily in a complicated pattern, racking up even more disputed points, singing to herself, "wonderful, sunderful, moonderful, family," over and over.

It was a moment that each of the sisters would remember with perfect clarity. Of course, when they had occasion to discuss it over breakfast some eleven years later, while eating greasy omelets with limp french fries in a booth at the Copper Kitchen on Chapel Street in New Haven, they didn't remember it the same way.

Amy thought it was the same day they saw the man with the spider monkey that got loose and went up a tree after stealing the camera from the Japanese tourists in Sheep Meadow, but Joanna was certain it wasn't even the same year, though she agreed that when it did happen, whenever it was, Soames had barked and barked, not at the monkey but at the comically hysterical group of Japanese tourists.

Joanna was pretty sure she was dressed in her ballet outfit and it must have been after a dance class recital, though Amy and Meg assured her that she had been dressed in ordinary clothing that day, and, in fact, hadn't even started taking ballet classes yet.

Meg recalled with absolute clarity her own red, polka-dotted dress with a wide belt and that she was wearing matching lipstick, while carrying the precious antique Chanel handbag that had belonged to their maternal great-grandmother, a classic black leather purse with a fourteen-carat gold clasp. Both Amy and Joanna were positive that Meg had received that coveted handbag for her twelfth birthday, which came a full three years after the afternoon in question, and the dress she described was one that had belonged to their mother before any of them were born and which they had admired in a photograph in one of the family albums.

So they didn't agree about any of the details of this day except the lady who said they were a wonderful family. They all agreed about that.

THREE

Leaving

Their sense of order had been annihilated. Restoring it was an impossibility. What had become of their wonderful family on that hot July night? Lou's refusal to admit any anger toward Janet, his refusal to join them in their disapproval and condemnation, was in some ways even more infuriating and inexplicable to his daughters than was their mother's original horrific offense. Nearly a month of bitter, largely unspoken discord had passed, during which time their parents were totally united in their complete unwillingness to engage with their daughters in further debate on this painful subject. The obvious solution became clear to Meg, Joanna, and Amy. They would leave.

They informed their parents perfunctorily. Joanna and Amy would move in with Meg. To the exceedingly rational Janet and Lou, it seemed at first like an absurd, teenage scheme, an adolescent storm that would blow over in a matter of days, with time to spare before classes at Warren Prep began, if the girls could finally exhaust their rage with a lot of perfectly healthy and dramatic leave-taking. They had absolutely no idea that as far as the girls were concerned, their family was truly shattered.

Reader's note: Why don't you show the actual moment when the three sisters decide that this is their solution? And why don't you show the confrontation, when they announce their plan to their parents? MG

Author's note: It didn't seem necessary to the momentum of the story to depict each moment in time. A narrative can indicate in all sorts of ways events that are about to take place or have already occurred. These are the choices a novelist makes on every page of a novel—what is left out as much as what is depicted. The uninvolved reader understands and accepts this.

Reader's note: But in the end, is there ever really such a thing as the uninvolved reader? MG

Author's note: The ideal reader has nothing personal at stake.

Reader's note: Oh no, not so. The ideal reader should have everything personal at stake. MG

Reader's note: When the author of this novel was a child, in all of her drawings the people always had their hands in their pockets. Although she would offer various psychological or symbolic explanations, there was a simpler excuse—she couldn't draw hands. AG

Author's note: Pointless interruptions in this text are as regrettable as they are unavoidable. Apologies once again to the reader who feels compelled to read these notes.

Reader's note: So you just couldn't write those scenes. MG

Author's note: I have my own reasons for not including those scenes. Those moments are implicit in the narrative. Every moment cannot possibly be described or every novel would be thousands of pages long. Readers accept the implied events of any story.

Reader's note: She had her own reasons for all those hands in all those pockets, too. AG

The morning Meg drove up to New Haven, the three sisters stood close together in the street beside the Subaru while Mike, the doorman who had known each of them from the day they were born, tied a few more superfluous, loopy knots in the stiff hanks of clothesline that zigzagged over their bicycles. Finally, having duly thanked the diligent and now perspiration-soaked doorman, Meg got behind the wheel and shut the driver's door. Rolling down her window and leaning out, Meg said in a low voice, "Guys, aren't you even a little worried about Janet and Lou? I mean, once they buy a clue? No matter how much they deserve each other, I'm anxious about them. I mean, one minute they're oblivious and everything is fine, and then the next minute they had some kind of anxiety attack that I didn't want them to come down the street to see me off, for God's sake, like I couldn't find my way without Lou's special advice about how to get to the Bronx."

"I think anxiety is very interesting," said Amy. No one said anything for a moment after that. Meg sat still for a moment in the baked heat, her eyes closed, a hand splayed on her forehead in a gesture that reminded both Amy and Joanna in an unfortunate way, they agreed as soon as Meg fastened her seat belt, started the car, and drove off, of their mother.

"That hand on the head thing really spooked me, you know?" Joanna said.

"Oh, my aching thoughts! My precious mind! My sensitive self! I can't believe how Janet that was," Amy concurred, mimicking the gesture cruelly.

Meg had to organize her schedule and get it approved, she had told them, and that wasn't a lie, though she had many days of what is known at Yale as shopping period to nail down her schedule. Mostly she was eager—anxious, really—to meet with their putative roommate Teddy Bell, the eccentric junior she had known only slightly the previous term in an American Studies seminar. She had phoned him at a number in Maine she was able to obtain from the Silliman Master's office by dint of deviousness and subterfuge, she was so wild with desperation, and for unknown and possibly not great reasons, he had agreed at the last minute to ditch his very desirable single room in Silliman and throw in his lot with the Green sisters.

Joanna and Amy were more than a little concerned about what sort of flake would agree to set up housekeeping with Meg and her two high-school-age sisters in an apartment on High Street on the strength of one phone call from someone he knew from across a seminar table. But even if he was completely gross or perverted, or merely crazy, Meg pointed out, though he had seemed none of those things in class, she promised, they needed him—they desperately needed his three-hundred-dollar share of the rent—and it was tremendously fortunate that he had been willing to do it, never mind why.

Meg had originally planned to share the apartment with two other juniors—Jennifer Goldsmith and Jennifer House, both known by Meg before Yale, as one had been in her class at Warren and the other had been on her Putney Student Travel trip to France that summer after graduation. But both of them had balked at the news that Joanna and Amy would be moving in. Within hours of Meg's call to each Jennifer to let them know of her family crisis and to check that it would be okay for her sisters to stay for at least a couple of months into the semester, Jennifer and Jennifer had bailed out on Meg and the perfect three-bedroom High Street apartment in the legendarily seedy Oxbridge Arms that they had all loved so much in June, leaving her entirely responsible for the rent. (Meg had, after all, been the one who had agreed to stay an extra day in New Haven to take care of signing the lease after finals, and Lou, who had driven up to New Haven to help her move her things down to the city for the summer, had been co-signer.)

But one of the Jennifers had at least thought of Teddy Bell, whom she knew from some singing group, so that was something. Teddy Bell was really okay, Meg kept saying, apparently attempting to reassure herself as much as her sisters. Meg was pretty sure he was from Maine or New Hampshire, or maybe it was a farm in Vermont—he had said things in class that made her think so, when they were reading Hawthorne. She remembered, too, that he could be funny. Beyond that, she couldn't really say what he was like.

"Leave it to Meg to be so spacey about someone who's going to be living with us," Joanna said to Amy at the nearest Starbucks on Broadway, where they tended to roost for hours at a time as part of their total parental avoidance strategy in those final desultory days, and where they had gone for iced lattes that afternoon, after Meg drove off. Joanna's job that summer was at a different branch of Starbucks, a dozen blocks farther south. She was highly critical of the inconsistently prepared iced lattes at this location.

"This Teddy Bell who is maybe, what, an amusing boy from Vermont, so, what, he's going to be our great maple syrup connection? Is that all we know about him? If he had been in a class with me," Amy said, dumping yet another packet of pale brown sugar into the dregs of watery coffee and ice cubes in her plastic cup, "for one thing, I would be able to describe him to my sisters. I mean, Meg can't even tell us what he *looks* like very clearly. Do you think she really doesn't remember, or do you think she knows and won't tell us what a weirdo he is?" Amy stirred her sugary sludge vigorously with her straw and then slurped it down.

"Maybe he's weird but in a good way," Joanna began, "like, you know, like us, the way we're weird. Maybe—"

"And I would know where he had gone to elementary school," Amy continued her relentless catalog. "And camp, and where his family spends their summers, and what his father does, and his astrological sign, and if he had a dog, and I would know who his friends are, what kind of music he likes, what books changed his life, what TV shows he watches. I would know a zillion things about him. I mean, what if he's some freak? What if this is the revenge of the Jennifers? What if he's a complete techno-geek with a homemade Star Trek uniform, or he's a Buffy freak, or he has terrible personal hygiene, or some completely bizarre personality disorder or deformity Meg never even noticed? He could be a total Diane Arbus person! And then everyone will think we're so nice for pretending we don't notice! How could she know nothing about this guy? Don't you think that's pretty shady?"

"I think we should just count on his being sketchy or maybe some kind of freak," Joanna said. "If he wasn't, why would he want to live with us?"

FOUR

High Street

🌿

Teddy Bell was not a freak. Crunchy-preppy, Joanna thought when he met them on the stairs that first time. A little too tucked in and crisp and mainstreamish to qualify as a trustafarian, though from Meg's vague reports about his background, he might be on the cusp. (Joanna was forever slotting people into pigeonholes, and she did it with the reckless speed and acumen of a postal worker, which is to say her percentages were good but she rarely got everything perfectly right.) She and Amy had just paid a disconcerting amount of money for a brief, urine-smelling cab ride from the New Haven train station, and though Meg had warned them that she wouldn't be waiting in the apartment because it was Yale's shopping period and she had to attend some classes that met at overlapping times, Amy, typically, just couldn't resist pressing the buzzer marked with a new GREEN / BELL label printed in Meg's block letters.

"But it's black," Amy said, after a moment of silent purposeless waiting on her part, while Joanna was in any case fumbling with the ring of indistinguishable keys Meg had given her. The small lobby was disappointingly dingy, and Joanna privately hoped its faintly urinaceous atmosphere had arrived with them as a lingering memento of their taxi ride and wasn't going to be an olfactory theme of their new lives.

"What is?" she snapped, irritated, not sure that any of the five identical-looking keys worked the lobby lock. Apparently, none of them did. She dropped everything she was carrying in order to try each key again with both hands free. Finally, one did work. It was one of those unwieldy turn-while-shoving lobby door locks. Their four heavy duffel bags and Amy's bulky drawing portfolio awkwardly filled the little tiled entryway. Joanna had a fleeting nostalgia for Mike the doorman.

"The bell. The bell button, anyway. It's a black bell button. It's a Bell bell button. If Teddy Bell lived in Bilbao then it would be a Bilbao Bell black bell button. And if it broke, the electrician who repaired it would send him a—"

"—Bilbao Bell black bell button bill," Joanna muttered in accompaniment, at last turning the correct key in the lock. Everyone in the family was used to Amy's echolalic habit, and it was customary to join her in the concluding chorus, which helped hurry the word attack to its conclusion. Joanna flung the lobby door open and with her foot she nudged the biggest duffel bag across the gritty floor toward the bottom of the stairs.

Unfortunate long-term cooking smells wafted through the building, which felt deserted. The aroma was of the type their mother called Body Odor Curry. Why would anyone willingly consume something that gave off that sort of stench? Joanna had the impulse to report to her mother on this manifestation. Then came the painful awareness, a little shock of rediscovery, the sort of reknowledge one keeps having when there has been a recent death, that her mother was no longer someone to whom her middle daughter reported about anything.

The bass line from somebody's over-amped stereo thumped faintly overhead. The building was not deserted after all. There were perhaps twenty apartments in the Oxbridge Arms, Meg had said, all occupied by Yale undergraduates except for a pair of little old ladies on the ground floor in the back, who had lived there since the Truman administration because of some law that allowed them to pay an infinitesimal rent indefinitely, much to the sorrow of the rapacious landlord, who preferred to rent to an ever-changing population of prosperous undergraduates with parents willing to fund the slumlike living arrangements that are a requisite element of any decent Ivy League education.

The Grouch Sisters, as they were known in the oral tradition of the Oxbridge Arms, were possibly a lesbian couple, or maybe they really were spinster sisters, no one was sure which. They were, in either case, presumably deaf. And deaf in the nose, too, unless they were the ones cooking up pots of foul-smelling stew as a passive-aggressive assault on noisy, inconsiderate students. They could probably remember when decent people lived in those apartments un-ironically, back when the hallway floor was clean and every other stair rail wasn't missing.

"Eew," said Amy, who was sensitive to odors of all kinds, a step behind Joanna.

Footsteps clattered down a flight of stairs overhead, then down a hallway, now down the stairs to the lobby. Although he had been on his way out, Teddy Bell flung himself to a halt on the bottom step to avoid a collision.

"Les autres sisters Verte, I presume? I'm Teddy. Was that you guys buzzing just now? Meg said you had keys. Hey, nice to meet you guys. Oh, good, you do have keys. Look, I'm terribly sorry, but see, there's this totally amazing class I'm supposed to be checking out, but wait, let me take that big one—"

Too bad about the goatish little beard thing on his chin, Joanna and Amy agreed, after he helped them carry their monstrous bags up the two flights before scampering off to class, late. Teddy Bell seemed friendly, civilized, rather pleasantly adult, actually— someone, in short, with whom it wouldn't be at all scary to share the apartment. And the bathroom. Amy was pleased, and said she thought he looked a lot like Meg, didn't he, almost the way a big brother would have looked if he had been born first in their family? And his mop of black hair seemed friendly, didn't it? Amy was practically babbling with relief. Joanna indulged her while noting to herself that she had liked him more than she could say, having been struck by something solitary and hungry in his eyes. Meg had done well after all, coming up with Teddy Bell for a roommate, when you considered all the possibilities of awfulness. The younger Green sisters were, they concluded, happy for what he was, and relieved for all he might have been and wasn't. They began to unpack.

Known for the occasional perfectly timed, carelessly uttered witticism in certain seminars, Edward Emerson Bell was secretly serious. Something about him—his posture, the tilt of his head, the flop of his hair, the way his perfectly ordinary clothes draped on his angular body—seemed of another time and place, though it would be hard to say what time and place that would be.

Contrary to Meg's vague impression from the seminar, he wasn't exactly a New Englander. His education before Yale had been at an international school in Paris, where he had lived most of his life, because of his father's work. (Alfred Bell, perfectly kind but utterly remote and formal as a father, had headed the Paris offices of a big New York law firm.) Yet Teddy didn't have the weirdly clipped and accentless English that is an accent of its own (the kind with which so many of his American schoolmates in Paris spoke, none of them having ever lived for very long in America).

Teddy's summers, after his mother's death in a terrible car accident in the Périgord the winter he turned seven (of which his strongest memory was his own broken arm, the unique sight of his father's tears, and the astringent smell of the hospital in Périgueux), were habitually spent on the coast of Maine, at his father's old family house. (Thus Meg's impression wasn't entirely wrong, just incomplete, as are, inevitably, most impressions.) There he had spent two months every summer until college, more or less alone with his widowed grandmother, the famously opinionated Avery Bell, feminist philosopher and writer of mysteries exemplifying those opinions.

Avery Bell's theory of boys was that they were not quite as bad as mosquitoes, though just as inevitable. Her theory of child management began and ended with benign neglect. And so Teddy, the only child of an only child, was left, happily enough, to seek out whatever company he liked. This was rarely his own cohort, once he outgrew desultory wasted hours of petty vandalism and pointless, boastful obscenity. Having become impatient with the local population his own age by the time he was thirteen, Teddy preferred to spend time with the lobstermen, the boatbuilders, and the crews who ran the makeshift ferries, most of them converted from retired lobster boats, which ran visitors out to the perpetually fog-shrouded islands that lay prettily on the horizon of the harbor view from his grandmother's porch. The last two summers in Long Harbor, Teddy worked regular shifts on the ferries, which he never would have been permitted to do had his father not died very suddenly of a heart attack in Paris the summer after Teddy's graduation from high school. The job would have annoyed his father as a pointless sort of make-work. It delighted his grandmother, who deplored the snobby tendencies of most of the summer people who populated Long Harbor on their predictable migratory schedule.

Teddy's speech habits, consequently, were like certain elements of his personality—an odd mixture of highly formal international diplo-brat correctness and coast-of-Maine colloquialism. Thus the occasional erroneous and unfair conclusion, reached by the occasional semi-observant person, that Teddy Bell was affected.

Sprinting across Old Campus that first afternoon, late for class, Teddy Bell had no idea, of course, that there had been anxious speculation about his possible freakishness or unfortunate motivations for wanting to live in the apartment on High Street with the three Green sisters. Why, indeed, had he agreed to it so readily at the last moment? Because of Meg.

Meg Green, calling him out of the blue, asking him to live with her and her sisters? It was like the manifestation of a daydream, like something he had willed into reality from his imagination. How could he resist that? Meg Green wasn't like anyone else he knew. He possessed very few actual facts about her. Something reminded him of old photos of his mother, but it was in a nice way, not a sick way, that he made this connection. Meg was old-fashioned, gracious, and competent, yet somehow not quite in her proper element as a college student, like someone Grace Kelly would play in a movie about a debutante who gets a job at a newspaper.

Meg Green, though not a bit of a flirt, had made eye contact with him for many lingering moments of connection, and she had somehow, without ever speaking directly to him, developed what felt to Teddy like a genuine (though intangible) sort of claim on him. He wouldn't have been able to explain this. Her term paper, "From Babbit to Rabbit: The Failed Male from Apex to Zenith," one of three chosen by the professor for discussion at the final class meeting, had knocked his socks off.

Just knowing that somewhere out there Meg Green was thinking her Meg Green thoughts, living her Meg Green life, had seemed sufficient to nourish Teddy's fascination over the summer. His intrigue was romantic in a sense, true enough, but not so very different from his fascination with Isabel Archer.

But then she had called him on the telephone and her Meg Green life had turned out to be quite unhappy and complex, and her Meg Green thoughts had turned out to be a tumult of worry and unhappiness that he, Teddy Bell, could assuage in an instant. It all seemed so perfectly inevitable. Would he really not mind living with her two younger sisters, was he certain? How could she even ask? What would be more welcome news than that there were two more Green girls, about whose existence he had known nothing until now? Ever since arriving at college, Teddy had fallen in love about once a month—small, brief flames that flared briefly and died in a quick blaze of hope, despair, and resignation. But his deep fondness for Meg Green was more enduring than that.

Meg knew this, of course. Girls have a way of allowing—really, encouraging—boys to develop all sorts of strong feelings of which they, girls, make satisfied note and then proceed to ignore most of the time, to the desperation or relief of the boys, depending on confidence levels. All through the previous school year, Meg had never really acknowledged Teddy's intensities, but from time to time there had been something between them—a casual gesture, a look, a slight touch—that she knew stirred him.

What was he thinking about on that still August afternoon, while Joanna and Amy were unpacking, as he hustled through Phelps Gate on his way to a music theory class in Hendrie Hall which he would presently decide, unimpressed by the last half of it as he would be, to drop from consideration on his schedule?

Teddy Bell was thinking of many things, as always. Often bothered by the stupidity of the world, he was, at the same time, quick to see and feel beauty of any kind. There was something beautiful and sad and precious about the Green sisters as an entity, and he hadn't even yet seen them all three together at the same time. He wanted to protect them from harm, from unhappiness, forever. He felt as if his life were beginning at last.

Teddy skimmed over the New Haven sidewalks, dodged the cars on Elm Street, and took the few steps of Hendrie Hall in a single leap, narrowly missing a collision with a lost freshman in a Yale T-shirt so new the fold creases still showed, gazing hopelessly at a Blue Book of course listings. Teddy was happy. Happy as Larry, the ferryman from Halifax, the one who rolled his own smokes and always called him Joe College, might say.

Reader's note: It seems strange "Teddy" isn't represented here with his own reader's notes in this manuscript before publication. AG

Reader's note: I urged him to comment but he declined. He disapproves of these reader's notes, in fact. MG

Author's note: I am especially grateful for the vote of confidence from all the interested individuals who read the manuscript at various stages and expressed their views directly to the author without resorting to demands for legal agreements requiring the public display of personal reactions to the text.

FIVE

Getting Along

❦

Joanna and Amy registered at Duncan High School on the following Wednesday, though Tuesday had been the official registration
day. That first morning, they had meant to go over to Duncan, but
as the hours passed, somehow they just didn't go, they just couldn't
make themselves show up. There had been so much to do in the
apartment, they persuaded themselves, to make it feel like their
own true home.

"Ambivalence, thy name is Jo-Jo and Amy," Meg reproved
them when she returned from class on the Tuesday afternoon of
what she had thought would be their first day of school, only to
find the two of them in the tank tops and shorts they had slept in,
bickering over closet space in their shared room and about where
towels should be stored and who should be the one to run out to
buy toilet paper, as there was none in the apartment. "Some of us
managed to take up our packs and get going hours ago," she
added, nearly tripping over the dark lumps that were her sisters'
backpacks, left carelessly in the hallway. "What have you been doing all day? Do I have to take you both over there myself?"

"We just weren't ready," Joanna admitted, emerging from the
closet with an armload of shirts. "We haven't rehearsed enough.

Amy and I weren't quite ready to face the hordes of New Haven. The hoi polloi."

"Is hoi polloi the rich fancy people or the common people? I can never remember which it is," Amy said.

"Common people, actually," Meg replied, flipping through the junk mail she had found stuffed in their mailbox. Pizza delivery and Chinese take-out flyers, coupons for a discount on one-hour eyeglasses at the dreary downtown mall. "Here," she said, thrusting the pile of flyers toward Amy. "This mess is all aimed at the hoi polloi. Oh, gross, special Hawaiian Pizza is only $4.99 with any other pizza. Tomato sauce, mozzarella, ham, and pineapple chunks. The hoi polloi special. Free delivery in our area."

"Eew," Amy agreed. "I guess I was thinking of hoity-toity. So it's one of those risky phrases, then," she continued, "because half the people you say it to think it means the opposite of the other half of the people you say it to."

"To whom you say it," muttered Joanna automatically. She had been folding shirts and sweaters and putting them away on the closet shelf and had just now completed the task.

"Janet talk!" Amy exclaimed in dismay.

"Sorry. Sorry. Bad habit."

"Isn't that my blue shirt I couldn't find a week ago?" Amy said, perusing the closet contents. "You thief, Jo-Jo. And you liar. You said you didn't have it."

"I forgot I had it, sort of," Joanna said guiltily. "Sorry. Take something of mine."

"I don't want your skanky clothes," Amy muttered.

"Fine, then forget about the green jacket you said you wanted to borrow," Joanna retorted.

"Stop it," Meg said. "Stop being babies. And you guys, we're completely out of toilet paper? Nobody on High Street ever has to buy toilet paper, we just take it from the women's bathroom in the basement of the British Art Center. Come on, empty that backpack and I'll show you where."

It was, after all that, shockingly easy to finesse their registration. Their Warren Prep transcripts had been sent, as per Joanna and Amy's somewhat imperious hand-delivered letters of request the previous week. Janet and Lou hadn't exactly agreed to this, but then Janet and Lou hadn't exactly disagreed with any of it either. Joanna felt bad about the tuition money already paid to Warren, a famously innovative school with a highly competitive admissions policy, and wondered if their parents would get any of it back at such a late date.

"Not our problem," Amy had said with a dismissive wave, but her eyes had grown round and her mouth had formed a silent little o when Joanna told her how much money their parents paid annually for her tuition at Warren Prep.

It was unlikely that the harassed woman behind the desk in the front office, or anyone else at Duncan, an overcrowded and decaying inner-city high school with an ongoing asbestos problem and three shooting incidents the previous spring, had scrutinized the transcripts with any care or interest on that Wednesday. In an hour, they were registered students at Duncan High.

Joanna and Amy, whose school lives had always, up until now, been the object of intense interest and involvement on the part of their parents and their teachers, had been needlessly concerned that they would have trouble without a parent to sign them up. The guidance counselor was in a hurry, there were lots of stragglers, and there were very few parents in view. It was all pretty disorganized. Nobody asked the questions the Green sisters had anticipated. They never got to use their rehearsed explanations about their mom's new job at Yale and the divorce and their move. Nobody even asked them why they were a day late.

Their claim of residency in New Haven was never questioned. Apparently, the photocopy of Meg's receipt for telephone service had been sufficient proof that some sort of Green family did in fact make its home at their High Street address. Perhaps Margaret Green was presumed to be their mother. Perhaps Margaret Green was presumed to be their crack-addicted great-aunt once removed who had custody of them because everyone else was in jail or rehab. It didn't matter. Nothing mattered.

"Duncan is just right for my mood," Amy said with angry conviction after school that first day. She and her sisters were at the table, picking at the refrigerated remains of their take-out Chinese dinner from the night before. Teddy was out, at a dinner meeting with some study group. "So first I walk through this totally sketchy neighborhood, then there are metal detectors at the doors, my classes are in these really horrible classrooms, there are kids saying things like 'Fuck your mother' in the hallways, some girl gang set a fire in a bathroom during fourth period, a weird girl was vomiting in the locker room—"

"Well, that was familiar, anyway," said Joanna.

"I'm not finished." Amy glared at her. "Don't interrupt me. You're always interrupting me. So when I left, when I was waiting for you out front, there was this skeevy guy standing right by the entrance saying 'smoke, smoke, smoke' with the stupid guard like two feet away acting totally blind and deaf. By the time you came out he was gone."

"Yeah, well, I didn't see the smoke guy, but otherwise, for what it's worth, that's pretty much my experience today, too," Joanna said. "Though when you think of it, there really always were girls vomiting between classes at Warren, too. That's all I was saying. That rich kids in New York probably vomit more than anyone else. But they do it more discreetly."

"God," said Meg. She was shocked (though not about the vomiting, as she herself had flirted with bulimia the spring of her senior year at Warren, though she didn't think Amy or Joanna knew anything much about that). Well, what had she thought it would be like? In her two years in New Haven, had she ever seen Duncan High? She had tutored a Duncan student last year as part of a

Dwight Hall program, but Marta, a shy Puerto Rican with very poor English who was now presumably attending the local community college she had aspired to, had met her on the Yale campus each time. It had never occurred to Meg to quiz her about the conditions at Duncan.

How could Meg have been so reckless as to suggest that her sisters could get an education in such a place? How would they ever get to college from here? Shouldn't Joanna be registered for SATs? Did Duncan even have a college guidance counselor? It must. But the local paper always had some headline about school budget cuts. Meg had never read the local paper. She read *The New York Times* and voted in New York. She suddenly realized that, like most everyone else she knew at Yale who wasn't a townie, she had treated New Haven simply as that space which one passes through to get from Yale to New York. She had no idea at all what Duncan was really like.

A cold wash of fear swept through Meg. For a moment, she doubted that they could do this at all—that *she* could do what was being asked of her. The burden of mothering her two sisters seemed suddenly overwhelmingly heavy. If life was as hard as this, she didn't see how they were to get through it.

"Are you guys totally sure you want to go there? It isn't too late to change your minds—Warren doesn't even start until after next week. I mean, you could try living at home and just not ever speaking to them, and you could come up here every weekend—"

Joanna was totally stunned, unable to make a sound at that instant. She felt as if she had been shot, Meg's easy betrayal was so sudden and devastating. She glanced at Amy, who had stood up from the table so abruptly that the flimsy bentwood chair tipped over behind her and clattered loudly on the bare floor.

"How could you say that? How could you even think it? Don't ever say that again!" shrieked Amy in a terrible, anguished voice. "Don't ever say it. Stop now. How could you even think it for one second? Take it back! Take it back! Oh, Meg, I thought we could trust you!"

"Amy—" Joanna wanted to remain calm, be the voice of reason, though in a funny way she was grateful to Amy for giving voice to the hysteria she felt. Meg looked miserable. Somebody was thumping up the stairs in the hallway, maybe Teddy. "Amy," Joanna began again, "please don't blame Meg."

Teddy's key rattled in the lock.

"Hello?"

He stood in the doorway, breathless from his sprint up the stairs. He liked to take the stairs two at a time. "Hey," he said. The air was thick with tension. He had an armload of apples snugged against his chest. "This guy brought a bushel of apples to the meeting." Teddy looked around the room questioningly and then, tilting forward from the waist, bowed in a gentlemanly gesture to drop the apples carefully onto the table. "They're from his uncle's or something, some kind of farm in Wallingford. Fucking Yale Co-op bag ripped on the street. No wonder they're probably going out of business with such crappy paper bags." He bent down to help Amy right her chair.

"Don't." Amy pushed his arm away rudely, as if he were an intrusive dog. Teddy backed up with raised eyebrows. The apples rolled and bumped against the Chinese food cartons.

"I think I'll just be in my room for a little while, now," Teddy said with exaggerated courtesy. "I'll just leave you little women to your delightfully atmospheric family get-together here. Carry on sharing and caring. Sorry to intrude."

"Yes, thanks. Great. Sorry, Teddy," Meg said over her shoulder to his retreating form.

"No problem." He stopped in the hallway. No one said anything. They knew he was still standing there. The three sisters looked at one another, waiting. After another moment, they heard his voice from the hallway.

"I guess this wasn't the moment to comfort you with apples."

"What's that from?" Joanna wondered. Janet would know. *Fuck.*

"Song of Solomon," Teddy said, reappearing momentarily in the doorway.

"Thanks, T, sorry we're so grumpy," Meg apologized again. "You're a pal."

"De rien, mesdemoiselles, pas de quoi, je vous en prie," he exclaimed in one of his several ridiculous accents, with a shrug. *"Je suis désolé de vous déranger,"* and he withdrew once more. His door closed a moment later and then they could hear the familiar sounds of Billie Holiday moaning softly about strange fruit hanging from the trees.

Joanna gave Amy a little shove on the arm and muttered, "You've a great want of manners, haven't you?" an ill-timed invocation of another of their mother's favorite lines. She knew the apples were for her especially, as she had an insatiable apple habit.

Meg wore an injured look. Amy glared at them both, first one and then the other, and then she shook her head and beat her fists on her thighs in frustration.

"Oh, Jo-Jo, don't you understand either? Doesn't anybody get it? It's just that I am so frustrated that I say something and I think I'm being clear and then everybody thinks it means the opposite. It's like the fucking hoi polloi thing. I'll apologize to Teddy in a little bit. Don't you understand what I was saying? I think Duncan is *perfect* for us," Amy said. "The disgustingness suits me just fine. And, Meg, please don't you go quoting Janet. Both of you do it all the time. All her little expressions. I just can't take it right now. Okay? All I'm saying is I think Duncan is perfect. I'll be fine. Joanna will be fine, won't you be all right with your classes, Jo-Jo? You're in honors French, right? With the smart kids? Tell Meg it's okay. And they said they would put you in honors English next term, right? And meanwhile you're probably the smartest kid in the class, so you'll get really good grades, which will be good for college applications, right? Make Meg see why this is exactly right for us!"

"Meg?" Joanna looked at her older sister questioningly.

"I'm just worried," Meg said. "There is just so much—"

"Don't be. We'll manage. We'll be okay with the school thing, really, but we can only do this if we stick together," Joanna said. "We know you're making a lot of sacrifices for us right now. We'll make it up to you someday, won't we, Amy? But if you bail on us now, without even giving it a chance—"

"I can't go back," Amy broke in fiercely. "I just can't. I won't. I can't. I just can't be with them right now. I want to stay here with you, Meg. I need to stay with you. So does Jo-Jo. We have to stay with you. We don't have anywhere else to go. I know you're not our mother, but you're all we've got right now. Don't you want us to stay with you?" Tears were running down Amy's face, and now Meg just couldn't stand it. She *would* shoulder this burden. She simply had to do this.

"So which is it, then?" Meg asked teasingly, taking Amy's hand and swinging it as if she were cajoling a toddler. She put her arms around Amy and hugged her. She uttered her question in a sly tone, invoking one of their mother's more despised philosophical inquiries—"A want or a need?"

"Oh, fuck you," Amy said, grinning now through her tears. "Fuck you very much indeed." She wiped her teary face with the heel of one hand.

"We'll manage, Meg, I know we will. We like adventures," Joanna declared, hoping desperately that what she said was true. "And we're going to find some."

Reader's note: When is something going to happen? This chapter is all very atmospheric, but if this is a novel shouldn't there be more plot by now? AG

 Author's note: Most readers appreciate the value of becoming intimately acquainted with the characters in a work of fiction.

Reader's note: Something has happened in this chapter—my sister has told the world about my bulimia. Thanks a lot. MG

Author's note: Do you want me to change it?

Reader's note: No, I want you to leave it in so your readers will know what sort of morality the author of this so-called novel really has, so they'll know who they're dealing with. MG

Author's note: With whom they're dealing.

Reader's note: There you go. MG

Reader's note: Whatever. I don't think it's so bad if the character has a history of bulimia, I mean, who doesn't? But I do think it's a perfect example of what's going on here. First there is a violation of a confidence and then the authoress justifies it with an intellectual theory, so any objecting to what she has done makes you and me look petty and unintellectual. Meanwhile, I don't see any major embarrassing revelations so far about the Joanna character. The middle sister is obviously the most mature and flawless member of the family. I can't wait for the reviewers to catch on to the whole self-serving and immoral strategy. AG

Reader's note: I doubt that reviewers can be counted on to right the wrongs perpetrated in these pages. MG

Author's note: Wilde said there is no such thing as a moral or an immoral book. Books are well written, or badly written.

Reader's note: I didn't suggest that the novel was immoral. I was referring to the author. AG

Author's note: In any case, the very existence of these notes in the published book is the remedy we all agreed to. You are both guilty of violating the spirit, if not the literal language, of the agreement, by persisting in making remarks that fall well outside the range of the intended function of these notes. The real repetitions and consequent failure to develop momentum in these pages lie not in the text of my novel but in your repeated accusations and my repeated explanations.

Reader's note: We can say what we want, when we want to, in these notes. The agreement guarantees that. MG

Author's note: Regrettably true.

SIX

Meg Finds Work

🌱

When your telephone doesn't ring, that will be me not calling you. Joanna couldn't remember where she had heard this. Was it a line from a song? Whatever. It was the message she mentally beamed at her mother and father several times a day.

Neither Lou nor Janet ever called or wrote, and Joanna thought this was a further example of their horrible behavior, though in truth, if either of them had phoned, she certainly wouldn't have been willing to engage in a conversation. Amy would probably just hang right up if she answered and heard one of those wise, familiar voices. Only Meg would probably listen, at least for a little while, to whatever either of her parents might have to say.

The silence from New York—which seemed self-involved to Joanna, and sanctimonious to Amy—made it all the more obvious to the three Green sisters that they would have to solve their money dilemmas on their own. Because with every day that passed, it became clearer how unrealistic they had been about managing their needs.

Meg had a monthly income from a small trust (established by the terms of Janet's mother's will) that had begun to provide a few thousand dollars a year when she turned eighteen. Though it would have just covered her living expenses if she had been on her own, now that Joanna and Amy were living in the apartment, with the additional expenses of groceries and a much bigger proportion of the rent and utilities, not to mention the countless other unexpected urgencies that seemed to drain their little reservoir of cash day after day, Meg had been forced to speak with someone at the bank to arrange a significant increase in her monthly check. She knew this meant she would have nothing left after senior year. But by then Joanna would have passed her eighteenth birthday and her trust would become available. Maybe that would last until Amy turned eighteen. And after they ran through Amy's money? Meg couldn't think that far ahead. They would have to stick together, that's for sure. There was just no way to ask Janet and Lou for anything at all, especially money.

Even with the plumper trust check, the money just seemed to melt away, with so much of it being reserved for rent, and in order to follow their strict budget, by the end of the week sometimes they really needed the money Joanna brought home from her after-school Starbucks job for their groceries. Was it possible to spend less? Joanna and Amy both thought they should give up the monthly space for the Subaru in the parking garage on Crown Street. True, it would save sixty-five dollars a month, but it would also mean endless time devoted to quests for street parking throughout the week, which Meg couldn't ask either of her sisters to do, since they didn't drive.

Meg had missed the deadline for applying for a Yale lot permit, which was almost as expensive as the garage, in any case. She knew people who moved their cars into the Yale lots every night when they were free, and then back onto the street again during the day when the lots were reserved for cars with permits, but it seemed like a bad idea to be enslaved to that schedule, especially with winter coming. Also it reminded Meg far too much of Lou's obsession with parking strategies on the Upper West Side, a skill that was a point of pride with him.

In any case Meg was reluctant to give up the garage. Something could happen to the car if it was perpetually parked on Lynwood or Edgewood, the streets with the best free parking. Dwight Street was also unmetered, but Meg had heard about two different daylight muggings in recent weeks, and it definitely wasn't a safe place after dark. And dark was getting earlier. And her Subaru had New York license plates, and she had heard that the New Haven police liked to make trouble for Yalies who parked out-of-state cars on the streets of New Haven. What's more, they couldn't afford the huge fine if the car were to be towed, and even one such episode would more than wipe out the money saved by parking on the street in the first place.

Teddy was persistently generous about his share of all the household expenses and he was also quite tolerant of all the pasta they consumed, but there were, after all, three of them and only one of him.

"But I'm a boy," he had pointed out to Meg the second week. "Boys are pigs, you know that. I eat a lot. I might just come in some nights and devour everything in the fridge. I might bring all my friends. Come on, let me kick in half the grocery tab. Why make this so hard? I've told you so many times now that I thought we should go halves in everything."

"Out of the question, Teddy, you've been so thoughtful with us as it is, and anyway, half of some of your things wouldn't suit me at all!" Meg had retorted lightly, touched by his kindness and anxious not to take advantage of his generosity, tempting as it was. She had never spent so much time thinking about money. She understood for the first time what people meant when they spoke of being "comfortable."

Meg spotted some job notices on the bulletin board over the copying machine in the English Department office when she was turn-

ing in a paper and had felt too neurotic about the paper going
astray to use the department drop box out in the hall, preferring
instead to put the paper directly in her professor's mailbox, although undergraduates were not supposed to do that. The notices
were there for the perusal of graduate students, but she realized
that she was qualified enough to make some money with little research jobs she could probably get done in a few hours of library
time during less intense moments of the semester.

"Can you really do that and still keep up with your work?"
Joanna had fretted. "Are you sure it's worth it?" It was a Sunday
afternoon, and they were walking on Chapel Street, window-
shopping and eating ice cream cones. The late September days still
had the feeling of summer and it was hard to stay indoors doing
schoolwork.

"You seem able to keep your Starbucks hours and get your
homework done."

This was true. Every day, Joanna went from her classes at Duncan to her afternoon job at the Starbucks right on their High
Street corner. Her New York experience had thrilled the manager,
who had put her to work the day she applied for the job.

"I would probably just waste those hours before dinner anyway," Joanna said truthfully. "I really don't mind the Starbucks gig.
It's kind of fun—it makes me feel as though I am in the middle of
Yale life, somehow. And anyway," she added, throwing her arm
around her older sister in a rough hug, "I am so glad that I can
contribute something to our household so it doesn't all fall on you,
Meg."

"Plus, it's literary," Teddy had pointed out when she told him
she had landed the job, and then in one of his bizarre voices he had
squawked, "No, no, it's a coffee pot, Mr. Starbuck!"

Meg asked the advice of the registrar in the English Department,
an especially kind and thoughtful woman who always had a smile

for her despite the ceramic jar on her desk labeled "ashes of prob-lem students." Mrs. Hurley assured her that she was qualified for lots of jobs and that she would keep her in mind if she heard of anything.

Only a day later, Meg had a call from a very sweet retired American Studies professor who lived out in Bethany. Right away, she did some simple library research for Professor Baldwin on a bibliography of the publications of the poet Richard Warren Bennett. Professor Baldwin's eyesight was failing and he was eager to complete the biography he had been slowly writing for the past few years. When her work was done, a quite simple bit of scholarship really, Meg thought he paid her far too generously. Professor Baldwin, whose edifying lectures on Hawthorne and Melville were still discussed, although he had retired just before Meg got to Yale, assured her in his courtly manner that she had worked very efficiently and had earned every penny.

Professor Baldwin had arranged to meet with her in the English Department office and he greeted Mrs. Hurley warmly, thanking her again for recommending Meg.

"She has been the perfect research assistant," he pronounced grandly. "Far superior to some graduate students I've employed in the past who thought too much and too little at precisely the wrong moments, worked too slowly, took their own ideas far too seriously, and were unforgivably careless with their citations."

Mrs. Hurley winked over his shoulder at the slightly embar-rassed Meg, and Meg had to stifle a giggle, recollecting just then that Mrs. Hurley had told her that Professor Baldwin's nickname on campus had been "Colonel Sanders," owing to the shock of white hair and the white goatee worn by both the professor and the fried chicken magnate.

Professor Baldwin's welcome money in hand, grocery shopping for the week ahead was an occasion without the usual sense of panic about the cost of everything. Meg savored the heady feeling of providing for her family. She let Amy choose a luxurious array of Pepperidge Farm cookies, and they had London broil for dinner that night.

Professor Baldwin was so delighted with Meg's excellent work that he phoned just days later to ask her if she thought she might undertake the completion of the index for the Bennett biography, which had been started by someone else, a graduate student of his who had recently left Yale unexpectedly for a better fellowship elsewhere. He rambled a bit, explaining far more than interested Meg about the graduate student's decision to go to Princeton to pursue his work on Thoreau, and Meg realized that he was waiting for her answer.

Though Meg had no experience at all with that sort of thing, she was able to get the hang of it pretty easily, and she quickly saw that the work was far closer to completion than Professor Baldwin had realized. Tempted as she was to string out the task and make it last, she was able to finish it in a few weeks of diligent effort.

"You can always become an indexer," Amy said over her shoulder one October afternoon, watching her proofread at the kitchen table. Amy was just in from school and Meg had a few minutes of work time left before a class.

"Right. Thanks for the marvelous career advice."

"Seriously, Meg, there are always ads for indexers in the back of *The New York Review of Books*. It's a real job."

"You would know, wouldn't you," Meg said, looking up at her little sister for a moment with a fond smile. "You little connoisseur of those classified ads. But, sweetie, don't you think 'Indexer' is probably a euphemism for being a left-handed Sagittarius amputee who likes John Coltrane, walking in the rain, and getting tied up?"

"So it seems I'm not the only one who ever wasted time perusing those ads rather closely," Amy said, hanging on the back of

Meg's chair and continuing to read over her shoulder. " 'Personal details of, philanthropy of, poetry of, politics of, possessiveness of, publishers of, Pulitzer Prize and, Puritanism—' "

"Who has the time to read silly personal ads these days?" Meg said impatiently, closing down her notebook computer and shuffling the stack of notated manuscript pages into order. "What time is it? Oh no, I'm almost late for class right now and I forgot to eat and you need to work on your homework, Miss Busybody, before dinner, okay, so we can go over it after?"

"When you're an indexer, the indexers' union will guarantee lunch hours, I promise!" Amy called after her sister as she flew out of the apartment.

The Sunday Meg drove out to Bethany with the final printout of her index work, Professor Baldwin's wife came into her husband's study to ask her if she wouldn't stay for lunch. Although chilly weather had descended, and consequently the Oxbridge Arms had suffered from several nights of *heatus interruptus* which had resulted in Amy's crowding into Meg's bed before dawn complaining of the cold, this day was strangely warm. Large, perfectly formed orange and red leaves falling continuously from the half-bare trees that flanked the Baldwins' screened porch were dazzling to Meg, who had hardly noticed autumn at all until that moment.

Halloween was just a week away, she realized. For the first time in her life she had made no preparations. She must be getting old. Not so long ago she would have anticipated Halloween with tremendous excitement and many plans. This time last year, she and her suite-mates had already spent copious time carving excellent pumpkins and planning costume strategies for numerous Halloween parties. She hadn't even noticed if there were parties this year. Meg thought of the aluminum foil "Never Forgive, Never Forget" coat of arms back in Joanna's childhood bedroom, and sighed. The previous weeks had blurred together.

Professor Baldwin and his wife, whose delicious lunch Meg devoured, quizzed her pleasantly about her studies, and then they quizzed her avidly about her sisters, and about Teddy, once she had alluded to her living situation.

"How fascinating to think of you all together like that," Mrs. Baldwin said. "Nancy Mitford said that sisters were a shield against life's cruel adversity."

"And her sister Jessica said in response that sisters *are* life's cruel adversity," Professor Baldwin added.

They were curious without prying, and Meg appreciated the way they did and didn't ask her questions. One of the most charming things about the old couple, Meg thought, was that they weren't just interesting, but they were so *interested*. It was a trait she knew well because people often described her own parents this way. In fact, the entire encounter had the ring of familiarity to it. Only here, instead of playing the part of one of the family's colorful children receiving a visitor, she was cast in the role of the admiring and grateful student being fed a delicious meal. She also enjoyed their marmalade cat, Tiggy Winkle, who flatteringly jumped in her lap.

By the time lunch ended they had discovered, to everyone's delight, that the Baldwins were acquainted with Teddy's redoubtable grandmother Avery Bell, whose writing they knew well. Apparently, they had spent time together one summer semester at Cornell some thirty years before, and the impression she made on them then had remained vivid.

Mrs. Baldwin left the table briefly and returned with a copy of *Outside Influences*,* Avery Bell's most popular and successful book. "For Judith and Edwin, who get it, with fond thoughts of many happy moments from your Avery," it was inscribed in a slashy script. Meg told them she and her sisters would be spending the Christmas break with Teddy at Avery's house on the coast of

*Avery Bell, *Outside Influences* (New York: Alfred A. Knopf, 1968).

Maine, and Professor Baldwin shuffled off to locate a copy of his most recent book, a collection of elegant literary essays,* for Meg to deliver to Avery.

"Have you never met Avery, then?" Mrs. Baldwin asked with a mischievous look in her eye. "No? Well, after your visit, you must come out here for tea and tell me all about it. I was pregnant with our son Henry that summer. Avery started off treating me as though I were just some sort of mindless breeder, though she warmed up after a while. A very challenging character, you will find. Unless she has mellowed with age."

"Nothing Teddy has ever said about Avery has made her sound the least bit mellow," Meg said. "She sounds pretty intense, actually." Meg was reluctant to be critical of someone she had never met, but at the same time she didn't want to sound too virtuous.

While the professor was pottering in his study, Meg began to help Mrs. Baldwin clear the lunch dishes and prepare coffee, regretting the end of her lunch with these terrific people. Not to mention that the interlude of earning terrific money had now ended, with no further work in sight. She would have to go back to Mrs. Hurley and see if she had any other adorable retired Yale professors with work to be done.

Reader's note: What's with the footnotes? AG

Author's note: Footnotes concerning publications referred to throughout these pages lend an air of veracity to the story.

Reader's note: Why footnote books that don't exist? Why give the illusion of documenting made-up books that represent real books by real writers who are thinly disguised for your purposes? AG

Author's note: The footnotes are provided, as you suggest, because they, like many other elements in this novel, are fictional representations of that which does exist.

---

*Edwin Baldwin, *American Scenes* (New York: Farrar, Straus and Giroux, 1989).

Reader's note: This is just silly. Are you sure the footnotes aren't just to show what a good little scholar you are? Are you trying to make your readers feel that they are reading a really intellectual novel? MG

Author's note: Every word on every page of this novel, including every word of these notes, is here for one reason or another.

Reader's note: You always do this. Your reasons are supposed to have more value and integrity than anyone else's reasons. AG

Author's note: This isn't the place to take that up.

Reader's note: This is exactly the place to take that up. You've written the novel—now take responsibility for it. Considering that you were not there and have had to resort to genuine fiction writing for a change instead of the mulching of reality that seems to be your more usual technique, I think you've actually done some very good writing in this chapter. But that said, your apparently guiltless appropriations remain troubling. MG

Author's note: Baudelaire said the only good parts of a book are the explanations that are left out.

Reader's note: I'm sure you think that's a satisfactory rationale. MG

Meg saw that Mrs. Baldwin was waiting politely for her to put down her pretty little polka-dotted demitasse cup, one of a set the Baldwins had brought back from a semester in Florence, Mrs. Baldwin had explained when Meg praised their sweetness. It had been such a delightful hour! Meg missed family meals with interesting conversations such as this one had been, and she enjoyed her lack of authority at the Baldwins' table. She had luxuriated in being taken so seriously by these wise people. She looked forward to her Avery-reporting tea with Mrs. Baldwin, though she had had an insecure reflexive thought that it might not have been a serious invitation she was meant to take literally.

As they carried the coffee things to the kitchen, with Tiggy Winkle mewing expectantly and escorting them anxiously, lest they forget the pathetic fact of a half-starved cat underfoot, Mrs. Baldwin asked her absently what sort of work her parents did.

When, after a brief description of her father's museum work and his more recent inventing phase, Meg identified her mother, Mrs. Baldwin called out down the corridor, "Edwin, listen to this! Our adorable luncheon guest is the daughter of Janet Green! You know, she's the one who did that presentation on *Wuthering Heights* that intrigued you so much."

Professor Baldwin returned to the kitchen, two copies of his book in hand. "If I'm not mistaken," he said, drawing a chair out from the kitchen table and sitting down heavily, as the exertions of climbing around the bookcases in his study had tired him, "she wrote that wonderful little volume on the childhood fantasies of the Brontë children, what was it called?"

"*Secret Places,*" Meg replied, caught in a complex cross-current of pride and sadness at that moment.

"Yes, that's it," Professor Baldwin said, fishing out a fountain pen from his jacket pocket. Even for Sunday lunch at home he was dressed as if for the classroom, in a tweedy jacket over a woolly sweater. "*Secret Places: The Imaginative Worlds of Angria, Gondal, and Glass Town.*[*] Marvelous book. I remember when it had just come out. Quite the controversy over that book, quite the controversy."

"Really?" Meg couldn't recall ever hearing anything about controversy.

"Oh yes. Much of it the usual sour sort of professional begrudgery over success, I should think. If you sell more than thirty copies of a book, everyone sneers and says you're not serious. I heard your mother give a presentation at the MLA. It was in Chicago that year, I believe. Was it Felice Rosen who was with her on the panel right after? The one who writes travel articles and celebrity profiles and such? Speaking of not serious? But she fancied herself the great authority on the Brontës for a few weeks, as I recall, after publishing an article in the *New York Times* Travel

*See chapter 2, p. 58.

section about a weekend in Haworth or something along those lines. And Vicki Cole was on that panel, that's right, and she got into that fight with her about, what was it, the gender issues? It's always gender issues these days, isn't it?" Professor Baldwin sighed.

"There was a terrific dustup among those three ladies, or women I suppose I really must call them—they could have charged admission for that one. People talked about it for months. Your mother didn't really knock over the water pitcher onto Felice on purpose, did she? That must be what, six or seven years ago now?"

"It was published in June of 1992. I remember because it came out right on my thirteenth birthday. But nobody talked to me about the gender issues, let alone a cat fight with water pitchers at the MLA."

"Edwin is exaggerating, Meg. Edwin, dear, you're getting carried away," Mrs. Baldwin soothed and tidied, as she often did. "But what a lovely birthday present," she added, shifting gracefully. "Edwin, did any of your book publications ever fall on one of the children's birthdays?"

Professor Baldwin was bent over the books on the table before him, intently inscribing something in first one and then the other. He finished with a flourish and capped his pen. He looked up blankly.

Mrs. Baldwin laughed and, addressing Meg in a conspiratorial tone, said, "The professor tunes the world right out whenever it suits him, and especially when he feels reprimanded!"

"Here is a copy for Avery Bell, and here, my dear, is one for you," Professor Baldwin said, pointedly ignoring his wife's remark. "I think you'll enjoy it. I would love to know what you think. There's quite a nice piece here that I'm rather fond of, some thoughts on James's novellas, or *nouvelles*, as he called them, which could intrigue you, given your paper on narrative voice that you were telling me about. I do hope you will take up the late, difficult

James before you leave New Haven. He'll teach you how to read and write for the rest of your life."

As Meg, touched that he had been so attentive to her lunch-time prattlings about her little paper, tried to find words of thanks, there was the jingle of the sleigh bells the Baldwins kept hanging on their front door. A male voice called out "Ahoy! Intruder warning! Permission requested to come aboard!"

"Granted, you silly man, just don't let the cat out!" Mrs. Baldwin called out cheerfully. A moment later Meg found herself being introduced to the Baldwins' houseguest, Mark Frank, a shockingly attractive man. She felt herself to be a bit flustered, inexplicably, as though she were about to get up and make a speech in front of an auditorium full of people. He looked to be in his late thirties, and as he threw himself into one of the kitchen chairs and took her hand warmly, she knew her cheeks were burning. She felt like a shy little girl and hoped nobody noticed in the dim kitchen light. His name was familiar to Meg. She tried to remember where she had seen it. Oh yes, the campus notices for his lectures. Mark Frank was the inaugural Shapiro Fellow.

The Shapiro Fellowship for the Study of Popular Culture had been endowed by a toy magnate, a loyal Old Blue who had made a huge amount of money with the Little Lucy dolls, a craze that had swept the nation during Meg's childhood, though she herself had never possessed one. ("Why don't they just call them Cute Fetuses, and be up front about the right-to-life propaganda they are?" Meg had once overheard Janet say to a friend on the telephone.) The early versions were worth a fortune these days to collectors. Meg had attended the Calhoun Master's Tea where the Shapiro Fellowship had been announced the previous spring. She had enjoyed the rather rough-hewn Marvin Shapiro, who was a far cry from the usual sort of speakers at a Master's Tea. He had given a slide lecture on the history of Little Lucy in the identical tones of reverent connoisseurship reserved by art historians for discussion of rare Chinese porcelains. The room had been packed with students.

Mark Frank's lectures—there had been two so far and Meg had missed them both—had gotten some great reviews from two girls in Meg's astronomy section. His topic had been "The Intersection of the Sacred, the Profane, and the Seriously Cool." Actually, it was the lecturer himself who had gotten the great reviews. She tried to reconstruct what they had said when she hadn't really been paying attention. He was British. His field was something very analytic and pop culture, with that High-Low thing going on, like the amusing but infuriating writing of Wayne Koestenbaum that Meg had tried to read for a women's studies class discussion of Jackie Onassis as a cultural icon. Meg thought of the way Amy used to think Janet had a friend named Herman Ootic.

"Meg here has just rescued me from a slough of despond," Professor Baldwin exclaimed by way of introduction. "Her research and her impeccable notes have saved me from myself, and she's only a junior."

"Really?" Mark Frank appraised her, well, frankly. He had startling dark blue eyes under jaunty terrier eyebrows. "What is that in human years? Twenty? I would have pegged you for quite a bit older, actually. Edwin has been telling me about your work for him, Meg, and do please call me Mark, but he failed to mention that you were an undergraduate. Everyone thinks Edwin Baldwin is the soul of generosity but, secretly, he likes to hoard his treasures like everyone else."

Meg was nonplussed and didn't have a clue how to respond to this line of chat. She didn't fancy herself a treasure being hoarded by anyone. Fortunately, Mrs. Baldwin jumped in with questions about his Sunday shopping experience in Middle America at some mall she had recommended. Meg took the moment to study Mark Frank. He had the look of an aging schoolboy, dressed as he was in a very old sweater revealing the frayed edges of an equally antiquated shirt collar. He wore threadbare corduroys and only his shoes were very new-looking—gleaming white sneakers that Meg imagined he had probably purchased that day as part of his mall expedition. Mark Frank had interesting rills of fine dark hair on his wrists, running down into his cuffs. Meg had to agree with those girls. He really was devastatingly handsome.

"Mark's a specialist in depictions of, what is it? Media?" Professor Baldwin began to explain. "Media in literature? Or is it literature in media? You explain it, Mark. I can't keep up with the lingo."

"I fool about with depictions of media in contemporary literature," Mark said with a shrug, ending his chat with Mrs. Baldwin about his observations of the behaviors of hideous family groups he had observed shopping at Wal-Mart. "How television and radio and film and the Internet are referenced in novels, that sort of thing."

"That sounds really interesting," Meg said truthfully. Every word he uttered sounded really interesting.

"It seems a popular subject for our times. There's always new material. Look," he said, interrupting himself and suddenly leaning forward, a bit closer than was comfortable, to stare into her eyes directly. "I don't suppose you know of anyone as miraculous as yourself looking for a bit of work from time to time? I could use a hand, and then there are the children, though I don't suppose spending time with them would be especially inspiring to the average ambitious Yale undergraduate whose mind is on higher subjects. Although anyone studying abnormal psychology might find them intriguingly useful, I suppose. They're perfectly sweet though a bit in need of taming." He stopped for a moment and got out a little pocket calendar, through which he began leafing.

"I'll be moving into a flat in Jonathan Edwards College next week, on, um, yes, on the Wednesday, the day before the family arrive." He jotted something down on the corner of a page with a little stub of a pencil that was stuck into the calendar, and Meg had to restrain herself from peering to see what he was writing. He put away his calendar. "There was some sort of problem with the previous person moving out late, some genius mathematician from China with nowhere to go who didn't make proper arrangements, and I've been a good sport about it, being on my own with the family not here yet. So I've been imposing myself like mad and taking advantage of my great good friends the Baldwins out in this bucolic retreat from the hurly-burly of New Haven."

Meg hardly thought of New Haven as a hectic place, compared, say, to New York, but perhaps, for all his intellectual sophistication, Mark came from a sleepy little town of some kind which made New Haven seem a cosmopolitan center by comparison. Or maybe he was just making socially graceful noise.

As if reading her mind, Mark said, "New Haven is a happening place compared to our little suburb of Birmingham, I assure you. In any event, the time has come for me to be getting organized as best I can. I am hoping to locate a student willing to do a combination of some research bits for me and some helping out with the kiddiewinks at the end of the day here and there. My wife hasn't been well and I'm concerned about her ability to manage everything on her own."

"Mark's children are very sweet," Mrs. Baldwin assured Meg. "Alice is seven and Wills is five, isn't that right, Mark? Do show Meg those adorable photos you showed me this morning at breakfast." Her words were effectively persuasive on Meg, on whom it was dawning that this meeting was no coincidence. "Mark's wife, Kelly, is just darling. And so bright. We met them last summer when Edwin and I were in Wales for the Dylan Thomas symposium and then we went on to Bristol for Edwin's lecture at the university, on the Concord transcendentalists. Mark and his family had been resident at Bristol for the year, and we knew they were coming to Yale, so we thought we should meet them."

This was too perfect! Meg looked at Professor Baldwin, who nodded his approval. Both the Baldwins were beaming at her and Mark Frank was looking at her with hopeful eyes.

"Well, you know, I'm sort of available right now," she stammered. "My work for Professor Baldwin is really finished after today. I was going to go look for something starting tomorrow." Meg had a further thought. "And my two younger sisters are living with me, so they could probably help with baby-sitting some of the time, if I can't do it. If you're in JE, we live really near you, on High Street, just the other side of the British Art Center."

"Mark, as it happens, Meg couldn't be located any closer to you in JE unless they lived in Skull and Bones," Professor Baldwin observed.

"Do people actually live in there, then? With no windows? Heavens! It must be very dark and awkward. How extraordinary!" Mark said.

"No, no, don't take me literally, I was just exaggerating the point, but don't you see, this is excellent!" Professor Baldwin thumped the table. "I hereby pass this treasure along, if she'll allow herself to be passed. Meg has a first-rate literary mind. You might say she feels in italics and thinks in capital letters!"

"Oh, that would be such a relief, Meg, if I could ring Kelly and tell her I've got this all sorted. She's really rather apprehensive. This is excellent. Whatever Edwin has been paying you, I am sure it's the fair and proper hourly wage, so shall we just go on from there?"

"Who's ready for a celebratory drink?" Mrs. Baldwin inquired.

"That was James, wasn't it Edwin?" Mark inquired. "The italics bit?"

" 'The Figure in the Carpet,' " Professor Baldwin replied.

"Whenever you speak aphoristically I know it can be only Hank J.," Mark said. "Not that I can read those long sentences anymore. Life's too short for such long sentences."

"No blasphemy in my kitchen," Mrs. Baldwin reproved Mark with a pretend rap on the knuckles and a smile.

"Excuse me, but really, Professor Baldwin, I'm not the least bit like Miss Erme!" Meg protested.

"A fine spice of intelligence on this side of the table, anyway," Professor Baldwin murmured approvingly. "Well done."

And so Meg was employed.

Reader's note: Needless to say, you weren't there. You seem to be laying all sorts of groundwork for plot development, and while that is a good thing for the novel, and while I applaud your ability to write real fiction as opposed to crafting fictionalized reports of actual events, you are still limiting yourself by loading the narrative with your theories and presumptions about how real people acted and felt. It's a dangerous game and ultimately I don't see how you can produce satisfactory results when your writing is limited both by what you cannot possibly know and by what you think you know. MG

Reader's note: This is the first chapter that feels like a real novel to me, as a reader who obviously knows too much and has too much at stake. AG

Reader's note: Maybe that's because you're not in it. MG

Author's note: Maybe you should both try to get a little more perspective here. And I must point out that just because you have the right to comment on any page of this manuscript doesn't mean you must comment when you don't have anything to say.

SEVEN

Homework

"Our mother believed that her love instructed us about how to be people," Amy complained bitterly, and certainly not for the first time. She was helping Meg make dinner in the haphazard little kitchen of their High Street apartment. "She thought she could just influence us by being so intimate and affectionate that we couldn't resist her."

It was a chilly evening in the middle of November, just before Thanksgiving, when each night darkness falls noticeably earlier with a surprising suddenness. The three Green sisters and Teddy Bell had fallen into something of a weekday routine—classes, early dinner, schoolwork, and sometimes a little television before bedtime, if a movie they could all agree on was showing on one of the two stations they could get on their pathetic Goodwill television set, which only worked at all thanks to the judicious arrangement of a foil-covered coat hanger rigged by Teddy.

On the nights Meg wasn't home until late, because of evenings with the two Frank children, Teddy often made dinner, though his idea of making dinner was usually to go out on his bicycle to get an assortment of delicious things from Jing's, the Asian grocer up on Whitney Avenue past the Peabody Museum. Amy adored those meals because he always stocked up on seaweed salad, cold sesame noodles, and her favorite, California rolls. Meg was hard on him about the expense of these meals.

"How much did you spend, Teddy, seriously?" she had asked him when she had come upon the evidence of their most recent Jing's feast.

"I don't spend it," Teddy had replied evasively with a guilty grin. "It spends itself, somehow, and is gone before I know it."

"And Janet was always so sweet and sympathetic and understanding and beloved by all," Amy added with sarcastic emphasis, as if this were a new observation, which it wasn't. "She always made *me* feel guilty for not being as good as *I* should be! Can you spell *hypocrisy?*"

Amy had become obsessive in her need to rehash the catastrophic events that had led them to this new way of life. Joanna, when present, would usually chime right in with her own grievances. Meg was never first to bring up the subject of their estrangement from their parents, and had grown quite weary of the subject, but she was nevertheless unwilling to deny Amy her right to a tenth grader's repetitive angst.

"Well, she did influence us, you know," Meg pointed out in her elder-sisterly fashion. "We couldn't resist her and consequently we did evolve into pretty decent people, after all." She had touched on the complexities of her living situation a few times in conversation with Mark, and those chats had left her feeling even less certain than she already was of the absoluteness of her sisters' views.

She turned from the stove, wiping her hands on a dish towel. "Hey, Ames, would you at least make an attempt to leave some of those string beans some middles at least, if you don't mind? I know I bought enough for all four of us but it doesn't look like it now with you snapping off a third of every bean there."

"I didn't say *we* weren't decent people," Amy said, picking through the remaining beans and nipping their ends with only slightly more generous standards for wilted ends and brown spots. Meg was such a nag about the cost of food—about the cost of everything, these days. "And I think you should stop trying to be the voice of reason all the time. I'm talking about the fuckbird. Janet. She's the one who's not a decent person."

"Maybe a bad person, or someone capable of being bad, anyway, can still have been a good mother?" suggested Teddy, seeking to introduce one of the standard variations on this familiar melody while captively eavesdropping and reading his philosophy assignment at the table.

"When Bad Parents Happen to Good Children!" Amy intoned, dropping the last mutilated bean stub into the bowl.

"When an Incompetent String Bean Assistant Happens to Dinner—Next on the Table in Five Minutes!" announced Meg, trying not to get burned in the cramped space as she seized what remained of the beans and threw them into the big dented saucepan (two dollars at Goodwill) in which she had sautéed some chicken breasts and shallots. The microwave pinged that the potatoes were ready and then obsequiously suggested in its programmed scroll that they should enjoy their meal.

"So where the hell is Jo-Jo? I told her dinner was at seven tonight and she was expected or she should call or leave a note, damn it. It's not so much to ask. Ordinary people do it."

"I hate ordinary people," Amy muttered.

"Teddy, will you get your books off the table so Amy can set it?" demanded Meg, ignoring Amy's remark. "Amy, will you set the table right now? And I mean right now?"

"Have you considered the irony," Teddy asked gently, closing up his books, "that while you three speak about the wonderful values you were raised to believe in, you've been totally harsh about your folks? I know it's not my place to comment—"

"He said, commenting away," Amy added.

"—But I really wonder if you have ever stopped to think about this. Was there no part of the famous Green wonderfulness, the loss of which you all mourn on a daily basis, that included compassion or forgiveness?"

Amy and Meg looked at him. There was a silence that might have gone on for quite a while had Joanna's key not rattled in the lock just then.

"Sorry!" she called out from the long narrow hallway. She dumped her books and draped her coat on one of their bicycles. Joanna rushed to her place at the table with mock urgency, which irritated Meg. Was it too much to ask that people show up for dinner if she was going to go to the trouble of making it?

"Sorry, Mom!" Joanna said. Meg gave her a look. They sat down and began to eat while Joanna, who was oblivious to the tension still lingering in the room, reported.

"So, there was this new guy who could not remember how to do a mocha and a whole bunch of people came in and ordered tall mochas just when I was ending my shift, I swear, it was like the Mocha Appreciation Club was having its monthly meeting all of a sudden. What a complete space cadet. The new guy, I mean, Mr. Rivetface. I think they must have pierced some part of his brain by mistake. Do you know, incidentally, you guys, I am about the only *barrista* in any coffee place in town without multiple piercings? It's a wonder they hired me, I'm so unpierced. I am so, so, *so* glad you talked me out of that nose-piercing thing last year, Meg, what the hell was I thinking? And everybody compares infections and they're always borrowing Neosporin from one another—"

"Overshare! Overshare!" bleeped Amy and Meg together.

"Sorry. So anyway, I must have showed him the perfect mocha like five times during the shift. I think he was high or something. Really. And then two of them were supposed to be decaf and he forgot practically while I was still calling them, you could just see it happening. His head just couldn't hold the information for more than two seconds. It was pathetic. I would still be there if I hadn't simply lied and marked two random ones decaf anyway."

Joanna looked around at her sisters and Teddy. Teddy was thoughtfully studying his plate. Only Meg met her eye. "Don't give me that look, Meg! They weren't old ladies with heart conditions or anything. They're just fussbudgets because they read too many magazine articles about caffeine. They thought it was decaf and that's probably the most important thing about how it affects you, right? What you believe it is?"

"Ah," Teddy murmured, "a Lockeian approach to the effect of un-decaffeinated coffee."

"Not more a Berkeleyan approach?" Meg challenged. "*Esse est percipi.* To be is to be perceived. To be perceived as decaf is to be happily sipped as decaf."

"So, as I was saying," Joanna continued, giving Teddy a friendly kick under the table but otherwise pretending to ignore both of them, "Anyway, they never tip. And they're not old or anything, I promise. I think they're graduate students, I see them a lot. And then there was this other new person being trained today, a townie, this girl who said she's never had a cup of coffee in her life. She told me she has Diet Coke for breakfast, with a PowerBar. So this girl was a total spaz also, and on top of that, she kept asking people if they wanted their beans 'grounded,' like electrically or something."

"Janet the Good would have kittens over what you did," said Amy. "Man, would she rake you over the coals about a million ways for the decaf thing."

"And then her husband, Mr. Integrity and Forgiveness, would know about some insane New Zealand study of decaf drinkers and their sleeping patterns versus a placebo group of people who only thought they were getting decaf," added Joanna.

"And then what would happen after that?" Teddy wondered.

Watching Joanna suddenly drop her gaze into her lap, he regretted the question because he was reluctant to cause pain, and his previous impertinent observation still hung in the air, unanswered. He had become so much more than a detached observer of the Green sisters. Participant observation, Meg, who had taken a class in anthropology, called his presence in their lives.

"Lou would probably have very nicely made me drink three big cups of strong coffee before bedtime so that I could have a totally restless night of caffeine insomnia, develop some empathy for people who have their own reasons for drinking decaf, and, thereafter, repent my careless ethical misjudgment," Joanna replied, subdued and less cocky, after this moment of reflection, which had started out as a witty retort but had then devolved into a genuinely thoughtful guess as to her father's likely response to her careless expediency with the truth.

"Right, and then Janet would have wanted you to write an essay about all you have learned about your inner sense of worth and your recognition of the selfhood of others, in terms of decaffeinated coffee, which she would have submitted to the Journal of Sanctimonious Goodness, and then the two of them would have made a contribution to a fair trade coffee organization in Guatemala in your name because they would have been so, so, *so* proud of you!" mocked Amy, who had a knack for simultaneous wit and viciousness, which she especially loved to display in front of Teddy.

"Sounds like you've all got some sort of internalized imperative from them irresistibly tweaking your conscience anyway," Teddy said lightly, after a long moment when the only sound at the table was that of cutlery clinking.

"Having a conscience is so inconvenient," Joanna remarked finally. "I can't help wishing at times that our mother and father hadn't been so particularly efficient with their, whatever you call it, their moral suasion."

"Oooh, moral suasion! Big vocab!" Amy exclaimed.

"Pay attention and you might learn something, dingdong," Joanna retorted, oblivious to the way they had circled around to a point quite close to the incompleted conversation that had been taking place just before she came into the apartment.

"Don't be hard on the staff, where is your familial teaching by example, Miss Efficient Moral Suasion?" Teddy came back cheerfully.

"Efficient suasion," chirped Amy. "Fish swish, Swedish, suede, swash, wash, cash, sash, sashimi, sushi—"

"SHUSH!" Joanna and Meg cried together. Teddy grinned and reached across the table to pet Amy on the head to show his sympathy.

"So, listen, you guys, we need to make a plan for Thanksgiving," Meg said a moment later, serious now.

"Can't we just skip it?" Joanna said. "I just knew you would bring this up again. I've been dreading this decision. My birthday last week was bad enough, and we got through that."

"But I love Thanksgiving dinner," Amy wailed. "How can we just not have a Thanksgiving dinner? I always peel the chestnuts for the stuffing! And then Joanna and I make the stuffing and the cranberry sauce while we listen to our old Pete Seeger tapes! I thought we were going to be a family on our own! Meg, Jo-Jo, you guys said we would be our own family. How can we just not do the most important traditional family things?"

"I wonder what Janet and Lou are planning?" Joanna said. "Since Lou's birthday is the same weekend this year. Not that it matters, I mean I don't really care what they're doing," she added, too late.

"Oh, November is the most disagreeable month in the whole year!" Meg declared. They all looked at one another. Amy's mouth was trembling and she roughly wiped the back of her wrist across her face as if to rub away her sadness.

"Since we're all going up to Maine for Christmas, I don't think Avery would miss me if I didn't spend Thanksgiving with her,"

Teddy said quietly. "We always go to the Langdons down the road anyway, that's what we do every year, so it's not as if it would change her plan in any major way. They're old friends and she and Diana Langdon have had a sort of competitive friendship for some fifty years, and I think George Langdon used to advise her on investments or something before he retired. Avery always makes the cranberry sauce from the directions on the bag of cranberries and spills sugar all over everything in the kitchen and then she presents it with great drama as if it was the most challenging part of the meal. And then George tells her the cranberry sauce is the best thing he's ever tasted and Diana always humors her in a sort of condescendingly gracious way that's pretty hilarious, considering the rest of the meal."

"What's that like?" Amy asked.

"The turkey is always desiccated, the stuffing is from a mix, and the gravy has lumps," Teddy replied in fond tones. "I mean, I love these people, but everyone has been drinking George's toxic eggnog for hours, waiting for the turkey to be overcooked, so body parts have started to go numb anyway, which is essential to enjoying the meal. It's all part of the tradition. But I've missed it before. The Langdons have their own family, in New York and Boston, and some of them come every year, so it's not like I'm essential."

"Are you sure, T?" Meg breathed. "Isn't that letting her down?"

"Christmas is really the more important holiday for Gran anyway," he reasoned.

"It sounds as though Thanksgiving is hugely important to your family," Meg said skeptically.

"I would love even that desiccated turkey," Amy said sadly. "Maybe you could bring some back and I can listen to Pete Seeger while I eat a desiccated turkey sandwich or something."

"Oh, please," Joanna groaned, swatting her impatiently. "We can do better than that. Don't be such a pathetic orphan."

"So if I tell Avery I'm not coming," Teddy persisted, "that way we could be together here. I'd really like to be here with you three," Teddy said. "It's a very long trip up and back just for those days, anyway. I could definitely use the time here, working, too."

"Would that really be okay, Teddy?" Meg asked. "Are you totally sure?"

"We can get a turkey at a supermarket," Joanna said. "Not that we have a roasting pan big enough. And not that I have a clue about how to roast a turkey. Janet always chased us out before the big drama of stuffing it and trussing it with those weird spikes and putting in the oven."

"Thanksgiving won't be Thanksgiving, no matter what," Amy said mournfully.

"Sure it will, Ames," Joanna said consolingly. "We can divide up the responsibilities and make it just right. We can figure it out."

"I was thinking maybe we should all volunteer to help serve Thanksgiving dinner at the downtown soup kitchen, if we're going to be here, together, that day," Teddy said hesitantly. "I mean, if that isn't just too completely virtuous and depressing. And it would be another good reason to give Avery for my staying here with you guys."

"No, it's just right," Meg said thoughtfully. "We could make our own Thanksgiving dinner the day before and make a lot so we have food to share."

"What does Avery think of us, I wonder?" Amy asked. "She said it was okay for us to come for Christmas, but I mean, does she know anything about us? I wouldn't want her to be mad that you were with us for Thanksgiving, but it would be so great if you can stay. I've been so afraid to bring it up until now."

"She thinks I'm sweet on all three of you," Teddy said with a grin. "Those were her precise words!"

Just then, the four girls who shared the apartment directly beneath theirs (it was very possible these four girls had actually met at a meeting of a support group for people with severe Joni

Mitchell disorders—one of them had told Joanna that the reason
their front room, which Joanna glimpsed when she had carried up
a package for them which had been lying in the front hall, was
painted dark blue was in homage to the eponymous Joni Mitchell
album) cranked up *For the Roses* for the fifteenth time that day and
possibly the three hundredth time that week.

Joanna exclaimed with unusual vehemence to the floorboards,
"Oh Jesus, again with the cold blue steel! So spike up and have your
smack overdoses already, for God's sake! The suspense is killing us!"

"Please, Jo-Jo," Meg said lightly. Although she trusted their
sensible judgment, Meg hated how casually her two younger sisters now spoke the lingo after just a few weeks at Duncan. "But
speaking of addictive substances, coffee, with caffeine, before
studying, everyone?" Meg offered (Joanna brought it home from
work in little unmarked brown sacks; Meg preferred not to think
about how it came into her possession), and, after all that, everybody seemed more relaxed.

*Reader's note: I hate this feeling I have of being an unwelcome guest at my
own party with every critical remark I make, but the way you depict Amy
seems condescending to me. You make her sound babyish and silly. Should
an author condescend to her characters in this way? Doesn't that keep the
reader from sympathizing adequately? AG*

*Reader's note: I don't agree. I think Amy seems adorable and touch-
ingly young at certain moments. Meg, on the other hand, seems like a
generic character, a grim and humorless older sister who carries the weight
of the world on her shoulders. MG*

*Author's note: Is it remotely possible that neither of you is able to read
objectively in general and specifically when it comes to these characters?
Just a thought.*

That evening, as was the case most evenings, all four of them worked diligently for hours. Meg had fallen a bit behind in her reading in the past three weeks, because of time devoted to the first task Mark Frank had given her, which consisted of going through his most recent essays and lectures, in anticipation of publication, and not only fact-checking in general but also specifically researching all the details of his quoted material in order to obtain legal permissions for the song lyrics, which was quite time-consuming, particular work. Meg was always conscientious about her work anyway, but she especially wanted to do a good job for him. She wanted to live up to Professor Baldwin's esteem, she was eager to keep this job for as long as she possibly could, and the time she spent with Mark was more important to her than she really wanted to admit to herself. And of course, there was the hourly wage.

Mark always had time for her. After they reviewed the work at hand, alone in his office on the fourth floor of Linsley-Chit— where he occasionally smoked unfiltered Camels, in complete insouciant violation of the campus-wide prohibition on smoking, which he had deemed "silly"—they talked about everything in the world, from Bill Clinton's effects on gender issues in the culture to the more subtle allusions in *Buffy the Vampire Slayer* to some thoughtful moments considering the nuances of the Green family estrangement. She could tell him anything and he would really listen, he would take her seriously (the thing we all crave the most), and then he would challenge her assumptions. When she felt herself fixed in the gaze of those intense blue eyes, Meg knew that Mark really saw her for who she was.

This was attraction. An adult attraction, not at all like the first and only serious relationship of her life that she had had with a boy on her Putney trip, Rob Chatfield, a self-assured lacrosse player from Baltimore who had promised all the way across France (she had finally slept with him in a youth hostel in the Dordogne) that their love would be undiminished by the miles between them once their summer idyll had ended, but who had almost instantly and predictably broken her heart just two months into freshman year when he wrote to her from Bowdoin to tell her he had become involved with a girl he had met on a squash court.

Teddy really saw her for who she was too, of course, and he understood her as well as anyone ever had, outside of her family. Teddy really had become family. Various of her Yale acquaintances and even one of the Joni Mitchell girls downstairs had, in fact, assumed they were a couple, she had recently learned. But Teddy was just good kind safe Teddy. Mark Frank was the exciting dangerous real world in which anything could happen.

Reader's note: This is infuriating and painful. I just wanted to make sure you knew. MG

Author's note: I had hoped that with the passage of time, you would be capable of taking a step back. Can you do that? Can you try to read this through the eyes of a stranger?

Reader's note: Why would I want to do that? MG

Author's note: Why wouldn't you be willing to do that? In the interests of comfort and harmony.

Reader's note: There is little evidence that comfort and harmony are any concern of yours. MG

Meg's basic work, they had agreed, would average out to about two hours every day in the library, or about ten hours a week spent on research tasks, plus another six hours, three afternoons of the week, with the Frank children after school. Any child-minding responsibilities beyond that would be negotiated as they came along, including those which might involve Joanna or Amy.

Time spent with his children was the exhausting part of the

job. Alice and Wills had taken to her so quickly Meg had found it worrying. Why were they so eager to consider her their intimate after just one meeting? Whenever she was with them, they crawled all over her. Wills would burrow into her lap like a puppy, while Alice would run her not-unsticky fingers through Meg's hair in nearly hypnotic fashion until Meg would finally, in a gentle way, ask her to stop. But Meg was sympathetic to them, and she felt that for whatever reason they really needed her in their lives.

Mark spoke fondly of Alice and Wills but didn't seem to spend very much time with them. Their mother was strange and reticent. Meg had at first supposed Kelly Howard to be his contemporary, but it was hard, really, to tell how old either of them were. She had wild hair and wild eyes and always looked as though she had a headache or was just waking up. Meg was never sure if she was dressed or not. ("I never know if she's coming or going, and I mean that literally!" she told her sisters.) Meg thought at first that Kelly was as British as Mark, based on the few syllables they exchanged, but then after the next encounter she decided that Kelly was, in fact, American. She couldn't figure Kelly Howard out at all. There was clearly a problem. She was supposed to be brilliant at something, everyone seemed to know this, but nobody Meg knew seemed to know what it was. Meg saw no evidence of brilliance or even basic productivity.

Several times, when Meg had arrived at the appointed hour in their dark warren of rooms on the third floor, Wills and Alice would have been home from school for perhaps an hour. But they would be waiting for Meg to make them something to eat, although their mother was there, lying on her bed reading, or, sometimes, just lying on her bed. Kelly would greet Meg languidly, with a slightly vague and confused look, as though she neither had been expecting her nor could quite remember who Meg was. Meg had begun to worry about Alice and Wills on the days when she wasn't with them.

The late arrival of the Frank children in New Haven had been problematic, but places for them in kindergarten and second grade had been found at Hand, a nearby private elementary school, to which they were driven every morning by a part-time art history lecturer whose daughter was in the kindergarten with Wills. A different Hand parent would inevitably drop them home after school. Apparently there was some sort of committee of parent volunteers that planned and scheduled to make this a certainty every school day, as though it were beyond question that Kelly could not be expected to take responsibility for the transport of her own children. Meg suspected that Mark's celebrity plus his charming English accent had gotten them quite far in their New Haven life. People were willing to do things for the Franks, and the Franks seemed quite willing to have those things done for them.

As there was never anything to eat in the kitchen, Meg would take the children down to the JE dining hall for a very early dinner. There was rarely evidence in the grim little apartment kitchen that anyone was planning to eat a real dinner or any other sort of planned meal. The kitchen cupboards contained little more than a few cans of soup and a depressing assortment of items pilfered from the dining hall—packets of crackers, small plastic tubs of apple sauce, and individual servings of cold cereal in little boxes. There were always dirty dishes and glasses in the sink when Meg arrived, and it seemed to Meg that Kelly never did the washing up, and instead simply counted on her to clean up.

Twice Meg had taken the children out for a snack at the counter at Atticus, the bookstore and café right on Chapel Street, which they enjoyed so much it was both gratifying and embarrassing. The expense was problematic and would have been very awkward to bring up to Mark, and Meg couldn't afford to take them to Atticus regularly. Perhaps she would ask him for some money to stock the kitchen with snacks for the children. Mark's lack of engagement with his family was not the most appealing thing about him, Meg would have admitted.

Wills had Mark's mouth and jaw, and the startling dark blueness of his eyes. The second time Meg was with the Frank children, she had been sitting on the big floppy sofa in their apartment when Wills settled into her lap with an almost heartbreaking sort of confidence, proffering a picture book, and Meg started to read it aloud. It was from the Hand school library, so someone must have picked it for him to take home for bedtime reading. It was one of Meg's favorite *Little Bear* books. She hadn't seen this book since Amy outgrew it.

Kelly was behind a closed bedroom door, perhaps taking a nap. The children seemed to know not to bother her or make noise. Alice was on her knees on the floor beside them, intently crayoning a castle she and Meg had been drawing together while Wills had been building a towering city out of books from one of the many packing boxes that were stacked through all the rooms. Meg had spent almost an hour brushing out Alice's hair, which had, beneath the outer layer of silky curls, been tangled in hard knots that had clearly been there a long while. Alice had been very good, though she cried softly for a moment when Meg had inadvertently yanked very hard on a particularly bad knot. Now she wore a red barrette of Meg's in her hair and seemed very pleased with her new look, interrupting progress on her castle every so often to scramble to her feet and check on her appearance in the bathroom mirror. Wills snuggled in more deeply and nuzzled his face into the notch above Meg's collarbone. The top of his head gave off a puppyish tang she quite liked.

Mark came home not so long after, when they were on their second reread of *Little Bear.* When he saw the cozy tableau, he murmured, "Lucky lad," and Meg pretended not to have heard him, though she lost her breath as she kept reading, and she sounded to herself like someone who had just run up a flight of stairs. She read to Wills with extra tenderness, in a voice she knew his father could hear as he walked about the apartment frowning, looking at the mail and glancing about at the mess. The world was larger than it had been the moment before.

Reader's note: I have a real problem with this whole development. I feel like a voyeur reading these scenes. Are they necessary to the novel? It seems so private. Why isn't the narrative staying in the point of view of the middle sister, after all, that paragon of sensitivity? Why isn't this novel more Joanna's story? AG

    Author's note: The novel's about what it's about. It's not about what it's not about.

Kelly, it turned out, was a former student of Mark Frank's. Meg had learned this fascinating news from one of her favorite teachers from freshman year, Claire Shipman, whom she had run into at Starbucks.

    "I hear you're working for Mark Frank!" Claire had exclaimed, by way of greeting. "How is that going for you? He's quite the wild man!" They had ended up sitting together for a few minutes to chat. It was the middle of the day, so Joanna was at school, which was good from a privacy point of view, but bad because Meg had grown unaccustomed to paying full price for her coffee. Professor Shipman had taught Meg's section of English 120, and she had been such a dynamic teacher, especially when they were reading Dickens, that Meg had written "Claire Shipman rocks my world!" on her course evaluation form.

    Although they touched on other subjects briefly, including Meg's current schedule of classes, Claire Shipman, who urged her to drop the "Professor Shipman" and just call her Claire now that Meg was a former student, seemed eager to return to the subject of Mark Frank, whom she had known when she was a graduate student at Duke and he was just making a name for himself with a series of provocative essays in *Rolling Stone.*

"Kelly was my student her first semester at college," she told Meg. "I was teaching my first class, too, so we were both neophytes. It was a section of the big introductory class Duke's English department prides itself on, something not unlike our own 114, and she was utterly original in a way that stood out, from her first paper, which was on existentialism and *Beowulf.* I was totally intimidated by her. She took Mark's seminar the very next semester, which was rare in itself, for a freshman, given what a hot ticket that class was, with juniors and seniors fighting for a place at the table, but apparently she had gone to see him in office hours to plead her case and he had been struck, as we all were, by her potential. Or by something, anyway."

"What was the seminar?"

"'The Interior Worlds of Henry James.' It was a nice class. Don't give me that funny look, the boy wonder of hermeneutics did start out on a traditional path before he reinvented himself. He was in transition when I knew him at Duke. You can probably look up some of his publications from that period. The seeds were already being sown if you know where to look. He wrote something quite good about James's fascination with vulgarity that in some ways was one of his first High Art–Low Art pieces. Mark also used to dress in a jacket and tie for class, if you can imagine that, like the Oxford intellectual that he was, before he started in with the bad-boy leather jackets and Mickey Mouse T-shirts."

"What was Kelly like when she was a student?" Meg was curious. "She seems very depressed now. Have you seen her since they've been here? She would remember you, don't you think?"

"You know, I feel bad about it, but I've been sort of avoiding both of them," Claire admitted. "I really shouldn't be telling you any of this." She burst out laughing as Meg leaned in with animation as she uttered these last words. "I suppose anything preceded by a statement like that sounds pretty juicy, doesn't it?"

"I really do want to know this," Meg admitted. "But only tell me if you want to," she added insincerely.

"Kelly was just brilliant. You know she was very successful for a while, when they lived in New York when he was lecturing at Columbia, right after they were married, doing these odd sort of performance readings?"

"What do you mean?"

"Oh, she would write these monologues that weren't exactly poetry and she would sort of inhabit them. She dressed up in weird clothing she found at the Salvation Army and had bizarre props. It was all very tongue-in-cheek sort of glosses on surrealism. It was performance art, very strange, but very funny and original and very, very intelligent. Full of arcane references to all sorts of texts. You know Harold Bloom laughed until he wept at one of those performances, when nobody else could ever figure out the joke. He told someone it was a pun in Greek about Walter Pater that made reference to James, Ovid, and Wittgenstein. But then he didn't want to explain it. 'My dear,' he said, you know, the way he always does, 'you simply had to be there.' That sort of thing. People say she was just amazing. I've only read small parts of those performances, in reviews. Everyone thought she was going to publish a collection but nothing has ever come of that."

"So then what happened?" Meg demanded, sounding to her own ears like a spoiled child who had to hear the continuation of a bedtime story.

"Well, then, having married her for her brilliance, he did his best to annihilate it, which he has done before apparently. Basically he proceeded to keep her barefoot and pregnant."

"Literally? And what do you mean, he's done it before, done what?"

"Well, you know what I mean. It's an expression. Found a

bright woman for a wife and kept her pregnant and on the side-lines. He does tend to marry the competition. There's a bitter first wife—have you ever heard of the mystery writer Joan Ritter? That's the one. And there are adult children who don't speak to him."

"How old is Mark?" Meg tried to seem curious in an impersonal way, though Claire didn't seem especially aware of Meg's avidity for information on this topic.

"Mark is fifty-one."

"Seriously?"

"I only know this because at Duke someone very close to me was involved with him. She was the person he left his wife for, and then he dumped her for Kelly. Believe me, I know more than I could ever want to know about Mark Frank, and he is definitely fifty-one."

"I'm really surprised," Meg tried to say this as mildly as she could. "I mean, about all of it. I mean, this just wasn't my impression—"

"Well, but aren't you minding those cross midgets?" Claire interrupted. "How are you managing? I hear they're a terror. You know they crawled out a window onto a roof the first night they were on campus? Mark and Kelly seemed somehow not to notice they weren't in their beds—it was a student walking through the quad who happened to look up and see them scampering around on the slates. I know, it sounds impossible, but it happened," Claire added, as Meg got the meaning of what she had just said and put her hand to her mouth to stifle her gasp of disbelief.

"Nightmarish, isn't it? What are they, on the fourth floor?"

"Third."

"Well, that's high enough." Claire looked at her sympathetically. "Nobody told you about this? Somebody should have warned you if you're responsible for those children. Who knows, they might think of doing it again. Although those are sort of tricky window latches on the old windows in those colleges. I hear they're replacing them in the next big round of renovations."

"Wills could probably undo those casement latches," Meg said. "In fact, I know Alice can. I've asked her to open a window myself."

"So now you can be on your guard. I am so glad we ran into each other! I feel much less guilty telling you all this now that the roof escapade has come up," Claire said. "I can't believe nobody warned you about that specifically. Are they little horrors to mind?"

"No, they're really sweet with me."

"Well, maybe they've begun to settle down. Anyway, from what I hear, after each pregnancy Kelly's gone into a serious depression, and maybe she wasn't too stable to begin with, you know? Though now I am sounding like a bitch on wheels. She hasn't done any work in years is the one thing I know for a fact. Not since before the first one was hatched. She's basically just disappeared professionally. There's a certain element of *schadenfreude* for my friend, as you can imagine, which is why she keeps track. Sometimes I tell her that if it weren't for Kelly Howard coming along when she did, those would have been her babies and her non-career."

"So how old is Kelly?"

"Well, if she was a freshman the first year I taught at Duke, she would be, what, twenty-eight now."

Meg thought this through. "Alice is seven!"

"And your point is . . . ?" Claire looked at her knowingly. "Yes, she was twenty-one when she had Alice." She looked at Meg again. "That's right, she didn't graduate."

Meg plowed through pages of English (*Canterbury Tales*) and history (the Crusades had been going on for what felt like an eternity), and she made a good start on her astronomy reading. She was taking an introductory astronomy class in order to fulfill a science requirement. It had been either the geology class known as Rocks for Jocks or this one, which was sometimes called Stars for Poets. Meg

had opted to study the stars because word had it there were divert-
ing nighttime field trips to the Yale Observatory out in Bethany,
but so far the trips had been canceled because of bad weather.

She had left for very last some revisions on the ongoing draft of
her independent English project, a hopelessly ambitious paper devoted to the impact of captivity on the narrative voices in *The
Catcher in the Rye* and *The Diary of Anne Frank*. She didn't have another meeting with Clayton Linton, her tutorial supervisor, until
the following week. Professor Linton was known for his hair
(a mysteriously achieved upsweep of the type Amy called "soufflé
hair") and for his passionate lecture style. Meg had never gotten
over the time in her sophomore year when he burst into tears in
the middle of a Dante lecture. He had fled the room, with an
apologetic, "Oh, I just can't go on, I just can't go on!"

Unsure of her ideas, and unsure that Professor Linton was going to be able to help her especially, as the material was outside his
usual range, Meg was becoming apprehensive about getting the
paper done. She decided she would ask Mark if he had any advice
for her when she met with him in the afternoon. She wondered if
there was any possible way he was related to Anne Frank. She tried
not to think about Claire Shipman's intelligence on Mark's family
life, but failed.

Teddy finished his philosophy reading (Sartre), and then made
some inroads on the vast quantity of Milton he had to finish before
the next lecture if it was going to make very much sense to him.
Schoolwork always came easily to Teddy, and it was common practice for him to let his mind wander a bit while he read, as he could
still be confident that the material at hand had been sufficiently
absorbed by some adjacent part of his brain. Pondering Milton's
blindness and its effect on the reading before him, Teddy also pondered the Green sisters' stubborn rage at their parents, about

whom he was, naturally, quite curious. Though he felt that Meg was the least self-indulgent with her anger, he wasn't sure she was any less certain of it. And Joanna and Amy were so brittle on the subject. Their insistence on the absoluteness of the situation was intractable! It was, in a way, Teddy realized (having at this moment one of those tiny ridiculous epiphanies one can have when reading a profound work of literature while simultaneously addressing a surprisingly parallel matter in one's life), another form of blindness and another paradise lost.

Joanna struggled a while with some irregular French verbs, with which Teddy was, as always, a tremendous help. She also dashed through some absurdly simple essay questions on *The Great Gatsby* for her English class. (Why does Nick Carraway think Jay Gatsby is "Great"? What is "the valley of ashes" and what does it symbolize? What is the symbolic meaning of Dr. T. J. Eckleberg's sign?)

Joanna had loved *Gatsby* when they read it the year before in her advanced English class at Warren Prep. She had written a paper on the meanings attached to Fitzgerald's depictions of honesty and dishonesty throughout the novel, for which she had been given an A, as well as an honorable mention for an English prize.

These irritatingly simplistic homework questions in front of her now could have come directly from the CliffsNotes she had seen openly displayed all around the classroom that day. Study notes such as those had been banned from classrooms at Warren.

Maybe the dour Mrs. Jacobson was relying on some teachers' version of crib notes as well. Her classes were just deadly, and they seemed to move at a glacial pace through the novel, which Joanna had taken to reading over and over while the so-called discussions droned on, which meant that she had practically memorized whole passages. She still loved it. Her copy of *Gatsby* was a tat-

tered and coverless specimen, one of the last left on the shelf by
the time she found her way to the class. (They had been spoiled by
Warren's tradition of providing each student with fresh copies of
books read for English class. When Amy saw the poor object, she
had exclaimed, "Ew! Think of all the eye-tracks on that book!")

This *Gatsby* was heavily annotated by previous scholars with
ballpoint-pen emendations on the text. Where Myrtle says of her
poor husband George, "He wasn't fit to lick my shoe," an enormous tongue lapped across the page. Jordan Baker's being a "slender, small-breasted girl" had provoked an obscenely enormous
pair of cartoon breasts, which drooped all the way down the margin of the page, and then again, at the end, a single specimen il-
lustrating "the fresh green breast of the new world" had been
literally rendered in green marking pen by the same generous
hand.

Many of the other students in Joanna's classes seemed to her as
if they were in some kind of trance. For the first couple of weeks of
school, Joanna felt as if she herself were not in a trance but in some
sort of never-ending improvisation for some very lame drama
workshop exercise of the sort devised by desperate substitute
teachers. Her days were nothing at all like any of her previous
school experiences and everything like certain movies and television programs about high school life. Joanna played her part as
best she could—the good kid trying to make her way under ex-
tenuating circumstances.

There was a dirty-looking boy who sat behind her in pre-calc
who actually put his head down on his desk and slept, day after
day. Sometimes the slight buzz of his snoring had a soporific
quality she had to work to resist. In her history class, most days
the teacher would hand out photocopied workbook sheets and
make them sit quietly answering endless multiple-choice questions on the material they were supposedly covering, while he sat
behind the desk at the front of the room, flipping through the

sports pages of the *New Haven Register*, and, unbelievably, listening to his Walkman.

Mrs. Jacobson was the worst, or maybe it just seemed that way because Joanna had always loved English class until now. A cranky old burnout with halitosis and varicose veins who was clearly counting the days until her pension kicked in, Mrs. Jacobson seemed not to notice what anybody did in her classroom, just so long as they were quiet. She didn't seem to care, really, if anybody was paying any attention at all, just as long as nobody made sudden movements or unexpected loud noises before the bell rang.

No other teacher activated Joanna's indignation so strongly as did Mrs. Jacobson, who had so far remained both totally immune to Joanna's obvious intelligence and uncharmed, as well, by her obvious eagerness to be engaged with the material. She seemed to feel that Joanna's comments and questions on the text, requiring deviation from the lesson plan as they did, were just one more obstacle between her and her retirement, just another form of trouble in her already burdened life. Mrs. Jacobson acted as if she had been sentenced to teach English at Duncan, Joanna thought, though for what crime? Callous indifference to young minds and great literature, perhaps.

But what crime had the students in the class committed, what had any of them done, even the potheads in the back of the room, to deserve such punishment as being taught by Mrs. Jacobson? *"Let the punishment fit the crime! Let the punishment fit the crime!"* echoed in Joanna's head sometimes during especially tedious moments in class—though not as badly as it would if she were Amy—as the Green sisters had over the years performed a lot of Gilbert and Sullivan in their living room musical entertainment repertoire. She couldn't exactly foresee an improvement in the classroom atmosphere when they moved on to their next required text, either. If Mrs. Jacobson could make *The Great Gatsby* stultifying, then

The Scarlet Letter, which Joanna had also read at Warren, back in ninth grade, held the promise of even greater desolation.

Joanna very much missed the feeling of loving school these days, but it couldn't be helped. Because she and Amy had registered at Duncan after classes had already begun, and though they were both qualified, according to their Warren transcripts, for placement in honors classes, there had been no room for them in any honors English class. Joanna was in an honors French section that wasn't bad, though the teacher had an atrocious accent and resented her for having actually been to France, and Amy had been admitted to a special studio art class, which also met so early in the morning that it still had a space.

Reader's note: At last, we learn something of the inner workings of the middle sister. MG

Author's note: I'm not sure what point you're making with that note.

Reader's note: I'm merely commenting on the way you have finally turned the novelizing machine on yourself. MG

Amy's homework was a snap. Every night, she could just zip through it and then draw and do some watercolor sketches or write in her journal. She didn't even want Joanna to know how little time her homework took her to complete, for fear that Joanna and Meg—and Teddy, too—might take it upon themselves to devise some more challenging work for her. Often, Amy lied and said she had worked all afternoon before anyone else came home, or she claimed she had used study periods to do homework assignments.

Amy felt as though she were just gliding through her classes every day at Duncan. She always knew all the answers, in every subject, and had recently begun to hesitate when called on in class, so as not to be the object of derision by the core clique of popular tenth-grade girls—at least, not any more than she proba-

bly already was. Her uncoolness had been identified on the first
day, in her history class, when Amy had been able to rattle off the
Seven Hills of Rome. This alone had probably labeled her as
a suck-up freak right then. Anna Scriven, the popular girl who
seemed to be the crucial social arbiter, the one girl in the class
whose approval or disapproval meant everything, had murmured
an undisguised, "Oh my God." But Amy had liked the startled
look on the teacher's face. She enjoyed feeling smart.

A haphazard student at Warren, which was a highly rigorous
school, Amy had always coasted somewhere in the bottom third of
her grade's class rank. Here, she was automatically the star of every
class in her schedule. Maybe the momentum from Warren would
wear off sooner or later, but at this point she felt not only very
brave and independent, but also almost magically empowered, as
if she had somehow become some kind of genius on the trip up to
New Haven from New York.

At sudden little moments, though, particularly on the long
walk back to High Street at the end of the day, when lights would
be going on everywhere and the billowing detritus of rubbish and
leaves swirling around lampposts and newspaper vending boxes in
the evening gloom would take on a sinister cast—during what
their mother always called "the blue hour"—Amy would sometimes feel a terrible pang, a sweeping feeling of panic and loss that
would just wash over her. It was a feeling that made her feel inexplicably fragile and sad and old. She knew she didn't just simply
hate her mother and father. She blamed them for the way she
missed loving them, the way she missed a much younger version
of herself. She blamed them for the way she missed being the Amy
Green who loved her parents so much and felt so loved by them
that it filled up her whole world without taking up any space at all.

*Reader's note: I feel that I should make a comment here, but I have noth-
ing to say. I'm actually touched that you know me so well. AG*

Reader's note: Beware. She doesn't know any of us as well as she thinks she does. She knows the characters she has made out of all of us very well. Don't confuse yourself with the character that is based on you. Don't let her revise your memories so that this novel takes the place of the actual events and experiences. MG

Reader's note: Give me some credit for having a brain, please. AG

EIGHT

Pilgrimage

❧

Even with Meg's steady income from Mark Frank, money was still tight. Reluctantly, she had cut back on her habit of giving a daily dollar to the Shakespeare Lady, a tragic and brilliant homeless woman who inhabited various doorways on Broadway. She had all of Shakespeare in her head, and insisted on reciting a sonnet in exchange for handouts from Yale students. When Meg lived on campus, she would often smuggle food from the dining hall for the Shakespeare Lady, and the previous winter, on a dreadfully bitter day, she had given her the really nice leather gloves her parents had sent the week before.

Meg and Joanna were in agreement that under no circumstances should Amy be allowed any sort of job—they wanted her to devote herself entirely to her schoolwork. Let no one ever be able to say that they hadn't managed well enough on their own or that their education had suffered.

Despite all of their budgeting and the fruit of their hard work, after the first cold weather utility bill coincided with the bookstore bill for Meg's course books, they realized they just weren't going to make it unless each of them dipped into savings. They simply had to do it, though it was a violation of their long-term plans, made in a family meeting three years ago. But wasn't this whole situation a huge violation of their long-term plans? They hoped they wouldn't need to take very much, just enough to get by. This was money that had been put aside over the years with the intention that it would pay for something really major someday after they had each completed college (which their parents had always told them would be completely funded, but now each of the three sisters was unsure in her own way if she could accept tuition money from them, though Meg was grateful that her Yale tuition had already been paid for both semesters, postponing that issue for many months). The really major something might be an amazing trip for the three of them together, perhaps, or cars, maybe even down payments on houses. This money had always been seen as something reserved for the start of their grownup lives. The Green sisters had always looked forward to their independence, but had never imagined it would come so precipitously.

The bank accounts had been opened when the girls were in elementary school. Lou and Janet had always emphasized that these accounts were the girls' own, to do with as they saw fit, though of course there was a great deal of moralizing talk about the virtue of saving the money for the future rather than squandering it on ephemeral amusements. At first there had been regular augmentations by generous birthday checks from their two grandparents. Then there had been small grandparental bequests.

Though they would have been shocked had anyone called them rich, the Green sisters had always lived very comfortably. They knew that Great-aunt Hodgson had left their father her estate, which was presumably a lot of money. Although finances had always been a serious subject, in their family it had been neither taboo nor a source of any particular worry. This had been fine while they were one big happy family. Each of them had assumed that the day would come when they would be on their own, but true financial independence had always been a vague concept for some future moment. Now Meg especially began to realize how naïve and ignorant they had been.

The three Green sisters had also always been pretty conscientious about saving any money they earned baby-sitting or on summer jobs. Added to those funds were the odd occasional windfalls or surprises (as for instance when Meg won five hundred dollars as part of an award for a philosophy essay on Prize Day just before her graduation from Warren, when she hadn't even known her essay was under consideration). Consequently, that autumn, each of them had a bank balance of something close to twenty thousand dollars.

They took the train to New York on the last Saturday before Christmas. It was a sharply beautiful day. The passing scenery, even ugly industrial yards, seemed possessed of some special clarity, as if rinsed of all summer haze and vagueness.

"You are absolutely positive that our bank is open on Saturday?" Amy asked for the tenth time since they had boarded the train. She closed her sketch pad and chewed absentmindedly on the eraser of her pencil, as was her habit.

"No, I'm sure it's closed. That's why we're here, idiot, going into the city for no reason whatsoever, so we can stand at the locked door and beat on it until mounted policemen come galloping up to chase us away," Joanna said crossly from behind her newspaper. (It was her newspaper now, though it had originally belonged to a businessman who left it on his seat when he got off the train in Stamford.)

"They're open until one on Saturdays. I told you already, sweetie. I called to make sure, too," Meg said more temperately from behind her history text, which she had been completely unable to read since boarding the train, though she had held the book open to the first page of her Crusades reading assignment for over an hour now, as if somehow the meaning of the words would flow directly to her brain through osmosis if she just stared at the pages long enough.

The train stopped at 125th Street and a few people got out.

The door closed and a conductor came through their car announcing the final stop in a matter of minutes.

"What time is it?" Amy asked for only the sixth occasion since they had left the apartment to walk to Union Station and the third time since they had sat down on the train.

"It's eleven-ten." Meg glanced at her watch and answered without looking up.

"Hey, Ames, we need to talk," Joanna said, bundling and thrusting the newspaper under her seat. It was *The Wall Street Journal.* Other than a pretty good movie review, it had turned out to be incredibly boring reading and, to top it off, very conservative. No wonder it had never been a Green family staple. And what was up with those drawings of people on the front page, as if *The Wall Street Journal* did not want to admit that photography had been invented?

"What, my dear sister," Joanna asked, "is your *problem* with the time thing? You are wearing a watch, aren't you? What time does your watch say?"

"Eleven-ten. I just don't trust it, I mean, what if it's not running right?"

"I think you can trust it," Joanna said. "Your watch is fine—look, same as mine. Same as Meg's. It's got to be more than coincidence, don't you think? Now it's eleven-eleven. That must be a lucky time. When you were little, you would make a wish."

"What did zero say to eight?" Amy asked abruptly.

"What?"

"Your belt's too tight!" Amy chirped with a triumphant grin. Joanna and Meg groaned appropriately. "So where does seaweed look for a job?" Amy asked, unwilling to relinquish her hold on them.

"Where?" Meg said wearily.

"In the kelp-wanted ads!"

One moment Amy seemed as mature and composed as anyone in her classes, but then at the next moment she was a little kid, Meg reminded herself, for whom this all had to be harder than

it was for her and Joanna. The train seemed to accelerate as it
whisked them out of the sunlight just then, entering the black-
ness of the Park Avenue Tunnel.

"Did you know bone china is made with real bones? Isn't that
gross?" Amy asked no one in particular and neither of her sisters
replied.

"What if the bank won't give us our money?" Amy asked as
she and Joanna stood up to put on their jackets. They rocked with
the motion of the train as it hurtled the final miles to Grand Central Station. People around them were stirring, gathering their
things, and could probably hear the conversation, though nobody
looked very interested. It was a Christmas-shopping crowd for the
most part.

"It's our money. They have to," said Joanna.

"What if they tell Janet and Lou?"

"What if they do?" Joanna nudged Meg, who was still reading
in her seat across from them; she was the only member of the family who could tolerate riding backward on a train. "Hey, we're almost there, Meg." She wanted Meg to join in reassuring Amy, and
she wanted reassurance for herself as well. This was the first time
they had left New Haven. It felt weird to be going into New York
as visitors, just for the day.

Amy plucked at Meg's sleeve, trying to get her attention.

"Don't pizzicato me," Meg said, swatting her hand away, still
reading. The door at the end of their car banged open and the conductor walked through again, a draft of dank New York underground air wafting after him. Joanna had a sudden intense stab of
something like homesickness that she hadn't felt until this moment. She let her leg jostle against Meg again.

"What?" Meg begrudgingly looked up from her book.

"Amy has a question."

"Like that's an amazing event?"

"What if they won't give us our money, and what if they tell
Janet and Lou?" Amy repeated.

Meg shrugged. "Why would they bother? Anyway, it's not really their business, is it?"

"How do you want it?" the teller asked Meg, stamping the withdrawal slip. They hadn't thought about this. They had worried about all sorts of other details and yet in the end everything went perfectly smoothly. They had anticipated all sorts of eventualities during the ride on the Broadway bus that took them uptown to their bank. What if someone saw them and reported back to Janet and Lou? What if they actually ran into their mother or father, or any number of other people in the neighborhood who knew them? Or friends from school?

Joanna and Amy had kept up with a few friends through e-mail and a little bit on the telephone, but neither of them was ready to see anyone from their old life, especially not on this Saturday, on this singular money mission. But those friendships were fading away rapidly. It was just all so embarrassing and complicated, almost beyond explanation. Being cut off from everybody from their old life seemed an inevitable and almost natural part of the cataclysmic shift their lives had undergone. The few friends with whom Joanna and Amy had promised to stay in touch had not really understood what they were doing, leaving home and moving in with Meg. And now that they were actually doing it, not just making angry noises about why they should leave, their new life would be all the more inexplicable.

Amy was well liked at school, but like Joanna, she had always felt so close to her sisters that she hadn't needed to make very many of those intense connections that most girls seek. The only close friend she had ever had, Emma Corrigan, had moved to Los Angeles with her mother at the end of the school year the previous spring, and Amy had felt the loss acutely all summer. No matter what anybody promised, she knew that they would never again have the same closeness, living so many miles apart. She and

Emma had gone to camp together for five summers, and Amy once spent a month with the Corrigans at their house in Sag Harbor. But that was before Emma's parents divorced.

Joanna had always been more of a loner, content to be well liked during school hours. The people she missed most acutely were certain Warren teachers. Mrs. Possick, the English teacher who told her she had the makings of a writer. Mr. Ryden, the British history teacher for whom she had written a huge extra-credit paper on Benedict Arnold. And she had been supposed to be managing editor of the *Warren Widgeon* this year. The adviser to the school's creative writing magazine, Mrs. Altschul, must have felt very let down. She had lobbied hard to get Joanna appointed to the position although it went against tradition to give it to a junior. And she had hugged Joanna so warmly on the last day of classes in June, telling her she was looking forward to working with her on the *Widgeon* in the fall.

It must have seemed to everyone at Warren as if Joanna and Amy had gone on an unexpected long trip, or taken a semester abroad. One of the last things Janet had said to Joanna was something to the effect that their places were being held at Warren, a school used to families who took semesters or entire years out of the country here and there. There had been a few sporadic communications with classmates, e-mails from the kind of girls who write to everybody they know, but after the beginning of the Warren school year, with everyone caught up with classes and sports and all the other preoccupations of school life, Amy and Joanna had simply slipped out of contact with every one of their New York acquaintances.

"We'll be those girls in the class pictures where nobody can remember their names," Amy said bitterly. "Look, that kid, I remember her, she was the girl who played the flute that time at the Thanksgiving assembly. What was her story? She and her older sister ran away from their parents and disappeared? I wonder whatever happened to them?"

"Oh, stop it," Joanna said. "More likely they'll look at their old class pictures someday and say, 'Why, look at that, Amy Green was in my class. I wish I had gotten to know her better before she left. And now she's so famous and successful, she would probably never remember me.'"

"Damn straight." Amy grinned gratefully at Joanna.

Reader's note: This chapter is amazing. It's completely accurate. I love it. Why can't the whole novel be like this chapter? It would be totally successful. AG

Reader's note: What you're calling accuracy is not necessarily a desirable feature. Some people might call it laziness. Is it really a novel when she isn't making up fiction at all, but is instead just reporting? I agree, this chapter is pleasant, so far, but I don't believe the accuracy is the element that makes it so. MG

Author's note: Amy—I'm glad you like it. Meg—Feel free to mention any parts of the manuscript you do like.

Although it was located so close to the apartment, they had elected to go to their own familiar bank branch where they maintained their accounts, out of a theory that they were known there, so large withdrawals were much less likely to be questioned. It felt unreal, like a dream, when they actually pushed their way through the heavy revolving door to the imposing bank lobby.

The bank in New Haven where Meg had her student account was dingy and plain, with a low ceiling and chipped fake walnut-grained Formica counters. It was situated just beside a community-center soup kitchen, and some of the people on the long lines at the bank looked as poor as the unfortunates who lined up waiting for the door to the soup kitchen to open at noon.

Joanna was struck for the first time by the beauty and elegance of this New York institution, with its soaring vaulted ceiling and ornate granite columns. Suddenly she understood for the first time why Lou would often launch into a horribly tuneless "I dreamt I dwelt in marble halls" when she was little and she would tag along when he did neighborhood errands. There had been an old-fashioned mechanical coin-counting machine at one time. Joanna recalled the sound it made counting the pennies from their big penny jar which they would bring in with great ceremony when it got full. She looked for it, but it wasn't there anymore, and in its place was a cluster of ATMs.

Cash? Large bills? The teller was growing impatient. How else would she get her money? Surely not traveler's checks. But cash? Meg looked at Joanna, and Joanna shrugged. They hadn't thought this through. Would so much cash be safe? A check? Yes, yes, a check, Meg agreed. Perfect. A bank check, then, was made out to Margaret Charlotte Green for the sum of twenty-five hundred dollars. In turn, Joanna and Amy each withdrew the same amount from their accounts. Prudently, Joanna also asked for her money in the form of a bank check. But Amy wanted hers in cash, in fifties and twenties. Meg and Joanna couldn't persuade her otherwise. With an important air, she took the thick sheaf of bills from the teller and stopped at a counter to organize it and tuck it away in her wallet. (She had a beautiful blue wallet of soft leather, one of last year's birthday gifts from Janet and Lou.)

"Do you think so much cash is safe?" Meg asked in a confidential tone a while later, when they were eating lunch at their favorite neighborhood sushi bar on Amsterdam Avenue, a place they had missed terribly, though sushi was a costly luxury these days. "We never have this much cash."

"This much cash. Dismiss crash. Isthmus bash. Christmas rash—" Amy started up.

"Oh, please," Joanna muttered, snatching the last *toro* morsel away from Meg's roving chopsticks. "Hieronymus Bosch."

"That's not close enough," Amy said crossly at Joanna's careless intrusion, which had spoiled the pattern. "Could we order one more dragon roll? I really miss dragon rolls. The ones in New Haven aren't the same."

"I'm just concerned about it, Ames," Meg said carefully, guessing that her youngest sister was both proud to be able to make a monetary contribution to their little household and also a little drunk on the excitement of having so much of her own cash in her hands. She nibbled on some little bits of pickled ginger from her otherwise empty plate. "So let me know if you want me to hold on to it for you, or anything. And no, we've already spent a fortune and you couldn't still be hungry."

"You're right, I am such a pig sometimes," Amy admitted. "I guess I'm not really hungry anymore. Anyway, here's a thousand dollars for the household," she added with grandeur, extracting her wallet from her bag and proceeding to count out that amount on the tabletop. The waiter had been approaching them with a pot of steaming tea for refills, but at the sight of the money on the table he skittered away. Perhaps, Joanna thought, he was used to cash deals on his premises and knew to keep a discreet distance.

"That's for our expenses for now, and I'll keep the rest." Amy pushed the money across the table and Meg took it and folded it compactly into an inner pocket of her knapsack. "Don't worry. I'll be careful. I know you think I'll waste it but I won't, I promise," vowed Amy. "This way, I can buy little things I need without having to come to you every time."

"Poverty enriches those who live above it," Meg said in a mock-Janet voice, and Amy and Joanna pelted her with the balled-up drinking straw papers that littered the table.

"Seriously, you guys, aren't you glad we did the work at the soup kitchen for Thanksgiving?" Amy asked. "Don't you feel really good about it?"

"I do," Joanna agreed, "though it made me so sad, especially those little kids. It also made me feel guilty for all the times we don't even think about people like that. You know, I see some of those people on Chapel Street almost every day. The guy who talked about chicken ghosts is always sitting out in front of Willoughby's. And the Shakespeare Lady broke my heart. We should work at the soup kitchen every week."

"You're right, I know," Meg sighed, "but I just don't have the hours in the day. I am so tired after classes and then the work for Mark, especially when I'm with Alice and Wills. But maybe you and Amy could go some nights. We should find out their schedule."

"How's that going?" Joanna asked. "You never say much about it. What's the work these days?"

"Oh, just a lot of different things getting his book ready for publication," Meg replied vaguely. "And we're working on a new project. Mark really liked my 'Babbitt to Rabbit' idea for a seminar he's thinking of proposing."

"When would he teach that? Isn't he only here for the year?" Joanna asked.

"He's thinking of extending his time at Yale," Meg replied distractedly, busying herself with their check.

"What do you think they tell their friends?" Amy wondered as they waited for the waiter to come back with their change. Lunch had been expensive, Meg noted, trying not to flinch when she read their total, even though they had not ordered with their customary abandon. She felt bad about turning Amy down on the additional dragon rolls. How many times had they eaten here in the past, blithely paying with easy pocket money handed out by Janet and Lou? She was, she had to admit, so fond of luxury.

"Who?" Meg said blankly.

"I mean," Amy continued, "do they lie about where we are and why? Do they just act like we're not home for the moment? Or do they tell everyone what wonderful selfless and sensitive parents they are being, indulging us in our fanciful little adventure?"

"Oh. Does it matter?" Meg asked with some weariness.

"Not really, of course not," Amy said. "But I mean, don't you wonder? I think about it a lot. Like when I practice my flute—"

"Which you should do more often," Meg interrupted.

"Anyway, I wonder if they care about whether or not I'm practicing, you know? Don't you think about it?"

"No, I don't think about it that way, actually," Meg replied carefully. "But then I left home to go to college two years ago. I'm not especially out of position the way you two are."

"Out of position," Joanna mused. "That's exactly right. That's what it feels like. I mean, I love living with you and I think the apartment is fine, but I do sort of feel out of position, like in a field hockey game when you're suddenly separated on the field from everyone else on your team and you have to figure out how to deal with it, you know?"

"Do you miss sports, Jo-Jo?" Meg asked suddenly. "God, I hadn't even thought about that! Not just the *Widgeon* thing, but weren't you supposed to be on the varsity team this season? You're right wing, aren't you? Oh, sweetie."

"Isn't that creepy old Kromesky from our building?" Amy said suddenly. "You know, Mr. no-neck science fiction writer guy?" It was. They sat in subdued silence until their erstwhile neighbor paid for his takeout order. He was never especially friendly to them when they weren't with their parents, and would have no reason to say anything to Janet and Lou, even if he ran into them while leaving one of those literary deposits on their doormat. That reminded Meg, she told her sisters, about a conversation she had the previous week with a guy in her history section who was obsessed with science fiction. He had been totally impressed that she lived in the same building as Kromesky, who, he had told her, had a huge success with a horror novel that had been turned into a cult classic of a horror film twenty years before, the residuals for which were probably supporting him now. They watched Kromesky with sidelong interest as he left.

"Close call, you guys," Amy said. "Let's eighty-six this joint."

"You've got that wrong," Joanna told Amy when they were back in the weak afternoon sunshine of Amsterdam Avenue, headed for the subway. Although they had spoken of going to the Museum of Modern Art, the way they had so often on a Saturday afternoon, it seemed like a drag now, and would probably be crowded. They were all three of them suddenly anxious to get out of the city and head back to New Haven.

"What do you mean?"

"I don't think that's right. I mean, as an active verb. I think 'eighty-six' is when you're thrown out of a place—you know, like you were drunk, so they've kicked you out—you've been 'eighty-sixed,' and then if you're banned you've been permanently 'eighty-sixed' from the place, and it's also when they've run out of something, like 'Eighty-six the tuna special.'" Joanna explained, with expertise only recently gleaned from Pearl, the waitress behind the counter at the Yankee Doodle, where she secretly repaired after school from time to time for a pig-in-a-blanket and a Coke before her Starbucks shift.

"It's also what you say when you're deleting some part of the order or some ingredient, like 'eighty-six the mayo on the BLT,'" Meg chimed in. She, too, had spent time in the Yankee Doodle. She was particularly impressed when, in order to accommodate two people together, the waitress would command "Doodle Shift!" and everybody wolfing down lunch at the tiny counter would slide over one place to make room without missing a bite.

"Jeez," Amy complained, "whatever, you guys. Go give a seminar on coffee shop lingo, why don't you."

"That's a good thought. I like it. '*Adam and Eve on a Raft: The Hermeneutics of the Coffee Shop in a Post-Chomsky World,*'" mused Meg. "There's a semester's credit for an independent project right there. I bet I could find someone to supervise it, too."

"When I was little I thought Janet knew someone named Herman Ootic," Amy confessed.

"We know. You've mentioned him before. The question is, did

he drive to work in a semiotic? Oh my God, there's Kromesky again," Joanna exclaimed. "Isn't he only supposed to come out at night? Why didn't he just go home and eat his sushi? Is he just carrying it around? What is *wrong* with him? Quick, guys, let's go in here, what is it, a gallery? Is the door unlocked, okay, go! Go! Move! Let him pass."

They ducked into a dazzling white space in which framed photographs were leaning against bare walls.

"Sorry—the gallery's closed until tonight at six," said a woman kneeling on the glossy oak floor surrounded by coils of picture wire and assorted bits of hardware. She said this cheerfully and without the usual sort of intruded-upon hostility one can encounter in such stray inadvertent circumstances, and the three Green sisters explained to her in a chorus of mutual interruption that they weren't there to look at the art but were hiding from someone and would only need to linger for just a moment more, if she didn't mind.

The woman laughed at this candid explanation, and, having finished wiring the frame over which she had been laboring, she got up to introduce herself as the photographer whose show was being exhibited. Everyone else had gone out to lunch, she explained, and she was here on her own until the gallery staff returned. A little embarrassed at their rudeness, they each felt obligated then to look at her work, and the photographer, who said her name was Harriet, told them to go ahead.

"They're lovely," Meg said perhaps just a little too quickly to have really taken in every one of the twenty or so images that surrounded them.

"It's all reflections, isn't it?" Amy asked, after another moment. Joanna had been studying the photographs one by one, and yet somehow had not noticed this, but it was true. Amy always saw the overall composition and connected structure of things so clearly and instantly, while sometimes Joanna felt as if there must be something wrong with her brain, she was so easily attracted to details that she often missed the more obvious patterns and larger meanings.

The photographs leaning against the walls of the gallery were a series of self-portraits taken in reflecting surfaces. Joanna was particularly struck by one showing the photographer, this Harriet, in what seemed to be a butcher shop window. There were all sorts of carcasses and pigs' heads and other dead animal parts visible around her and even through her face. It was savage and beautiful at the same time, as if it were a declaration that behind Harriet's almost sweet expression there were dark and unpretty—perhaps even murderous—thoughts.

"Is this how you see yourself?" Joanna asked, without turning around. "I know that feeling, but I've never actually seen it before."

"It was one of the ways I saw myself that summer," Harriet said. Joanna turned to look at her. She had gotten back onto the floor again and was intently screwing little eye-hooks into the sides of another frame. Joanna thought she seemed marvelously comfortable, this thirtyish woman in old jeans and a baggy sweater who had somehow come to possess certain knowledge about the world. Joanna yearned for some further connection with this fascinating person, but couldn't imagine how it would ever come about. She often discovered people and was excited by them in this fleeting way, harboring brief but intense curiosities, but she had not yet learned that other people had been known to respond to the discovery of her existence with a similar intensity.

"I've seen that picture somewhere," Meg said, coming up behind Joanna. "I know I've seen it very recently."

"There's another print of that image in the big survey show at the Modern that just opened last week," Harriet said. "'Black and White and Shades of Gray'—Have you seen the show? Or maybe a review? It's been all over the place."

"Oh, you mean MoMA? No, but actually we were talking about going today," Joanna replied. "But—"

"That's it! The same photograph was on the announcement for the show. I saw it in Janet's mail pile at the end of the summer," Amy contributed. "You're Harriet Rose."

"Yes, that's right," Harriet agreed. "And you're—?"

"Amy Green." The chatter had stopped abruptly with the mention of Janet's mail pile. Harriet looked at them expectantly.

"Oh, sorry, and this is Meg, and that's Joanna. Green also. I mean, our names are the same. We're sisters," Amy added unnecessarily, with her usual zest for blurting information haphazardly.

"Well, thanks, really, sorry to bother you, and good luck with the show," Meg said then. "Come on, guys."

"You're sure the coast is clear?" Harriet asked with an amused look on her face. Clearly, the three girls entertained her immensely. She was kneeling on the floor, coiling up some wire.

"He's gone," Amy confirmed, having made a second circuit of the group of photographs. She peeped out the door to be sure and then turned back inside and walked over to Harriet, who was now threading wire through the eye-hooks on another frame. "Um, excuse me again, but I just wanted to tell you that I really love the ones in the bucket of water, with the flowers," she said, a little self-conscious to be making a declaration of what was probably boring and obvious to the top of the head of the actual creator of the photographs.

"The way the stems of the flowers were going into the water break the line right there, you know? The way they come right through from one side of the reflection to the other, dividing the image? It's wonderful. And with your face just sort of there but not there? It's like a perception of a perception."

"You should be an art critic," Harriet said to Amy, putting down her pliers and getting to her feet. She stretched, and rolled her head around, unkinking her neck. "You're incredibly observant. No, that's not fair. I take it back. I know lots of unobservant art critics and some of them will be here in a few hours. I just wish art critics were as observant as you are. That's what I meant to say.

And by the way, the title of the show is 'Objects in Mirror,' which I have really mixed feelings about because it's kind of obvious, but the guy who promised to do the lettering on the door hasn't shown up yet, so now I really want it, but I'm trying not to panic one way or the other." Harriet got back down on the floor and reached for the next frame. Over her shoulder she added, "So, Miss Amy Green, are you a painter?"

"We've got to go," Meg said impatiently, holding the door open. Street noises underscored her determination to leave the peaceful little gallery space. "Sorry. Really. But, you guys, it's getting late—it'll be dark soon, and we have a train to catch."

"She plays the flute like a charm, but she is a *great* painter," Joanna pronounced, ignoring Meg for another moment. They had no specific train to catch, after all. Meg was just being bossy.

"Well, I'm really glad you ducked in here, you three, but don't let me keep you," Harriet said, scrambling to her feet and putting out her hand to shake each of theirs as they departed. "Meg, Joanna, Amy, goodbye, Green sisters! I'm sure we'll meet again."

They were subdued on the train ride home, oddly exhausted, but they had the satisfied feeling one does after a mission has been accomplished. Amy leaned heavily on Joanna's shoulder and slept most of the way home, while Joanna daydreamed out the window. The afternoon had grown gray and chilly. Meg, sitting across the aisle from them in the near-empty train car, attempted with a little more success to penetrate some of her history reading. As they pulled into the Milford station, Amy stirred and sat up.

"Look, you've drooled all over my jacket," Joanna complained good-naturedly. "Don't worry," she added, as Amy scrabbled for her bag, which was, after all, stuffed with an uncommon quantity of money. "I've got your bag over here with mine."

"She noticed about our names, but she didn't say anything," Amy said.

"Who did?" Joanna asked.

"The woman in the gallery. The photographer, Harriet. I could tell. She made a little smile when we told her our names, but she didn't make any of the usual stupid remarks. Do you really think I'm a great painter, Jo-Jo?" Amy asked, and snuggled down against her again. "That was such a nice thing for you to say to her."

"I really do," Joanna assured her. The train started rolling again; they would soon be in New Haven. "You have a wonderful talent. You were great teaching painting to those little kids at the Y in the summer, but I mean you have something that's really there, not just technical skill. You're incredibly skilled with a pencil but you also have an eye. Like the way you could really see those photographs today. I hope you keep up with your drawing even though everything else, like your painting class, is messed up right now."

"Maybe someday I can travel and be a great artist and have a show in a gallery," Amy said contentedly, and she closed her eyes again.

Joanna looked out the window at the rushing scenery. Mud flats, strange, mysterious, municipal structures of the sort visible only from trains and airplanes making final approaches to airports, and large dilapidated factory buildings all streamed past. The particular factory window from which, over time, it appeared that many different colors of paint had been spilled flashed by.

Joanna had first noticed this window the year before, when she had taken the train alone up to New Haven to visit Meg for the weekend, and now she reflexively looked for it whenever she rode the train. It was a private pleasure, a secret she shared with whoever it was who had been discarding paint out the back window of whatever sort of establishment it was, without, in all probability, having any awareness that the multicolored spills had made a splendid splashed pattern down the grimy concrete block wall. It was wonderful, Joanna felt, even though the window overlooked a hideous barbed-wire fence and a thicket of rusting metal drums and discarded fence sections and a solitary abandoned supermarket trolley canted at a useless angle. (How did it get there? It would have to have been hoisted over the high fence, and for what purpose? Another of life's mysteries.) The train rocked and another desolate factory building blurred by and Joanna continued gazing out at the darkening landscape, and saw, now, instead of the outside motion of the world passing, the stillness of her own pensive reflection in the window, with Amy's sweet head tucked under her chin.

NINE

Couch Potatoes and California Rolls

🌱

"Your father really invented the Couch Potato? That is so cool!"

Amy was nonplussed. She hadn't meant to say anything, but Anna Scriven had pulled out a Couch Potato during lunch, and it had been passed around her group with many giggles and whispers. Amy, eating her peanut butter and banana sandwich and a yogurt alone at the end of the same table as she did day after day, had blurted out that her father was the inventor of the Couch Potato before she could even consider the opprobrium she risked by attempting to initiate conversation with the Scriven crowd.

The Couch Potato was a molded plastic potato—an Idaho baking potato, more or less—with a button at one end resembling a potato eye. Pushing the button activated a chip that played a variety of responses in an accented, Dr. Ruth–ish voice of indeterminate gender which was a deliberate parody of every Viennese psychiatrist ever depicted in the worst jokes and movies about psychiatrists.

The Couch Potato repertoire of some thirty randomly generated replies ran the short gamut from "And vat comes to mind ven you zink of zat?" to "And does zat make you zink of your muzzer?" In between were such bits of wisdom as, "But vat is ze real qvestion here?" and "You must be kiddink!" Amy's contributions (the entire Green family had brainstormed the Couch Potato's responses) included "I zink you already know ze answer to zat qvestion," and, her personal favorite, "Zat's very interesting but ve vill speak of it anuzzer day because now our time togezzer is opp!"

"Yeah," Amy said, uncertain as to the extent of any appropriate reply to La Scriven, the Imperial Empress of the tenth grade. At Warren, Amy had always been able to negotiate a narrow perch at the edge of the popular group. She knew better here than to fall into the easy trap of presuming any right of intimacy on the basis of one possibly falsely extended olive branch.

"So, is your dad, like, some kind of shrink?" Anna asked. Her entire group now turned toward Amy expectantly. Amy regarded them warily, not sure what their smiles actually signified. This could be a breakthrough. It could also be a vicious game. Perhaps they weren't sure which it was going to be, either.

"No, he's an inventor. But he's really funny about shrink things. His college roommate is a shrink." She paused, not knowing whether she should say anything else. Talking too much would be a fatal error. *Fatal, natal, ladle, label, able Mabel, strong and able, keep your elbows off the table.*

"So, what's your name? Amy? Amy, do you ask the Couch Potato for help with your problems, or do you go to a real therapist?" This was from one of the Ladies-in-Waiting, Dana Snow, a loud, confident girl with a horsy laugh who drew prosaic rainbows and unicorns in art class.

"No," Amy replied coolly, looking her in the eye, trying not to show how wobbly she felt up here on the high wire with them, under the bright lights, the crowd roaring below. "Why do you ask? Are you looking for professional help? Maybe I could get you a referral." As she said the words, she regretted it.

"Ding ding ding!" approved one of the other girls, a paler sort of Anna Scriven copy, distinguished chiefly by her raccoon-like rings of dark purple eyeliner. Whenever Amy saw this girl—they had two classes together—she thought of her as Not Quite Anna Scriven. She didn't know her name. Not Quite made a little show of applauding Amy with fluttering hands over her lunch tray as she brayed in a carnival barker's voice, "I think we have a winnah heah, friends, a definite winnah!"

Dana glared at Amy with a hard, hateful look. At this game, where there was a winner, there was also a loser.

Anna Scriven was actually very funny and generous in her compliments, once she liked you. By the end of lunch period, Amy found herself laughing loudly with the girls at the table over countless little jokes and impressions of teachers and stories about some of the pathetic losers in their grade. There were seven of them in the core group (Teddy had dubbed them the Scriveners after listening to some of Amy's vivid descriptions of their unpleasant ways during the first week of school; she would have to correct the erroneously negative impression now that she was getting to know them better), and these girls always saved each other places when they met for lunch during sixth period.

Amy had noticed and envied the way they took turns bringing in delicious-looking lunch treats to share, while she sat nearby pretending to read and eating her sandwich. Before lunch on this day ended, Amy had first been given a generous handful of nachos to dip into the communal container of guacamole by Katia (the girl formerly known as Not Quite), and after that, Alexis passed a homemade brownie down the table to her as if she had always been part of this group.

The bell rang and they gathered up their things. Anna put her arm through Amy's as they made their way to the hall. Amy did her best to link arms casually. A stream of jostling bodies filled the hallway, and the roar of noise made it impossible to converse. The knot of girls dissolved into the greater mass of students. Now Amy was alone with Anna, who stopped for a moment and put her backpack down between her feet so she could re-do her ponytail. She held the elastic in her teeth while she scraped her hair off her face with both hands and then re-bound it with an expertise Amy had never had the patience to develop. When she put her hair up she was forever getting her fingers trapped in a band that was too tight or else she left the elastic too loose and her hair spilled out in a matter of minutes.

"I've got history, and, shit! It's Wednesday, so that's a double period of bio, and then basketball practice, so, I guess I'll see you tomorrow at lunch?" Anna acted as if they had been best friends since nursery school.

Amy nodded noncommittally, secretly jubilant.

"I could call you later, or wait, you call me—here's my number." Anna took up Amy's hand and proceeded to inscribe the precious numbers on her palm with a thick blue marking pen. "Okay, gotta go—call me!"

Amy stood in the middle of the hallway stupidly looking at her written-upon hand. Something tugged at her sleeve. She ignored it, and she felt the plucking again, this time augmented by a sharp pinch.

"Don't pizzicato me," she exclaimed in irritation, whirling around.

"Don't think you're so smart," Dana hissed. "And don't think I won't pizza-whatever you whenever I feel like it." She stood blocking Amy's way for a moment and then stalked past her. The warning bell rang. The corridor was suddenly deserted.

"Twenty-four divided by eight is three apiece," Amy said. "Right?"

"What?" Joanna looked up from her *Scarlet Letter* and marked her place with her finger. They were each lying on their beds in the room they shared, reading for a few minutes before sleep.

"Nothing."

"Twenty-four whats divided by eight whats?" Joanna asked in irritation. "I thought you were reading."

"Never mind."

"God, I hate it when you do that. Fine, I will." Joanna resumed reading about the conflicted Arthur Dimmesdale, whom Pearl refused to kiss. What a wuss! She tried to like him but just couldn't stay sympathetic for a moment. It was also hard not to envision Pearl growing up to be Pearl the waitress at the Yankee Doodle.

"California rolls."

Joanna threw down her book. She was a hundred pages ahead of the class anyway. "What?"

"Shh, I don't want to discuss this with Meg. She'll just be cross. I want to bring California rolls for lunch with my friends. If I get twenty-four for the eight of us, that would be three each."

"Oh God, those girls. I am so sick of hearing about them! First they were awful and you couldn't stand them and now they're so splendid you want to impress them with your sophisticated little palate. Why in the world should you spend your money for a parcel of girls who don't give a rat's ass about you? Why don't you just make sandwiches for them?"

"They do give a rat's ass! They're my friends now. And nobody eats sandwiches."

"That's crazy. Sandwiches are a great food. How can they not eat sandwiches? What do you mean? Everyone eats sandwiches."

"We just don't."

"We?"

Silence.

"Hey, Ames, correct me if I'm wrong, but you used to love sandwiches, I mean, like in the distant past, you know? A really, really long time ago, like last Thursday, you used to eat peanut butter and banana sandwiches every single day. Not now, of course. I understand. Times have changed, you've matured. Only nerds and dweebs and babies eat sandwiches."

Silence.

"So, Ames, tell me about these California rolls?"

Amy sighed, swallowing her impulse to make a barbed response, knowing that tolerating her sister's teasing would be in her best interest. "I would get them where Teddy goes—Jing's. We pass it on the way up Whitney Avenue, you know, next to the Laundromat."

"The ones he gets come five pieces to a package, I think, Ames. Does that mess you up?"

"So I would need, let's see. I could get—"

"And I think they're three dollars, if you care."

"So if I spent fifteen dollars that would be—"

"An insane waste of money."

"Fifteen dollars would be five packages for a total of twenty-five pieces of California roll. So there would be one extra if we each have three pieces," Amy concluded. She wrote all this down on a page in one of her school notebooks. "Soy sauce, ginger, wasabi," she murmured, writing.

"Remind me why you need to do this?"

"Oh, Meg, every day the others bring in really wonderful things to share and I just feel in debt at this point. I didn't dare do it before now because it would seem as though I was being aggressive, you know, assuming I was part of the group, but now I really am. Two different girls, Alison and the one I think still doesn't really want me in the group, you know, Dana Snow, have said something a little mean about my taking food from them without bringing in anything of my own to share. I really feel like I owe them."

"As if," Joanna corrected automatically.

"Well, whatever. I thought you wanted to hear about this."

"No, I mean 'as if' instead of 'like,'" Joanna said.

"Oh. As if I owe them, I mean. So what I was sort of hoping was that you would approve of the expenditure," Amy said hopefully, not rising to the usual bait of the Janet-like correction. The sisters had agreed that any unusual expenses had to be ratified.

"Surimi is just fish baloney, you know," Joanna commented in her superior, big-sister manner, which Amy knew meant she would approve of the California rolls, in the end. "They don't use real crab meat. Lou showed me an article about how they make surimi. It's not the worst, but it's really just a paste made with pollack and the orangy color is—"

"Lou's theories about California rolls or anything else are of no significance to me," Amy declared impatiently, and then stopped. She continued her calculations, hoping her outburst hadn't spoiled Joanna's decision about the fifteen dollars.

"Paprika," Joanna finished.

"So I'm not saying you should eat them if you don't want to. But I really need to bring them in this week, because after that it's Christmas break and I so, so, *so* need to pay people back right away. It's important, or I wouldn't ask. I just don't want to mess up my being part of this group. Will you agree that I can spend the money, please, please, please? What time do you think Jing's opens?"

"I think they won't have California rolls before your first class, no matter when they open," Joanna said. "They make those for the lunch crowd, mostly. But yes, I suppose I support this, if this really is a debt of honor."

"Thank you, Jo-Jo, I knew you would come through for me. It must be so nice to have lots of pocket money the way we used to! To think how I used to spend money without a thought! I'm going to tell everyone. We'll have such a grand feast!" Her eyes sparkled merrily.

Joanna enjoyed seeing her little sister looking so content. "All this talk has made me hungry," she said, getting up. "Do you want me to make you a peanut and banana sandwich? That's definitely what I'm having."

"Yes, please," Amy said in a small voice. "With a glass of milk."

The day she brought the California rolls to school, Amy was late for her first-period class, which ordinarily would not have mattered, because it was art, and not only was Miss Cunningham lenient in general but also she really liked Amy. Sequestered as she was down in the flaking art room under the sweating steam pipes with her hoard of underbudgeted art supplies, she wasn't really supervised by administrators and she tended to indulge her favorite students quite a bit.

Amy was late because the smiling but otherwise impossible-to-communicate-with proprietor of Jing's—perhaps this was Jing herself, Amy had no idea—had insisted on wrapping the freshly made California rolls very, very carefully and precisely and slowly before putting them all into a moist brown paper parcel. Teddy had placed the order for Amy, as he was a good customer whom they recognized and trusted about an advance order. But when Amy arrived, Jing, or whoever she was, wanted Amy to see them, to admire them, to revel in the glory of their freshness and plump perfection. She had displayed them with pride, and Amy had praised the California rolls to the skies while proffering her money in the hope of speeding things along.

Precious further minutes were expended while Amy pantomimed the necessity for plenty of pickled ginger, many slices of her beloved oshinko pickles, eight packets of soy sauce, and a few little cones of the powerful green mustard paste, wasabi, for the most adventurous palates among them. All in all, the transaction had taken almost fifteen minutes to complete, and this was time for which Amy had not calculated.

"Cleverpig's not here!" Paul Walker, a pleasant, dorky boy distinguished chiefly by his painful-looking acne and his technical

skill with a Radiograph pen, whispered to her as she slid into the
back of the art room. "You're totally screwed."

"And you are?" An alien substitute teacher, an elderly man,
was sitting at Miss Cunningham's desk. He surveyed his thirty
charges irritably, with none of the urgent *joie* of every art teacher
Amy had ever known. He glared in her direction expectantly.

"Amy Green."

"You know the rules, don't you, Amy Green? Where is your
late pass? You did stop at the dean's office for a late pass, didn't
you?"

"I am so sorry I am late, but I had to pick something up on the
way to school, something that was very important, and it took
much too long. Normally I am always on time for this class, I love
art, you can ask anyone—" Amy babbled. She had never been
asked to go to the dean's office. She didn't even know where it was.
She resented being mistaken for one of those bad students who
would know the protocol for breaking the rules.

A soccer ball rolled past one of the classroom windows, which ran
at eye level along one wall of the classroom and offered a peculiar
vista of disembodied feet on the immediate patch of grass outside
the window at the edge of the playing field. Amy had sketched the
limited perspective a few items—a series of her drawings were
tacked to the board behind the teacher's desk. A thundering mob
of legs ran in pursuit of the soccer ball.

"And the something you had to pick up? Perhaps you would
like to enlighten us as to the significance of this very important
item which has delayed your arrival at our lovely institution of
lower learning this fine morning?"

"Look out, idiot," Paul Walker hissed at her. "That's Slattery,
he just retired. He's about a hundred and ten. He flunked me last
year in geometry and fucked up my summer. He hates kids. He
must be really poor if he's being a substitute now. It's crap money.
My aunt is a substitute."

"Mr. Walker, perhaps you would be interested in a detention? No? No desire to have an extra study hall to work on your pathetically inadequate geometry skills? Pity. Very well then, now shut up and see if you can stay inside the lines in your coloring book." Mr. Slattery studied the class attendance book and frowned, then he looked up and counted heads and frowned, then went back to the attendance book, ticking off the results.

The rest of the class bent over their work on the art tables. The room was silent except for the abrasive sound of someone filling in a big area of his rough sketch paper with a charcoal stick. Dana Snow got up and sharpened a pencil for so long that Amy wondered if her ambition was to grind the entire pencil away. She looked up and saw that Dana was trying to catch her eye. Dana signaled with a tilt of her chin and a raised eyebrow an inquiry that Amy was able to answer with a nod to the affirmative. Dana made a silent "Yes!" gesture with a raised fist and returned to her seat. Amy opened her sketch pad to a drawing of the New Haven skyline she had started at a table in the café on the roof of the A&A Building, hoping that Mr. Slattery's attention might have drifted away from her. She began to work on the shading.

"Well, Miss Amy Green?" His imperious voice pierced her concentration a short moment later. No such luck.

"Yes?" She looked up.

"You're very industrious. I see you have a certain amount of talent, though of course, talent isn't genius, and no amount of energy can make it so."

Amy wondered if he thought he was complimenting her or putting her down or just giving pompous advice to a young person.

"You have two options," he said, looking pleased with himself the way certain teachers do when they think they are being original and fair in the way they enforce their authority. He stared at her hard over the tops of his half glasses. He probably had a theory about dominating students through aggressive eye contact. "You will either remove yourself and your things from this classroom, which you have arrogantly entered when nearly half the period had already elapsed, and take yourself to the dean's office, or you will display for the class your very important personal artifact, the obtaining of which you claim has delayed you, and the presence of which seems to delight at least one of your classmates already."

Very slowly Amy bent down to pick up the paper bag which she had placed with care at her feet. She carried it up the aisle toward the front of the room, holding it in front of her with both hands with an almost ceremonial reverence.

"What have you there?" he asked sharply.

"California rolls. For lunch. With my friends."

"California *whats*?"

"Rolls. You know, like sushi. Sort of Japanese food," Amy said, as apologetically as possible, not wanting to sound any more arrogant than he already thought she was.

"Raw fish in my classroom! And at this hour! What, exactly, makes them Californian?" he sneered. "Have you imported them from California? Are they the food of surfers and Hollywood stars? Open the parcel, I want to see these California rolls."

"It's just what they're called," Amy said, trying to undo the carefully folded paper. "There's no raw fish. It's seaweed and rice and avocado and crab meat, well, imitation crab meat, but it's cooked." The folded paper around the layered trays had been arranged so prettily, she saw now, it would be so important to get it back the way it was so she could unwrap the California rolls with a ceremonial flourish at lunchtime.

She thought a moment. "I guess it's the avocado. But then they could be called Florida rolls, and they're not," she added logically. "Maybe they were invented in California. I don't think they're really what people eat in Japan or anything." She folded back the paper and exposed the top layer of her delicious little morsels, all nestled together in a cunning arrangement, ornamented by the tracklements she had labored to obtain for her friends.

"Avocado," Mr. Slattery observed authoritatively and incorrectly, as a perfectly formed cone of bright green wasabi caught his eye.

"Actually," Amy began, desperate not to appear too much of a know-it-all in her correction. As if in a dream, Amy said, as she recounted the tale to her sisters and Teddy that night at dinner with a bitter sense of wrong, she watched Mr. Slattery's spotted claw swoop down and pluck the tempting morsel from its artful place in the center of the arrangement.

"No—" she started to say, "that's—"

But of course by the time she uttered the word "hot" it was no longer necessary for her to inform Mr. Slattery any further about the incendiary nature of a large lump of very powerful green Japanese mustard.

Its effect was instantaneous. He howled in shock and danced backwards as if he had been struck in the chest before spluttering incoherently and trying to spit into the wastebasket what remained in his mouth. The entire class burst out laughing, adding to the teacher's rage and humiliation.

He reached for the coffee mug on his desk, and as he swigged down its contents, Amy could be heard to say in a faint voice, "Liquid only makes it worse." The class roared. This was better than anything on Comedy Central.

Mr. Slattery was wiping his tongue repeatedly with his pocket handkerchief. There were tears running down his face. Amy felt sorry for him, but she also felt sorry for herself. She had done nothing wrong.

"Open the window!" Mr. Slattery commanded to the room at large. Two boys leaped to push up the sashes of the row of windows just above their heads.

"Now, Amy Green, you take these disgusting things two by two and throw them out the window!"

"No!" Dana cried out softly. Her indignation, faint as it was, irritated the irascible teacher, and he repeated his command.

Miserably, Amy complied with his order, pitching the morsels in pairs with reluctant hands into the spaces between the metal security bars, up and out, over and over until they were gone. As she performed the grim task, Amy bit her lip to keep from crying and concentrated on the words to one of Lou's silly rhymes: *Higgledy piggledy/My black hen/She lays eggs for gentlemen/Sometimes nine and sometimes ten/And throws them out the window/The window, the window/The second-story window/High-low, low-high/She throws them out the window.*

Amy could hear a whistle blow, signaling the end of gym class. Several students slowed as they passed by the window and she could hear someone say, "Gross!" before the many pairs of feet trampled the beautiful maki rolls into the dirt.

"And now, Miss Amy Green, perhaps you have begun to regret your arrogance and misjudgment? No? Well, then, don't sit down," Mr. Slattery said, not giving Amy a chance to reply. "You come away from the window and go right up to the front of the room and explain to your classmates all about your poor judgment and your disruptive behavior."

Amy slowly walked to the front of the room. What did he have in mind? Mr. Slattery was smiling strangely. All of the students had abandoned their work and were now just watching the two of them. She stood there. Before she could even think of what she was supposed to say, he added, "No, don't speak, sing. Not mere words but a lovely melody which I am sure you can manage, given your great cultural expertise."

Amy didn't think she understood what he had said.

"You must sing your explanation. Don't look so puzzled. I am sure you have a lovely voice. That is what I said and that is what I meant. Yes, that's right—let's hear it—a song of remorse, if you please. Class, Amy will now sing for us."

Several girls burst out in nervous giggles. A boy in the back called out, "Sing it, sister!" and began to clap slowly. Other boys began to clap along with him, and then some of the girls did, too. Amy looked beseechingly at Dana but couldn't catch her eye.

"It was just one of those things—" Amy began to warble desperately. "Just one of those terrible things—" The long harsh tone of the electronic bell marking the end of the period sounded just then, and there was a spatter of applause as she ran to her desk and gathered her books, trembling but proud that she hadn't actually cried. But Amy's humiliation was far from over.

By the time Amy arrived at lunch, almost everyone in the group was assembled at their table, clearly waiting for the much-heralded treats. Dana sat among them, her eyes glistening with a curious sort of delight. Amy's heart sank at the realization that not everybody might already know what had happened to the California rolls.

"Sorry, you guys," Amy sighed as she slid into her chair at the end of the table. They all stared at her expectantly.

"Didn't Dana tell you about the disaster this morning in art class with that cretinous substitute? It was funny, when he had smoke coming out his ears, I guess, but what a horrid waste. Oh, I could have just cried when I had to throw every single one of those beautiful California rolls out the window. He is such a fossil! He must be older than dirt! And he was so mean, the way he tried to make me sing! Wasn't it just a nightmare, Dana?"

"Wasn't what just a nightmare?" Dana inquired, looking innocently puzzled.

"The whole thing! The way Mr. Slithery, Splattery, whatever, Slattery, made me throw away all those beautiful California rolls."

"Oh," Dana replied very slowly, looking into Amy's eyes with a cold stare, "I didn't see it. I have no idea what you're talking about."

"You didn't bring anything to share *again*?" Alison asked derisively. "I don't believe this. I told you she was lying when she said—"

"I am not lying!" Amy shouted. "I went to Jing's this morning and I spent fifteen dollars, which is more than I can afford, for a wonderful treat for all of you today! It was going to be the best ever!"

"Right, whatever," Dana said, turning away dismissively. "So, who's got something else?"

"I knew we couldn't count on her," Katia muttered with deliberate volume so Amy could hear her as she rummaged some flattened granola bars from her backpack and passed them around. "She's too out-of-it and weird. She's just not one of us."

"Amy, you promised you would have California rolls to share with the group," Anna said in a measured voice that stopped all other conversation dead. "And now you don't have anything. That shows disrespect for the group. That's not the way we do things. It's not acceptable."

"But I *did* have a huge parcel of California rolls for us!" Amy cried, desperately. "They were the most beautiful things. There were twenty-five of them! But I was late because it took so long to wrap them and then the shitty senile substitute teacher made me open them so he could see what they were, and he took a piece of wasabi and burned his mouth, and then he got mad, and he made me throw them away, and he made me sing—"

Anna turned to Dana for confirmation. "Dana, you're in that class, right? So what happened? Did you see all this drama and these allegedly fabulous California rolls?"

Dana shrugged a little shrug and said, "I don't know how I could have missed that. It was a pretty quiet class this morning. Though Amy's totally right," she added generously, "we did have a substitute. And maybe I did hear Amy singing to herself after the bell rang."

"Pathetic," Alison pronounced.

"Amy," Anna said coldly, "this is not the way to treat friends.

How could you think lying would work? Did you think we would all just pretend to eat your imaginary California rolls, like some little-kid tea party?" The girls at the tables snickered appreciatively and a couple of them mimed with exaggerated gestures of delight the eating of invisible morsels with invisible chopsticks.

"If you can't contribute your share, then you shouldn't have sat and eaten with us all these days, that's all," Anna concluded. "It's dishonest."

"I can find some other kids from that class who saw it!" Amy cried out in desperation. "That boy—Paul Walker saw what happened!"

"That loser! The Specimen! Perfect! A great friend for you. Spess would say anything to get attention." Alison snickered.

"You've got to believe me! Or come out on the field—you can see where they got all messed up after I threw them out the window—"

"Whatever," Anna said with a weary gesture of dismissal. "It's okay. Forget it. You don't have to keep going with this. Just, from now on, you probably shouldn't sit with us, since you can't keep up."

"Can't I bring California rolls again after vacation?" Amy begged. "I can get them again, when classes start, right after vacation."

"I don't think that will work," Anna said with a shake of her head, avoiding Amy's eyes. The other girls also looked away. Only Dana met her gaze, a triumphant smirk just curling the edge of her lip as Amy picked up her things and fled the cafeteria.

Amy was in a sad state when she got home. She contained her sorrow as best she could, concentrating on her homework until Teddy and her sisters had all assembled for their meal of Meg's garlicky spaghetti and broccoli, and then she poured out her tale of grief.

"Indignation meeting called to order!" Joanna declared. "What shall we do with Mr. Slithery-Slattery? Making her throw personal possessions out the window like that just because he made a fool of himself? I say he should be arrested without delay! Or at the very least we should send away for a lot of magazine subscriptions in his name."

"Ames, I am so sorry! I'd like to do to him what I'm doing to this piece of Parmesan," Meg said with her sisterly loyalty, as she violently grated a lump of hard cheese over the big bowl of steaming spaghetti in the middle of the table.

"Actually," Teddy said thoughtfully, while tearing a baguette into chunks for them to share, "the one I would like to see the Karma police bring to justice is that little viper Dana. When you think about it, the teacher was just being an asshole, but what she did is really cruel. But all these girls sound pretty vicious. They deserve each other."

"I agree," Meg said. "What made you think this girl was your friend, Ames? I mean, what made you think that any of these princesses were really your friends?"

"I don't know, Meg. I guess I'm not a very good judge of character. I wanted to think they were my friends," Amy said mournfully. "I've never really had friends like that before. I feel like some kid who grew up in the 1920s on a farm ten miles away from the nearest neighbors or something. I'm like Anne of Green Gables in *Up the Down Staircase*. Even though we're sophisticated New York kids in some ways, like we know the subways and stuff like that, our whole life was our family, you know? Are we just really, really weird? I think we are. Maybe it's abnormal, but I've always had you guys, so I never thought I needed other people, not the way most kids do."

"I know just what you mean," Joanna said. "I've never thought about it exactly that way, but you're totally right."

Meg nodded.

"So we're just three big freak weirdo sisters with no friends, I guess, but we'll always have each other," Amy snuffled. "Not that I think you suffer as I do. But thanks, guys. Without you I would be nothing."

"So just how *Little Women* does it get?" Teddy asked.

"What kind of remark is that? What do you mean?" Joanna challenged him.

"I mean just that. Up to now, you three seem to have lived in some sort of hermetically sealed family life as if it were the nineteenth century. All that's missing is Beth, and yes, I know about the turtle, but seriously, what were your parents thinking?"

"They liked the names, and they liked the idea of three sisters in a close-knit family, I guess," Meg answered. "What are you suggesting? That we took on the attributes of the claustrophobic March family because of our names? Don't you think that's a little too simple? What was that, the CliffsNotes explanation of our family?"

"I don't think you took on all the attributes, by any means," Teddy answered evenly. "But I do think that you have more in common with those girls than their names. And," he added, after a thoughtful pause, "you're not going to like this, but it came to me the other day, when you guys were obsessing all through dinner again about the fucking e-mail from whatshisface, Philip Hart. Because if you think about it, you sort of do have a Beth."

"What are you *talking* about?" Amy cried impatiently. "I'm trying to tell you about my horrible day and we just agreed that Mr. Slattery is an asshole and none of us know how to have friends and now you're talking in riddles about our family. What are you saying? Just say it."

"Okay—the death of your imaginary family perfection is like Beth's death in *Little Women*," Teddy said.

"What the hell does that mean?" Meg exclaimed in irritation. "This isn't some lit crit thing for some paper for some seminar.

This is our family. This is our lives! This is *us*, Teddy. And will you guys please eat before it gets cold?"

Nobody lifted a fork. Steam curling up from the bowl in the middle of the table was the only motion in the room.

"I know that, Meg," he said tenderly, reaching out for her hand after a moment. "I know it's serious. But think about it, okay? Don't get mad at me. You guys know I will stand by you all the days of my life, right? This isn't a criticism, okay? Just an observation. Which is this: the death of your belief in the perfection of your family is your Beth. Beth was too good to live. Your family's theory of itself as perfect was too impossible to sustain. See what I mean?"

There was a pause. They all looked at one another.

"Oh my," Amy muttered after a while.

"By George, I think he's got it," Joanna whispered.

"Will you all please eat now?" Meg insisted. "Pass the bread around, will you, Teddy? We may be the most dysfunctional family on earth, living our lives under some weird literary spell cast by our witch of a mother, but we still have to eat."

"In Hartford, Hereford and Hampshire, hurricanes hardly happen," Amy enunciated softly. She helped herself to a piece of bread.

Reader's note: This chapter has some very good writing. But it's such a horrible reminder of an awful moment in my life. What does it do for the novel? I don't see why you're telling this story at all. AG

Author's note: It's an incident that elucidates Amy's experience in the public high school in New Haven turning out to be far more difficult than anyone anticipated. It advances the story and it gives the reader a sense of Amy's issues as she tries and fails to fit in.

Reader's note: I didn't "fail" to fit in. That's an exaggeration. I wasn't as much of a loser as you want me to be for the purposes of your stupid novel. AG

Author's note: Readers won't conclude that Amy is a loser by any means.

Reader's note: I don't see how you can be so confident about what readers are going to think, one way or the other. You're always talking about how people read fiction like a Rorschach blot. You know you can't control how people interpret what you have written. You say that all the time. AG

Reader's note: She says it but she doesn't necessarily mean it. MG

TEN

Doodle Meeting

🌿

Teddy, in his irresistibly persuasive tone, had suggested quietly that he and Joanna should have a private rendezvous at the Yankee Doodle for lunch. It was the day before the long drive up to Maine for Christmas with Teddy's grandmother. New Haven had an empty feeling, with the Yale campus deserted until January.

"What's up?" Joanna said as she swung onto the stool beside him, a few minutes late. She had ducked out of the apartment with a claim that she was going for a walk, and she had felt mildly guilty about her maneuvering to keep Amy from joining her. Joanna had pretended not to hear Amy asking her if she would wait for Amy to get dressed, and then she had hurried out of the building and up the street and across the Jonathan Edwards footpath so that Amy wouldn't have been likely to catch up to her if she tried. Meg had left the apartment very early, as she had told them she would, in order to put in a few extra hours with Mark Frank's children in anticipation of her week away. The Franks apparently had no specific Christmas plans, and Meg was worried, she had said at dinner, that the children would just sit around while she was gone. She had bought them a pile of inexpensive card games and puzzles, which she and Amy wrapped economically in pages from the color comic section of a Sunday *New Haven Register* someone had abandoned at Starbucks.

They had made their plan at bedtime the night before, and Teddy had already gone out by the time Joanna had woken up. He had probably worked out at the gym or gone for a run before spending some time in the library before lunch. Joanna could see through the steamy window of the Doodle that Teddy was reading a three-day-old *Yale Daily News* with great concentration, and he finished the article he was reading before he looked up. Joanna had found Teddy unusually preoccupied in recent days, and she was somewhat apprehensive about this mysterious summons.

"The squash team is really circling the drain," Teddy said. "Blake, this guy I know, he's really good, but he can't do it all by himself. Anyway. So. You're here." He folded the paper and pushed it aside. "I thought we could talk, just the two of us. I've already ordered for you—we're having five pigs."

"Four of them are yours," Joanna warned demurely while simultaneously gazing with delighted greed in the direction of the grill. There they were, in all their bacony splendor, sizzling in a row. She was ravenous, having had no breakfast.

Teddy snorted. "I know about you and pigs-in-a-blanket," he replied, "and the word on the street is that you can eat two without a blink, and maybe three under certain circumstances."

"Busted," Joanna said, looking at Pearl, who winked at her as she wiped the counter and served her the usual Diet Pepsi. Teddy was drinking milk. There was one other customer down at the end of the short counter, a tired-looking black man wearing a Yale maintenance uniform who was drinking coffee and reading a newspaper. His double cheeseburger was the only other order on the grill.

"So?" Joanna prompted. Ordinarily she felt completely comfortable with Teddy, who, she noted with a detached, almost scientific interest, hadn't shaved in a couple of days. She resisted the urge to fuzzy the bristles on his chin, where his little underlip chin-beard came and went from one week to the next.

After living in the same apartment for nearly three months, they were accustomed to seeing one another in various states of dishevelment and personal untidiness, and she had grown so used to his presence, whiskers and all, that at times he just felt like family. She had never known a boy so well—Lou didn't count—and something about knowing Teddy made Joanna feel more at home in herself. She envied him his easy and uncomplicated boy body. Why weren't they all boys in the first place? she often wondered. It all would have been so much easier.

Sometimes the four of them would watch television all piled on the decrepit old sofa together in what Amy called the puppy pile. But being just the two of them on their own by prior arrangement, out in public, seemed very different from the way it felt when the two of them happened to be alone together in the apartment, and Joanna felt oddly self-conscious.

She was also still preoccupied by an unsettling encounter at Starbucks the afternoon before, near the end of her shift. Joanna had been wiping up spilled coffee grounds around the bar area and restocking the sugar, stirrers, and napkins before signing out. She had started to chat about the endless rain with a woman with short spiky hair and big dangly earrings whom she knew as a regular customer, maybe a lecturer or junior professor, someone who was notable because she spoke with a faint German accent which was almost imperceptible at times. Also, she always had a friendly smile, she always said hello to Joanna, and she tipped generously. (As it turned out, she was then an editor at Yale Press, though she was soon to depart for a better position at Random House in New York, but Joanna wouldn't learn this until they met again in New York at a time more than a year after the events that have inspired this story.)

The customer made a reference to something involving an umbrella on an episode of *Ally McBeal* that had been on television the night before, but Joanna was not an *Ally McBeal* watcher. The conversation shifted quickly to movies, but went nowhere fast when Joanna couldn't express a preference for *The Sixth Sense* or *American Beauty* because she had seen neither.

Joanna had seen no new movies at all in New Haven. Another thing she missed from their New York life! Their whole family had a habit of going to movies together every week or two, after agonizing deliberations, with *New Yorker* and *New York Times* reviews in hand, about what they would see.

"Sorry, I just haven't gone to the movies in ages," Joanna confessed to her while bagging the rubbish under the counter. "But the reviews of both sound excellent."

"I'm trying to figure out your taste, that's all. I was thinking maybe we could get together sometime and go to a movie," the woman said. "And hey, after all these weeks how silly is this? I know you but we don't even know each other's names. I've never even seen you out from behind that counter before. I'm Ursula. You're—?"

"Joanna. Um, sure, maybe, that would be nice, it's just that between the expense and the time—"

"I'd love to take you," Ursula said. "No problem. I'm talking about a real date, which you don't seem to be making any easier. You know, dinner, a movie, whatever. What do you say?"

"Oh." Joanna suddenly understood. "You're asking me out."

"Yes, I am," Ursula said. "You're not just cute, you're incredibly perceptive."

"Oh," Joanna said again. There was a roaring in her ears that she knew was her own blood rushing about in her head, rearranging itself, moving from here to there in a blink, everything was being rearranged, everything, everything, constantly moves and changes, every cell is the same and nothing remains the same, that's what blood does, changing itself constantly, always.

"I'm sorry," Joanna said, finally. "I don't think I can do that."

"Okay, well, no harm in trying," Ursula said, putting her hand on Joanna's arm. She had very kind eyes. "I understand, no problem. Really—I'll get over it. So listen, do you have a partner? A group of us like to meet at this bar over on Orange Street about once a month and play silly games of pool for money, and maybe you—"

"No, no," Joanna said, taking a step back, shaking her head. "I'm sorry. Just—"

"Okay then, no big deal," Ursula said a little stiffly, withdrawing her hand. "Don't get all upset, all right? I thought you were cool, and I apologize if I've made a mistake. I didn't mean to put you on the spot. Not everybody's comfortable being right out there, and I can respect that. You're young."

Joanna nodded.

"Well, sorry again if I made you uncomfortable," Ursula said.

"No problem," Joanna had replied, wishing she were anywhere but there. "Hey, my shift is ending and I'm supposed to clean up all the dirty dishes and stuff on the tables every ten minutes, so I better finish up," she said somewhat apologetically, hoisting the bagged trash.

"Okay then, see you around."

"Yeah, see you, and, uh, thanks," Joanna said awkwardly, before escaping to the back, where she had to fill in her shift times on the Operational Excellence Deployment Board.

"We need to talk about some things," Teddy said.

Oh no. Did he want to move out? This was, of course, inevitable. How would they manage? And she would miss him! But why was he meeting with her instead of Meg to break the news?

"Things?"

"I have a list." Teddy fumbled in the pocket of his zippered sweatshirt. "Here it is." He smoothed out a wadded sheet of yellow lined paper. Joanna peered over his shoulder. He reflexively covered the paper with his hand, and then uncovered it again to let her read the short column of words that were neatly printed in his familiar blocky writing. A list was good. And his letting her read it was good, too. It wasn't long, only some four lines, the first one of which read *monthly thing*. Teddy drew the scrap of paper away before she could read the next line.

"Sorry, no offense. But if it's okay with you, I'd rather tell you what's on my mind than have you read my notes."

"Sorry." She waited apprehensively.

Their pigs were served on two plates, three in front of Teddy and two in front of Joanna.

"Okay." Teddy drew a deep breath. "I need to say this, and it's a little embarrassing. I thought I could talk to you about it more easily then either of the others."

Joanna nodded for him to continue, her mouth full. She hoped she would be flattered that she had been selected for whatever this was about. Probably not.

"See, I know Meg in a different way from the two of you, and she's my same age and everything. I just didn't feel comfortable talking to her about this, and I know it's silly. I don't want to embarrass Amy, who's way mature for her age but she's still young and easily weirded out. So that leaves you. The sturdy one in the middle, I guess."

"Okay," Joanna said cautiously.

"It's a bathroom thing," Teddy blurted. "It's not very meal-ish. A sort of personal hygiene issue. I'm sorry, I should just be able to say this." Teddy was blushing now. He took a drink of his milk and wiped his mouth with his sleeve in his unconscious, little-boy way. Joanna began to relax. This would be manageable.

"Okay, look," he said at last. "It's one of those strange things that women living together all start to menstruate at the same time."

"Tell me about it! I read an article about this about once a year, it's some kind of entrainment thing, I think, and I know it's so, anyway, from experience."

"I mean, I realize everyone knows about this. I remember the guys on the ferry crew joking about it, when three of them, whose girlfriends shared a house, realized that the girls were all, what did Ben call it? 'riding the rag,' at the same time and none of them were getting any that weekend. Not to be gross, but that is how guys talk when there aren't any girls around. Anyway, I thought I'd be cool with all the, you know, female things that living with you three would involve. But it is a little overwhelming to be the only guy using the bathroom at the time of the month when, you know, the um . . ." He trailed off this awkward soliloquy and looked at her hopefully.

"God, you mean the whole bathroom wastebasket thing when we're all flowing at once?"

He nodded, looking chagrined. "It's no big deal," he said. "It's just—"

"No, it's not something you should have to see," Joanna said apologetically. "I can speak to Amy and Meg about it. Teddy, you have no idea how worried I was about whatever you wanted to talk about. I'm so relieved that it's only this. Would it help if we got a better wastebasket?"

"One with a lid would be nice."

"Oh, Teddy, I am so sorry that you had to make a whole thing out of asking about this! You should have said something."

"There was never the right moment. I didn't want you to think I was some kind of fusspot, you know? And every time I thought of it was exactly the wrong time to say anything, trust me. Though I must say it's been a relief a couple of times when you're all snapping at everything anyone says or does, and everybody is in everybody else's way, and then a few days later, there's the evidence that it was just another huge PMS festival."

"Are we that bad?"

"Only sometimes. And on the same subject, since I really hope we won't be having this conversation again, could you all keep your, um, supplies somewhere where I don't see them all the time? I'm sorry to have to ask this, I wouldn't have expected to be so bothered by—"

"And you grew up in a house without sisters, and then your mother—" Joanna stopped.

"And my mother died when I was a little kid. So I never saw a lot of sanitary napkins and Tampax and whatever. It's okay to say it, Jo-Jo. My mother died when I was seven."

"Your mother died when you were seven," Joanna said softly. Her eyes began to brim with hot tears from nowhere. She had become something of a crybaby these days, although easy tears were usually Meg's specialty. "And then your father two years ago. No wonder you're so cross with us for rejecting the two living parents we've got, Teddy."

He patted her on the shoulder awkwardly, and she put her hand over his and held it there. It wasn't really clear who was comforting whom. After a moment, Teddy leaned forward and took a big bite of a hot dog, and Joanna fumbled some paper napkins out of the countertop dispenser so she could wipe her face.

They ate together in thoughtful, comfortable silence for a while.

"Split the last pig?" Teddy offered, seeing Joanna eyeing it there on his plate.

"You bet." Joanna watched Teddy's expert bisection. "You know, when we were little, Lou devised the perfect way for us to share anything fairly, like cake. One of us would make the first cut, then one of us would make the second cut, and then the third one would get to choose who got which piece."

"Did Amy have a set of calipers for these moments?" Teddy asked, laughing fondly. He took up one of the dripping hot dog halves and spread some pickle relish on it. "I can just see it. Amy would be triumphant that she got the piece half a millimeter bigger, and then Meg would be noble about having the smallest piece." He took a big bite of his hot dog.

"So she could bludgeon us with her nobility, you mean. You really do know us, Teddy," Joanna agreed, expertly applying a fine stripe of mustard to her hot dog half before rotating it in the bun.

"Why did you turn it?" Teddy asked curiously, his mouth still full.

"It's a family thing. Really a Lou thing, I guess, from when we were little. If you turn it, the mustard and ketchup are on the inside and that way it doesn't drip or get all over your face."

"That's ingenious. Your father sounds really really clever."

"I should make you some of his Zepto coffee sometime."

"*Qu'est-ce que c'est* Zepto coffee?"

"Coffee made with coffee," Joanna explained. "You make coffee, and then you use it to make coffee."

"Sounds intense."

"It's nothing if not cromulent," she agreed.

"So, anyway, what about you? With the cake? Where were you?"

"Me? I'm the one in the middle. You know that."

"But you like crusts. I sincerely hope you aren't scarred from a childhood spent only getting middles and never getting edges," Teddy said with mock solicitousness.

Joanna was touched that he knew about her and crusts. It was like the way he recognized her insatiability for apples. She ate the cores, too, and had a bad habit of leaving little piles of seeds and an occasional stem here and there in the apartment.

They smiled at each other comfortably. Teddy mopped the last of the relish from his plate with the last bite of hot dog bun. The guy from Yale maintenance paid and left. Joanna looked out onto Elm Street. The moist heat from the grill by the window blurred the reds and greens of the Christmas decorations on the lamp post.

"So." She drained her soda and gazed down at her empty plate with regret. Two and a half pigs was really disgusting. "Next item on this list of yours."

Teddy unfolded the list once more and she had a quick glimpse of the words *parking, Amy and school, Meg's secret life* before he folded it up again.

"Coffee?" Pearl asked.

Joanna was torn. She was spoiled by Starbucks (where she had been given a small and most welcome raise the previous week for her conscientiousness and expertise). She had also been drinking really good Kenyan coffee all morning while getting some of her homework out of the way. But it would be offensive to go across the street for better coffee, especially since Pearl would probably watch them. (Pearl had once expressed enormous irritation to a sympathetic Joanna about certain Yale girls who accompanied their cheeseburger-eating football player boyfriends to the Doodle but who brought with them salads and fruit smoothies from Au Bon Pain across the street.) Anyway, it would be wrong to interrupt this moment. They both nodded yes and Pearl brought them two mugs of the Doodle's weirdly burnt yet diluted-tasting java.

"When water's boiled too hot, the air bubbles go out of it, they're probably using robusta beans, and they really need to scrub out that urn," Joanna whispered. Pearl was talking on the phone and her brother, who manned the grill with the seriousness of a jet pilot, had finished scraping who-knows-what off its surface and had now stepped out onto the sidewalk for a break.

"So. Next item," Teddy said, calling the meeting back to order. "Nothing else quite so sensitive, I promise."

"Parking, I see?"

"Yes. Do you realize Meg is paying sixty-five dollars a month to park the Subaru in that crummy garage on Crown Street? I know she missed the Yale permit deadline, but she should apply again. And otherwise I know lots of people who get by with street parking. You just have to know where to go, and you have to move the car on a schedule. But I could help. I just thought you guys ought to consider that. I've mentioned it to Meg a few times, but she isn't very receptive."

"That might be a great idea, but it's sort of Meg's decision, isn't it? I mean it's her car and all. And I know she is worried that something could go wrong that would end up costing more money than we'd be saving, if someone breaks in or if it's towed."

"Hey, I don't have a clue how you guys work out all the little details of your financial decisions. I just thought you ought to know about one way you could save some specific dough. Meg seems phobic about it, I don't know why."

"Well, the garage is just down the street, and I think Meg likes the convenience and knowing she can just go get the car whenever. Plus there's the whole Lou parking obsession she might have absorbed osmotically. We hardly use the car, except for big grocery expeditions to Hamden and stuff like that, or her drives out to see Professor Baldwin, so maybe it is a crazy expense. Things were so much simpler when Lou and Janet paid for everything!" Joanna exclaimed in frustration. "It's not just the parking, it's everything. We thought we were independent but we had no idea how much our lives really cost, with every little thing. It all adds up. God! We were so spoiled! Are we still spoiled? We are, aren't we? Are we just big babies? How do you stand us, Teddy?"

"Very easily," he replied gently. "You know that. So, Lou's parking obsession?"

"It's like a family joke but it isn't a joke at all. Lou is just obsessed with alternate-side-of-the-street parking. He knows all the Jewish holidays, like Shavuot, when alternate-side-of-the-street parking is suspended."

"Shavuot?"

"It's in the late spring or early summer. It's a sort of a harvest pilgrim festival that's always fifty days after the second night of Passover. There are traditional meals with wheat, wine, pomegranates, dates, olives, figs, you know, stuff like that."

"Oh, of course," Teddy said, "I used to see all that Shavuot-y stuff in the Shavuot aisle at the supermarket all the time. And of course Avery had such great Shavuot recipes. It's a wonderful family tradition."

"Oh, shut up, you just like saying the word. Anyway," Joanna continued, "I had a friend in kindergarten whose mother was one of those leftover hippie Birkenstock Jews who brought the same homemade mandelbrot for every bake sale. They always had a Shavuot party. So I actually do know what it is beyond its implications for parking."

"Seriously, I'm impressed at your encyclopedic knowledge of an obscure Jewish holiday. I'm also glad Amy's not here to start perseverating on the word *Shavuot*," Teddy said. "Though I might start. "Shavuot. Shavuot."

"Stop it!" Joanna nudged him hard. "In New York it's not obscure, it's a huge big deal because alternate-side-of-the-street parking is suspended. That's major. Anyway, when it wasn't Shavuot or some other holiday, which was most of the time, we spent lots of childhood Sunday nights cruising around the West Side with our father looking for a parking place that would be good until Tuesday morning. And one of the worst fights I ever remember Janet and Lou having was over parking, when Lou didn't want to drive to a funeral in some deep dark part of Brooklyn because he didn't want to give up a great parking space. The dead person was some old twice-removed aunt of Janet's whom she hadn't seen in ages, but she really wanted to go anyway, to see the other relatives or something. We have so few relatives, I guess she wanted to see them even though they were never close. I mean, if not then, when? Anyway, Lou really didn't want to go because it was some kind of trifecta fabulous parking space that was good for a whole week or something because of holidays and street-cleaning schedules and whatever."

"Like a seven-letter Scrabble word with a 'Q' and a 'J' on the triple-score square, I get it. So what happened?"

"Janet took the subway to the funeral and they didn't speak for three days."

"Wow."

"Yeah, pretty intense but not intense, you know? I feel nostalgic for the days when something like that was the worst problem. So anyway. What else have you got on your list?" Joanna peered in the direction of the folded scrap of paper.

"You know what's on my list. I saw you see it," Teddy said with a laugh. "Amy and school." He put down his empty coffee mug and twirled on his stool to face her.

"Look, I am really concerned about her attitude, now that the Scriveners have turned on her. We need to watch her carefully in January, after the vacation. Let's hope it will all have blown over by then with those little bitches. I think she's really discouraged and could start to screw up, maybe cut classes or just zone out, which would be a disaster. I just wanted to get that on the record."

"You're right," Joanna said, peering into the glass case across the counter. "Do you think the pie is worthwhile? No, you're right. Anyway, Amy doesn't want to talk about it at all, but she was really hurt. Whenever I bring it up, she just says she dreads going back and wishes she could stay home and be home-schooled, God help us. And to think that I used to feel that Amy got the cream of everything. She sure hasn't got a lot going her way right now."

"Maybe I can get Avery to talk with her about new strategies for being her own woman while we're in Long Harbor," Teddy mused. "The two of them will either love each other or be at each other's throats after the first day. You'll see—they're very alike in some odd ways."

"And we should be having this conversation with Meg," Joanna added, "because she needs to pay a little more attention to Amy. She needs to pay a little more attention to a lot of things. I feel as though Meg has been a million miles away in the past couple of weeks. I know she just handed in that big paper she was working on forever, the Anne Frank meets Holden Caulfield thing, but she's just so disconnected lately, don't you think?"

"Which brings me to the last item on my list—Meg." Teddy screwed up his face and closed his eyes for a moment, with a look as though he had suddenly remembered something painful.

"Meg's secret life," Joanna prompted. "That's what your list says. But I have no idea what it means."

"Something's going on," he said.

"Something?" Joanna was apprehensive again, feeling suddenly that this was the real reason for their meeting. A policeman came in and ordered three cheeseburgers to go. Pearl bustled around organizing his food while his cheeseburgers were on the grill. Joanna idly thought she could eat a cheeseburger.

"Yes. I don't just mean how distracted she seems. I saw her. I saw something," Teddy said.

"Sometimes we're all pretty distracted. You've been distracted lately," Joanna pointed out. "So what?"

"No, I saw something," Teddy repeated.

"What do you mean? You saw what?"

"A couple of days ago I was walking in a nice Yale-free part of New Haven, way over on State Street, because there's a shoe store over there that has Docs in my weird wide size, except it turned out they didn't, except in purple, so forget that, and I passed by a bakery café on the corner, and people have told me about this place, Marjolaine, where a baker named Gretel bakes amazing things. So I was going to go in and get this famous plum cake they have, for a treat for us, you know, to celebrate the end of the semester, but then I saw that Meg was there with someone. I saw her at a table in the window. So I didn't go inside after all and she didn't see me."

"Teddy! Stop speaking so cryptically! I can't stand it! You saw her with someone *what?*" Joanna gripped his arm urgently.

"Ow! Let me explain! They were being very affectionate. And he was this older guy."

"Define 'very affectionate' and 'older guy,' please," she said impatiently.

"They were holding hands and sitting together, and they were just, I don't know, looking at each other in a certain way. I can't say exactly what it was I saw, it was just a quick glimpse and I wasn't expecting to see Meg in the first place," Teddy said, rubbing his arm where she had squeezed it. "But there was an intensity. A vibe. And he was really a lot older, like in his fifties."

"When was this? Do you think it was Mark Frank? It must have been. I don't know who else it could be." Joanna didn't know what to think. "But Meg says he looks a lot younger than he really is. I've wondered if she had some kind of crush on him. She's sort of reticent on the subject, if you think about it, and even though she said we would take turns baby-sitting, she's never asked Amy or me to do it, not once. What did this guy look like?"

"This was day before yesterday, and I can't really say what the guy looked like. I guess he could be an academic, I didn't really get a good look at him, you know? I registered that he was this older guy, kind of big, in a big sweater anyway, and he had a head of gray hair, and big eyebrows, but mostly it was just the whole effect of the two of them together."

"Wow." Joanna still didn't know quite what to think. "This wouldn't be so strange if she had said she was meeting him for coffee or something, but she never mentioned anything like this, plus, what were they doing all the way over on State Street? It's not like there's a good reason for that. I thought they hung out in his office and had their little ultra-literary chats together there. Sometimes Meg comes in to get coffee for the two of them. He always gets a tall latte."

"So you agree it's odd," Teddy said. "Unless they went there for the plum cake. But think about it. It's a place to meet that's kind of private and away from campus. What's that about?"

"Oh dear," Joanna said, sloshing the last of her coffee around in the chunky white mug with an unconscious rhythmic intensity. She could use some plum cake. "What are we going to do? I don't think we should let her have this relationship, if that's what it is."

"It's not up to us, actually, and I don't know that we need to *do* anything," Teddy said. "But I wanted to tell you about it, is all. And maybe Amy doesn't need to hear about this right now."

"You're right, she doesn't. Especially since we don't even know what it means. Oh shit! Teddy, Teddy, Teddy," Joanna said with a burst of feeling, "this is *so* disturbing. But I'm glad you told me about it. I know you're looking out for us. Thank you. Really." She put her hand on his arm again, but gently this time, and rubbed the spot she had abused a moment earlier.

Teddy didn't answer but she could see his eyes fill with feeling as he leaned over and put his cheek on the top of her head and drew her against him, putting an arm around her.

Joanna stiffened and then relaxed. Why didn't she feel what she secretly believed she ought to feel at a moment like this? She was fond of Teddy, to be sure, but she just didn't have any sensations of attraction, even though she liked the idea. She *loved* the idea. She had felt for weeks now that she wanted to want Teddy. But it wasn't there. What did she want? She thought about Ursula's assumption at Starbucks the day before. Did everyone know this about her? Was she the last to figure it out? Maybe Ursula was only half-right. Maybe she just didn't have a sex drive at all. Would she ever feel genuine intensity of physical feeling for another person? Did everyone else in the world? It was hard to imagine.

So many novels and magazine articles made Joanna feel that everyone around her maintained a constant inner struggle against animal urges to rub and touch and press his or her body against someone else's, that everyone walked around trying to keep in check a profound desire to copulate with members of the opposite sex. Joanna had never kissed a boy and wondered if she ever would.

"Do you think of me as a girl, Teddy?" she blurted. "I mean, I know I'm a girl, one with Tampax and everything, but that's not what I'm asking. You know what I mean."

"I think you're a wonderful person," Teddy answered, giving

her shoulder a squeeze that made her heart sink. "Not like anyone else I know. Really. But I'm not sure what you're really asking, how serious you are. Do you think of yourself as a girl?"

"That's what I'm trying to figure out, if there's an easier way, you know—" she started, but then she lost her nerve. "It depends on what 'girl' means," she replied, and immediately regretted the words. "Hey, some other time, you know? This is too serious for right now. Never mind. Sorry, I know I started it."

"But I do mind, actually," he said, startling them both. He turned and tilted her chin with a finger until he had forced her to meet his gaze. He smiled with the sad superiority of one who knew that his fidelity, like his love, was unalterable. "Oh, Jo, can't you?"

"Teddy, I wish I could," she said, with a little shake of her head.

They sat without talking. Pearl refilled their coffee mugs.

"So what do we know about this Mark Frank?" Teddy asked presently.

"Mr. Verb Adjective, as Amy likes to point out? I don't know. Not much. English, handsome, brilliant, needy kids, dysfunctional wife, smokes despite the rules. Sounds like a recipe for trouble, doesn't it?"

"It is, of course, none of my business really—"

"Shut up, Teddy! I mean it! Of course we're your business! But do you think we're just totally the weirdest people ever, really, the three of us, each of us with our unique neurotic tendencies plus the synergy of us together plus our whole family mess?"

"You know, you keep asking me to define you. I think you're— unique," he replied after a moment's hesitation. "But sometimes I think there's something that happened in your family that make you all, I don't know, somehow convinced that you spring from Platonic conceptions of yourselves. Do you know what I mean? Nobody can live up to that. And you expected your parents to be in uniform and at a sort of moral attention forever, which is a Gatsby reference you should recognize, incidentally."

"What time is it, anyway?" Joanna broke in. "I've got to get back, there's a ton of laundry to do before we can pack. But I was listening, really." She scrabbled on the counter for the check but Teddy had hold of it and snatched it away.

"Can't we split it?" Joanna asked.

"How about I pay for this and you do my laundry?"

"Deal."

Reader's note: So that's how you met "Ursula"! I had thought you met in New York. But meanwhile, what was the purpose of this chapter? I know what you'll say—that it establishes more conflict and sets the story up for the events that follow while illuminating the relationship between these two characters. I know how you rationalize. I'm sure there's a quote from some famous writer for the occasion, too. Couldn't you have achieved this without just sitting them down to talk to each other? That's all they do. You always complain about novels where characters do this at convenient moments. MG

Author's note: First, you don't really know what I would say. Second, which proves the first point—ironically enough, given my antipathy toward authorial choices defended on the sole grounds of their connection to actual events or circumstances, the simple response to this query is that it happened this way, that this was the circumstance of the reality from which this moment in the fictional narrative is derived.

Reader's note: So you don't like it when someone else writes your lines for you? And remind us again—what makes it fiction? AG

Author's note: What makes every word on every page fiction is that this is a novel.

Reader's note: But that's really crap. You know you're playing a game here, going back and forth over the line of fiction and real-life incident. Why can't you just admit it? AG

Reader's note: Do you really expect our sister to start admitting that at this point? Haven't you figured out by now that she will play this game, with as many moves, for as long as it takes, until she thinks everyone agrees with her? MG

Reader's note: *I don't see how even ordinary people reading this novel can fail to see what she is doing.* AG

Reader's note: *The ordinary people who read this novel will be happily entertained by what she has done. You might as well get over any hopes you have of winning people over to our side.* MG

Reader's note: *Then why are we writing these reader's notes? I thought that was the whole point.* AG

Reader's note: *We're writing these notes because we can.* MG

Author's note: *You're writing these notes because you are both angry at me over the publication of this novel and because you have forced me into an absurd agreement. It's disappointing that you needed to do this. I had thought the three of us had a decent relationship these days, but neither of you has enough respect for my artistic integrity to trust me. Neither of you understands the nature of a novel, what it is made of, where fiction comes from. So you have ganged up on me, which is nothing new, and made me feel like the outsider looking in, like some kind of emotional burglar. And the two of you wonder why I have always felt like the family narrator?*

ELEVEN

Christmas Mischief

❧

"Christmas really was Christmas, even without very many presents," Amy said contentedly, lying on the rug in front of the merry little fire that burned in Avery Bell's parlor fireplace. Avery's sleek tortoise cat, Miss Demeanor, purred beside her. Amy had rearranged and balanced yet again the assortment of small painted wooden tree ornaments, each with its own particular Bell family history which Teddy and Avery had taken turns providing, and she was proud to gaze upon the big Christmas tree which glittered with symmetrical perfection in the firelight. It was three days after Christmas and the girls had been outside most of the day, walking on what they could find of the snowy paths in the woods on a slippery hike over hill and dale that Teddy had promised would be far less strenuous and half the distance it turned out to be.

"This has been an excellent Christmas," Joanna agreed contentedly from the cushiony recesses of the marvelously deep sofa. "I'm ahead ten thousand points in Blink—"

"Because you cheated with the extra dominoes," Amy interrupted. "And you changed the rule of slap clap nines halfway through. *And* you kept changing secret partners. So your points don't really count on the grand tally list, only for the duration of our games in Long Harbor—just remember that."

"And we've got Teddy, and Avery, and each other," Joanna continued, ignoring her completely, "even though Teddy is a terrible liar who should never be trusted again about estimating the duration of a freezing slippery walk in the woods. When we complained, he just laughed like an irresponsible fetus. Oh, my poor feet will never be the same again," she added, wiggling her striped socks. "But it was very beautiful, so I guess I'm not sorry we went. Plus we were entitled to make pigs of ourselves at dinner again, after all that. I don't know about you guys, but I'm stuffed."

"Me too. But is there any more hot cocoa?" Amy asked from her position of utter comfort on the floor. "I can't get up without disturbing Miss D."

"There is plenty indeed," Avery said from her habitual place on the couch, an Irish blanket over her knees, where she had been alternately dozing and perusing a battered Angela Thirkell novel. The moment they laid eyes on her, Avery Bell had instantly reminded the three Green sisters of Mrs. Roth, their favorite teacher at Warren, now retired. She was a marvelous Latin teacher, given to throwing chalk at the heads of inattentive students, who all adored her anyway. Like Mrs. Roth, Amy had pointed out as they carried their bags up to the bedrooms, Teddy's grandmother was hard and soft in interesting ways, like a cross between a nuclear physicist and a chicken.

"I'll go put a flame under the hot chocolate pot," Avery said. "But first tell me if your 'me too' was about being stuffed or about the frozen feet or about the suspicion of my grandson's outdoor leadership capabilities."

"Oh, all of those things," Amy replied honestly. "But especially Teddy. He's really terrible. He always says he can get somewhere in a few minutes even though it really takes an hour, or that a walk is just a couple of blocks when it's six miles."

"It's a form of optimism that runs in our family," Avery pronounced, putting her book down and warming to her topic as she slipped her feet into her downstairs house moccasins. (She was a woman of many precise habits.) In the six days they had spent together, they had adapted to Avery's habit of taking any stray remark as a launching point for a philosophic ramble on myriad topics. "His father certainly had it. It's an essential flaw in the Bell family character. 'He won't be a bit of trouble, you'll hardly know he's there at all,' is what he said to me that first summer. Can you imagine? A seven-year-old boy who had just lost his mother. He was shattered, though it hardly showed. And of course, there I was, optimistically thinking he was absolutely right, how much trouble could a small boy be? Ha!"

"Gran, I don't think that's optimism, exactly," Teddy said from the doorway, where he stood with a fresh armload of firewood from the pile by the kitchen door. "I think the word for it is 'denial.'"

"Oh, don't start using your fancy Yale terminology on this old lady," Avery scolded crossly. "I suppose you think your old grandmother is just too, too turnip truck, but I know a thing or two about how human beings are."

"Of course you do, Gran," Teddy soothed, dropping the wood into the big copper tub on the hearth. "It's in all your books." He left a trail of snow worms that had formed in the patterns of the soles of his sneakers. Amy swept up with her hand the ones she could reach without stirring from her cozy spot and crunched them into a single lump, which she offered to the cat, who sniffed at it for a moment and then turned away.

"And speaking of how human beings are, I believe our friend Meg is having yet another secret telephone chat in the library with a love interest of some kind," Avery said with a sly look of triumph. "I may be an old nuisance, but I still notice what goes on."

"You're not a nuisance, stop that! You're just trying to provoke flattery and you know it. But what makes you say that about Meg?" Teddy asked, catching Joanna's eye. Amy had stopped stroking the cat and was clearly listening as well.

"It's a tone of voice a woman uses only when she is speaking with a man," Avery said with authority. "I went in to get my reading glasses, which I remembered I had left by the telephone just before dinner, and I could not help but hear her. There is a kind of laugh, a way of responding—well, I just know." She cocked her head to one side and murmured, " 'How silver-sweet sound lovers' tongues by night, like softest music to attending ears!' "

"Hey, you guys," Meg said, coming into the parlor, buttoning her sweater. "More cocoa? I can heat it up."

"How was your phone call?" Amy asked with candid interest. "You said you were going upstairs to get a sweater, not into the library to make a telephone call."

"What? Oh, fine," Meg answered, startled. "I, um, just needed to check with someone about, um, something for the reading for the art history class I'm taking next term. Oh, I'm sorry, Avery, I should have asked! I'll pay for any calls we make while we're here."

"Don't speak of it," Avery dismissed with a wave of a hand. "But that's quite commendable, Meg," she said, fixing her with the gimlet gaze over her half-glasses that Teddy had long thought of simply as "the look." "Planning your reading for a class that hasn't even started yet. I wish Teddy were half as diligent as you."

The next morning, Teddy and Joanna found a moment to confer in the laundry room.

"What the hell, Teddy?"

"We've got to talk to her," he said. The laundry room was a place that would have ordinarily interested Joanna very much. She could see that the cupboards and shelves were stuffed with old picnic hampers, retired toasters, soap flakes in a box so old it was probably worth something to collectors, baking tins, vases, thermoses, straw hats, all sorts of interesting objects. She made a mental note to prowl at a later point. She wanted to ask Teddy at another moment about the poignant row of worn dog collars on hooks that had obviously belonged to several generations of Avery's spaniels.

"How can we?" Joanna said in frustration. "I tried to get her to talk last night but she was buzzing around brushing her teeth and flossing and plucking and moisturizing and then after we turned out the light she went right to sleep, or pretended to. You know how hard it is to talk to Meg about something when she sort of vaporizes. She hates talking about feelings anyway. You know what she used to say when we were little? 'I don't want to discuss about it.' That's such a total Meg expression. But she's been *so* out of it since we got here, don't you think?"

"We'll just be honest and tell her that we know about her and whatshisname, the dashing Professor Verb Adjective," said Teddy, concentrating on tracing a jagged crack in the red linoleum floor with a socked toe. "And, obviously, it's not okay, we're concerned about it. We'll just tell her we know something's going on with him and we can just try to talk to her about the whole thing. We don't even have to get into the feelings part of it. I mean, what sort of future does she think this can possibly have?" Teddy looked up to see what Joanna was thinking.

"Oh, that will be a very relaxed conversation," Joanna said bitterly. "Trust me, I've had family conversations like that, you know? This is where you came in, remember?"

"Okay, fine, how do you want to handle it, then?" Teddy asked. He leaned against the ironing board and the iron sitting on one end wobbled dangerously until Joanna steadied it.

"Look out," she said crossly. "I don't know! Just let me think about it, okay? Boys always want to *do* something. Girls like to analyze."

"I think of you as someone who prefers to do something," Teddy said.

"Maybe. Okay, here's a thing I can do. I'm supposed to go grocery shopping with her in a little while. We said we would make dinner tonight. So if you can keep Amy busy here, maybe I can find a moment if it's just the two of us in the car."

"Fine. That might work. Suit yourself."

"Are you mad at me, Teddy?" Joanna asked anxiously. "I mean, we don't have a problem, do we, you and me? I would hate that more than anything."

"No, it's not you. It was you, for a while, but it's not you anymore," Teddy replied cryptically. "So fine, let's try that, that's a good idea," he said, moving toward the door to the kitchen, suddenly impatient with the conversation. "Let me know how it goes."

It didn't go. Try as she might, Joanna could find no easy way to work the conversation around to Meg's telephone call or to Teddy's having seen her at the bakery with Mark Frank. On the way to town, Meg had twiddled the radio until she was satisfied with a blaring song called "Weird Science" that she said was by a group called Oingo Boingo. Conversation was impossible. Joanna had never heard of either this song or the group and thought it very strange that Meg had developed a sudden and mysterious affinity for this awful music.

Shopping for their groceries, Meg had taken charge of the wagon and had distractedly consulted their list over and over, motherishly sending Joanna on one mission after the next throughout the store. Vanilla extract, check. Lemons, check. Pork roast, check. Eggs, check. No, not small ones, large ones, check. The least-haggard-looking green vegetables, check. Tapioca, after a prolonged search as neither of them could think where to find it, check.

On the return trip, Meg took the opposite tack, talking a blue streak about how much she liked Avery, how prickly but secretly kind Avery was, how she really wanted to read Avery's novels now, how beautiful her house was, how charming the village of Long

Harbor was, how wonderful the view of Stark Island was from the upstairs bedroom windows, how sweet Amy was with Miss Demeanor and maybe they should think of getting Amy a kitten for a surprise, and before Joanna knew it they were back at the house, unloading groceries from the back of the Subaru.

Amy had gone with Avery to town in the ancient Volvo called Edna, ostensibly to the post office but really for a conversation about taking her art more seriously over coffee at a place next to the post office, a plan engineered by Teddy. He heard the car in the driveway and came out to help Meg and Joanna carry things in the back door to the kitchen. Joanna gave him a negative shake of the head when he looked at her expectantly.

A few moments later, when they had taken off their coats and were organizing the food in the pantry and refrigerator, Teddy said to Meg in a casual tone, "Oh, you had a phone call."

"Really?" Meg looked surprised. "I didn't give anyone this number."

"Well, it was a man. He didn't leave his name. Who knows, sometimes people get a number from their Caller ID thing."

Joanna tried to intercept Teddy's gaze but he kept his eyes on Meg's face, which had gone a little pale.

"What did he say?" Meg asked, folding the brown paper grocery bags vigorously and putting them in their slot under the counter. She looked out the window. "Pretty snow on those bushes. What a beautiful place this must be in the summer. Lucky you, spending your summers here every year. Does it get hot? I suppose it does, but probably not humid, since we're right on the shore, right? Are there many mosquitoes?" Meg began to empty the dishwasher, and busied herself finding the right slots in the kitchen drawers for a fistful of cutlery.

"Your message, Meg? Do you want to hear it or not?"

"Oh, sorry, Teddy, yes, yes, go ahead," Meg said, opening and closing drawers while she hunted for logical homes for a spatula and a measuring spoon with unnecessary urgency.

"He said he really wanted to see you as soon as possible," Teddy said. "He said he had made up his mind about something."

"What? Are you sure that's what he said?" Meg asked, dropping her pretense of nonchalance. "He had made up his mind about something? But we agreed that we weren't going to be in touch until after the new year. Are you sure he didn't say anything else?"

"Who?" Joanna asked. "Who is this 'he' person?"

"He said you would know what he meant," Teddy said.

"Was there anything else?" Meg was a little breathless and had developed two small pink spots on her cheeks, like someone who has just come in from skating on a brisk winter day.

"Um, yes, he said it would be best if you waited to get in touch, to, um, make a plan, when you're back. He said you shouldn't call him until you're back in New Haven."

"Teddy?" Joanna asked. "When did this telephone call from . . . *him* come exactly?"

"Just before you got back just now," he answered easily. "I was reading, Amy and Avery had just gone out. I thought it might be you guys at the Big Valu"—he pronounced it the perverse way Avery did, "Valloo"—"with a question about what to get for dinner."

"He said I shouldn't call now?" Meg asked uncertainly. "I should wait?"

"You got it," Teddy said.

"Was there really a phone call for Meg when we were out, Teddy?" Joanna asked at the first moment when she could get him alone, having propelled him back into the laundry room for another powwow. The dryer was running and provided a pleasant mechanical whir. Joanna always loved the smell of hot laundry. It always made her feel taken care of.

"Do you come here often?" Teddy clowned. "People will say we're in love."

"Teddy?"

"Call it Plan B," he replied. "I've sprung the trap. Let's see what develops."

"What could possibly develop? What are you thinking? This is cruel. I should tell Meg you lied to her about the call," Joanna whispered hoarsely. "She totally went for it."

"But you won't," Teddy soothed her, putting his finger to her lips. "Because we have something in common, Joanna. Neither of us is entirely nice when we need the truth of a situation."

"Force it out into the open, you mean?"

"Sure."

"What happens now? I mean, if I don't tell her you lied."

The dryer buzzed and stopped running. The little laundry room became still and almost instantly chillier.

"You won't. We watch her. She'll insist on going back to New Haven early, which is okay with me, I hope you don't feel cheated out of New Year's Day here, but it would actually be better for me to get back anyway. I'm sort of reaching my limit with Avery right now. I mean, I love her, but you haven't heard every single story ninety-nine times the way I have. Plus, if you have any of those insane millennium breakdown concerns, maybe we shouldn't be on the road."

"It's not the millennium. I thought we agreed about that. And will you please tell me about these dog collars?" She reached up and fingered one. The tags jingled faintly.

"That was Ezra. He came from the pound," Teddy said, touching the collar. "And this one was Milne. He was originally called Barkley but his name changed because of a bad habit he had that resulted in what we called the pooh corner, if you really want to know."

"Does Avery miss having dogs now?" Joanna wondered, taking clothes from the dryer and folding them into separate piles.

"Sure, probably, but she's probably better off with a cat, in the winter especially," Teddy said. "Though I miss Milne. He used to like to go out in the kayak with me. And Thurgood, this is his collar—he was tremendous, a really witty dog. So anyway, where were we?"

"The millennium. Is this your shirt?"

"That used to be my shirt but I gave it to Amy," Teddy said.

"Look out for Amy borrowing your stuff," Joanna warned. "She's sly. If she wants something you've got, she uses borrowing as the first small step toward possession and the next thing you know you don't have the heart to ask for it back."

"Don't worry about it. So you and I know when the millennium really is, but Amy and Avery are millennium believers. Meg seems to flip-flop," he added. "But my guess is she'll use it as an excuse to go back to New Haven early. So anyway, we'll just wait and see what happens when she calls him. Maybe he'll set up another rendezvous at the bakery. Whatever, we're forcing his hand, don't you see? This will precipitate a confrontation of some kind, since she thinks he's made up his mind about something."

"Hmm," Joanna said, emptying lint from the dryer trap, the laundry done. "It's awfully complicated, isn't it? Can we sit?" They both slid against the wall until they were side by side on the linoleum floor next to a pile of laundry baskets. Joanna began to gather up some stray clothespins into a neat pile.

"But isn't it cruel," she began again, "sort of getting her hopes up in a pointless way? And how did you know there was a something for him to be thinking about, anyway?" She slid her small hand under the dryer and felt around, and was rewarded with two more lint-covered clothespins.

"There's always a something, isn't there? And it's no crueler than what she's doing, potentially messing up a family. She's playing with fire and she's going to get burned. I thought you'd be pleased, Jo-Jo!" he cried out in frustration. The day had been both unprofitable and unsatisfactory and he wished he could live it over again. He looked sorrowfully at the dear face beside him. "I thought I was helping bring this mess to an early conclusion!"

"Maybe you are," she said, leaning against him. "I just hate this! Oh, Teddy, I don't want to be mad at you on top of everything else!" She put one arm across his shoulder and hugged him awkwardly for a long moment. They sat together for a while with their heads touching in a sad communion, their eyes closed as if against some harsh light.

A change seemed to have come over Meg. Although they had planned to stay in Long Harbor with Avery until New Year's Day, she had, as predicted, insisted on returning to New Haven the day before, citing vague concerns about chaos on the roads and millennium problems with computers. Avery insisted that it made no difference to her, as her New Year's Eve habit of many years was to be in her own bed asleep by nine.

"It's not a sacred tradition or anything?" Meg asked worriedly.

"Certainly not," Avery assured her. "Nothing is at last sacred but the integrity of your own mind, for goodness' sake. Never forget that."

"Emerson always did have such a way with words," Teddy footnoted helpfully, which caused Avery to swat him.

They would be leaving first thing in the morning in order to make the long drive to New Haven in what there was of the watery winter daylight.

It had snowed most of the past two days, and in that time, when they were all together incessantly through the days, reading, eating endless meals, listening to Django Reinhardt and Le Hot Club of Paris through the hiss and crackle of Avery's dusty old records, playing marathon hands of Blink, Meg had been quite unlike herself. She started when spoken to, blushed when looked at, was very quiet, and was often found sitting over an unread book in her lap, with a timid, troubled look on her face.

"So, my dear, you've become very quiet," Avery said to her as they tidied up the living room before bed.

"I'm sorry, Avery," Meg said, piling newspapers neatly next to the kindling basket, which brimmed with pinecones she and Amy had collected that afternoon. "I didn't mean to be such a bore. You've been so welcoming and generous to us, letting us overrun your house for the most wonderful Christmas."

"I've loved having you three girls in the house, with your richness, your enjoyments, and that absurd card game. I look forward to my work and my solitude, but I will also miss all three of you, and of course I always miss Teddy. It's been a nice change from the wilderness of my books in this lonely house. And you're not what I would call the least bit boring, Meg. The secret of being a bore is to tell everything, as our friend Voltaire so wisely pointed out. You, on the other hand, tell very little. Nothing, in fact. Hardly boring, that."

Something in Avery's kind and honest eyes made Meg wish she could blurt out her deepest worries, and if they had been truly alone, she might have.

"Love is the difficult realization that something other than oneself is real," Avery said gently.

"How do you know that?" Meg asked.

"A very wise woman called Iris Murdoch said so," Avery answered.

"It is all so difficult—" Meg began hesitantly.

"Dishwasher empty, everything put away!" Amy announced to

Avery, appearing at just that wrong moment. "And I hope it's okay with you—since it's our last night, I gave a little bowl of cream to Miss D."

"On the table, no doubt. In one of the best dishes, I assume. I won't know what to do with her when you leave, Amy, she'll be so spoiled," Avery said with an indulgent chuckle. "Where are the others?"

"Teddy's gone to sleep, Joanna's reading in bed. So come on upstairs to bed, you," Amy said with impatience to Meg. "Don't just stand there in the dark. I did all the dishes myself while you were just lurking in here. You're the one who wanted to get an early start tomorrow and you're driving."

"Don't be cross with me, Amy," Meg said. "You were great to do the washing up, really. You've been great. Don't mind me."

Avery reached over to turn off the big reading lamp by the couch. The three of them stood together and admired the glowing Christmas tree for one last look.

"I don't want to go back to school," Amy said. "Can't I just stay here with you?"

"But you must get your education," Avery reproved.

"Sometimes I feel as though there isn't anything to learn in high school," Amy said. "The subjects are all so stupid and boring. Sometimes I wish I could study real things."

"Ambition, Distraction, Uglification, and Derision," Avery said.

"Reeling, Writhing, and Fainting in Coils," Meg added.

"It's the best Christmas tree, Amy," said Avery, noting the solemn face on her little friend. "You did a splendid job arranging every ornament perfectly."

"I hate it that time passes," Amy declared. "I want it to stop."

"In sweet times, yes," Avery said, "that would be splendid. But surely the many advantages of time passing should not be overlooked."

"Whatever," Amy said begrudgingly. "I just know that I want

to be here and now, and I don't want to be back at that egregious
school next week."

"But remember our talk," Avery reminded her. "You can make
the most of it. And you can stop time in your own way whenever
you want—you have a marvelous ability to preserve your moments with a pencil or a paintbrush. You don't have to give up
your moments. Joanna, I suspect, has words with which to do just
that, if she gets around to it, the way I have had good strong words
for company all my life, and Meg here"—she gave Meg's shoulder
a friendly squeeze to soften her words—"I'm not quite sure what
Meg's gift is, actually, she's so full of secrets, but perhaps that is
her gift—holding secrets safe. However, Miss Amy Green, I see in
your future that you will be a great artist. It is a gift in which I
know you will find much comfort."

"In ten years, let's all meet here and see how many of us have
got our wishes," Amy whispered.

"If we are all alive ten years hence," Avery said dryly. "Ahoy,
it's late," she said, suddenly businesslike. "Shadrach, Meshach,
and to bed we go!"

She sighed a little sigh as she bent to switch off the Christmas
lights and then fumbled in the sudden dark for her glasses and
book and her cardigan sweater, which was draped on the arm of
the sofa. Waiting for her out in the hallway at the bottom of the
stairs, Amy and Meg each thought at that instant that Avery suddenly looked very old and small.

The house creaked and settled. The furnace rumbled on. Upstairs, radiators knocked. The day was over. The interlude in Long
Harbor had come to an end. Miss Demeanor emerged abruptly
from the darkened room, having been dislodged from her perch on
the sweater, startling all three of them, and darted past them to
run swiftly up the stairs, as if she had an urgent appointment that
she had almost forgotten.

———

Reader's note: I'm learning terrible things about events in my life as I read these pages. MG

Author's note: I'm sorry you feel obligated to read so literally. There are many meanings in the story of The Little Women, and not all of them pertain to your experience.

Reader's note: Do tell, what exactly is the meaning of this story? MG

Author's note: Flannery O'Connor said it best: The meaning of the story is the story.

Reader's note: It's bad enough that you have the Avery character spouting literary chestnuts. Can't you explain yourself in your own words instead of perpetually hiding behind the words of authors you happen to admire? Are you consulting some anthology of defensive literary quotations? MG

Author's note: This novel is how I explain myself in my own words. Ideally, it would speak for itself. Ideally, readers will allow it to do just that.

Reader's note: You feel absolutely no obligation to honor reality? MG

Author's note: Wallace Stevens said reality is not what it is. It consists of the many realities which it can be made into.

Reader's note: How handy for you that Wallace Stevens said that! MG

Reader's note: Are there any more scenes with the Avery character? AG

Author's note: No.

Reader's note: I think you should have her come back into the novel. I was hoping she would play a larger role in the story than this. AG

Author's note: Understandably, you miss the person I call Avery in this novel since her recent death, but the events of the story are limited by necessity and she simply doesn't figure again in the narrative. Reference to Amy's trip to Paris with Avery the following summer existed in an earlier draft, but that has been cut.

Reader's note: Why? AG

Author's note: The entire chapter set in the following summer was dropped. It wasn't essential to the story.

Reader's note: Is there no place to work it in elsewhere in the manuscript? AG

Author's note: It is unwise for an author to take advice from a family member about how to construct a novel.

Reader's note: "An" author? "A" novel? AG

Author's note: This author. This novel.

TWELVE

New Year Troubles

❦

As it turned out, although there was much excitement around the world about this particular New Year's Eve, because many people thought it signified the start of a new century, although many others held out for the year 2000 being the final year of the old century and reserved their excitement for the next New Year, there was little festivity in the Green-Bell household.

It was a long and tedious drive. Amy alternately slept and complained, no conversation seemed to last very long before breaking down into unpleasant disagreement, Teddy was critical of the way Meg stayed in the left lane even when there were impatient drivers trying to pass her, and finally, after a lunch stop in New Hampshire, they listened to the radio without speaking for the rest of the way to New Haven.

Teddy closed his eyes for the last three hours in order to give the impression that he was sleeping, but he was thinking. He felt undependable, capable of changing directions as easily as a weathercock, and he hated himself for it. What did he really imagine would come of that malicious telephone message? It had seemed reasonable, even amusing, at the time but the closer they sped toward New Haven, the large and darker the falsehood loomed. Stupid, stupid, stupid.

Sitting in the front seat beside the stony-faced Meg, he had tried to catch her eye several times since Long Harbor, but she would only stare at the road ahead, and he felt injured by her unwillingness to acknowledge him just as he felt a gnawing certainty that he had harmed this dear girl immeasurably and she had every right to treat him as the worm that he was.

He sat up and looked over his shoulder when Meg slowed for the entrance to the Mass Pike, and saw Amy and Joanna tilted against each other in the back seat, sleeping like puppies. Amy looked especially fragile. As he watched, Amy swiped at a strand of Joanna's hair that was brushing her face without opening her eyes. Joanna rearranged Amy's head on her shoulder and opened her eyes for a moment. She saw Teddy and smiled before closing her eyes again and drawing Amy more snugly against her. He felt a surge of helpless love for both of the sleeping girls. He sighed heavily and Meg patted him unexpectedly on the leg. He looked at her and she granted him eye contact for a moment before readjusting her gaze.

"We're too much, aren't we?" she said quietly.

"What do you mean?"

"We're too much for you. We're overwhelming with all of our neurotic this and that. It's okay. You can be sick of us. You're entitled."

"I'm sorry, Meg," Teddy said soulfully.

"What are you apologizing for?"

"I'm sorry I can't make everything perfect for you," he said desperately. "You deserve to be happy. I'm sorry you aren't happy. I'm sorry I'm not your—"

"Don't!" Meg said fiercely. "Just don't." She turned the radio on and jabbed at the buttons to find a station. She settled on some staticky Coltrane. "I can't have this conversation with you right now," she said over the music. "I just can't."

————

Meg declined to pull the car up in front of their building so they could unload their things, because she didn't want to take the time, with all the one-way streets, to circle around several blocks in order to park the car in the garage on Crown Street. Nobody wanted to argue with her, so they drove directly to the garage and carried their bags up High Street, picking their way through the refrozen ruts of unshoveled sidewalk slush.

"I hate frozen footsteps," Amy complained.

"What?" Teddy asked irritably over his shoulder.

"Other people's footsteps in the slush that have refrozen. You can't really walk in them, even though you're tempted," Amy explained. "They look nice and easy but they're like a booby trap to trip you unless you have really little feet that will fit inside the footprints, but if your feet are that little you probably can't take big enough steps to match—"

"Just go faster and stop bumping me with your bag," Joanna interrupted crossly.

From the moment they climbed the cold stairs to their apartment late in the afternoon—where they discovered that the heat and the electricity had been out for an indeterminate number of days, resulting in a hideous stench emanating from the refrigerator—Meg had been agitated and snappish. Before she even took off her coat, she grabbed the telephone and took it into her room, closing the door on the cord. She burst out of her room moments later, still in her coat, with a wild look in her eye, before exiting the apartment, slamming the door behind her so hard it bounced open again and Teddy had to go shut it properly.

Teddy heroically filled and carted out two trash bags full of the freezer contents, much of which consisted of bagged quarts of homemade soups and stews, foil packages of leftovers, and large quantities of Meg's beloved bargain chicken parts from the Stop & Shop. Amy and Joanna spent an hour cleaning out the refrigerator and swabbing it with disinfectant to try to overcome the eye-watering odor.

"Id sbells like subthig died id here," Amy said mournfully.

"I don't think I'll ever eat chicken again," Teddy said, slumping against the doorway. "Man, you can still smell it on the stairs. But at least the building's warming up now. I could hear the radiators banging all through the hallways."

"Where did you leave it?" Joanna asked. "Not in our trash cans, I hope—someone will report a murder before the garbage is collected next week."

"I'm ahead of you," Teddy replied. "I dumped the bags in the bin in the British Art Center parking lot. And if I hadn't been so desperate to get rid of them, I would have stopped to rescue some damaged posters the gift shop had just thrown away, but I just had to toss those putrid bags in there right on top of them. I think I saw a Stubbs."

"So where did Meg go, do you think?" Joanna asked.

"Yeah, what was that about? The mystery phone call last night, right?" Amy chimed in.

"She made a call when we came in, but it didn't sound like she talked to anybody," Teddy said. "So I don't know. Maybe she went to Mark Frank's."

"He's away until next week," Amy said with certainty. "He left this morning." Meg and Teddy both looked at her.

"And you know this how?" Joanna asked.

"Well, since you ask, and since you seem to be willing to include me for once in the ongoing conversation about Meg instead of sneaking around in laundry rooms behind my back, I'll tell you. I read a letter he wrote to her the day before we left. It was in her bag. I read it one time when she was in the shower a couple of days ago."

"Amy Green!" Joanna exclaimed.

"Amy Green what?" Amy retorted. "Is reading a letter any worse than making up a phone call?"

"How do you know about that?" Teddy demanded.

"Duh, I'm not as dumb as I look, okay? She was talking about it before dinner with Avery, when I was setting the table and Avery was making the salad and cutting up all that fruit to go with dessert while Meg got dinner ready. I heard them."

Amy was spreading Nutella on a cracker with her usual demonic precision for such tasks, and she stopped to square off the edges with professional symmetry.

"Don't stop!" Joanna demanded. "And that's really disgusting, by the way. Nutella on a Stoned Wheat Thin?"

"You have no palate for one of the great pleasures in life," Amy retorted with dignity.

"It's the combination," Joanna said.

"As opposed to the perfect combination of Nutella and a spoon?" Teddy offered.

"She told you about that?" Joanna said. "For God's sake, I was in eighth grade."

"But it was the whole jar," Amy pointed out. "And the Larkins, those people whose kids you were baby-sitting and then they came home early, they must have looked under the sofa and found the empty jar sometime—"

"Continue!" shouted Joanna and Teddy together.

"Okay, so now you really want me in this conversation after all! See? So maybe the young innocent child does have a little something to contribute," Amy said sarcastically. "So, any old hoo, she told Avery how upset she was because she wasn't supposed to call him—she wouldn't say his name—and then she did, but it was really awkward and he couldn't speak for very long, which was probably the call Avery overheard, and apparently now she was worried that he was upset about it and called back to yell at her or something. She was scared that she had done something really wrong, somehow, and she was afraid about what he had made his mind up about. She said something bad had happened that was her fault and he was all upset. And she told Avery he was supposed to go away this morning with his family to stay with some people in

New York for five days, so she wasn't expecting to hear from him until next week, because they had a plan. So the call you told her had come while she was out had her all upset. She didn't say you made up the phone call, but that was my guess and I can see I was right!" Amy concluded her soliloquy with slightly breathless triumph.

"Well, aren't you the little font of info. So she told Avery she's involved with someone who has a family?" Joanna asked with curiosity. "Even though she wouldn't say his name she sort of admitted she was involved with a married man? What did Avery say about that?"

"Meg was worried that Avery would judge her, but Avery just laughed and said"—here Amy drew herself up and managed an uncanny duplication of Avery's fierce yet kind visage—"'My dear, the older one grows, the more one likes indecency!'"

"Woolf," Teddy said. "One of Avery's favorite remarks, actually."

"So, Amy, what else was in the letter?" Joanna asked.

"Are you sure it wouldn't be immoral for me to tell you?"

"Oh, it's definitely immoral. But do tell us, Ames."

"Do you want me to go look for it in her bag? You two can be lookouts."

"Absolutely not! Just tell us what it said, if you don't mind," Joanna said impatiently.

"Well, he said he would miss her but that given the recent unfortunate drama—those were his words, 'the recent unfortunate drama'—their time apart was all for the best, and that his family would be in New Haven for most of the break, that they were going to a professor somebody's house in Bethany for Christmas dinner, and then that they were leaving for New York today, in the morning, so he would see Meg in the new year and they would sort things out—his words. And that no matter what happened to their relationship he valued her—what was it? her fine splendid mind, I think, something like her spicy intelligence."

"So where could Meg have run off to, if he's out of town?" Joanna mused.

"I saw her take keys off the hook as she left," Amy offered. She dipped the tip of her knife into the Nutella and licked it pensively.

"Don't do that," Joanna said automatically.

"So? We all take our keys when we go out," Teddy said.

"Not just her house keys. Some other keys." Amy nibbled another defiant glob of Nutella from the knife tip.

"What other keys?" Joanna wondered.

"Mark Frank's office in Linsley-Chit," Teddy said. "She's got all of those keys. But what would there be for her to do in there if he's away? Ransack his lecture notes for clues to his true feelings? I wonder what the recent drama was."

"She wouldn't be able to get into the building. It's New Year's Eve, remember?" Joanna pointed out logically. "Every Yale thing is locked up and dark."

"Not everything," Amy pointed out. "She could get into the Franks' apartment in JE."

"You're right," Teddy said, "but to do what?"

"Read through his stuff, rummage in their drawers, read other people's letters, boil a rabbit, who knows, I'm tired of this," Amy said crossly. "Are we going to eat dinner or what?"

Some rather grim omelets were consumed that evening, made with basic ingredients procured at the unpleasant twenty-four-hour grocery situated incongruously beside the fastidious J. Press shop on York Street. This was the one place on campus where cigarettes and junk food could be obtained by bleary Yale students all night long. After they ate, when there was still no sign of Meg, Teddy had rung the Franks' number, but it just went straight to voice mail—Mark's voice—saying they were out of town until the fourth of January.

"Strange," Teddy had remarked, "I knew he was a Brit, so that's no surprise, but his voice was plummy, somehow, in a way that just doesn't go with his face at all."

"What should his voice sound like? Big sweater-y? We've never even had a glimpse," Joanna pointed out.

"She definitely had it worked out that we would never go over there to baby-sit once they hooked up," Amy mused. "Or maybe Meg just wanted to keep us away from him because she knew we would see something."

"See something like what?" Joanna asked. "You mean see the way they gazed into each other's eyes, or see how irresistibly charming he is so that we, too, would want to fall in love with him?"

"Ick," said Amy.

Teddy went out for a walk, he said, but when he came back a while later, he admitted he had loitered at the entrance to the JE court-yard in the hopes of checking to see if there were lights in any windows, but the gate was firmly locked and nobody had passed by to let him in.

They were watching New Year's celebrations around the world on their crummy television set when Meg came home, shortly before midnight.

She was panting, as if she had been running, and she stood in the doorway observing the three of them sprawled in front of the snowy image of the Eiffel Tower fizzing like a giant sparkler.

"Looks festive," she remarked breathlessly, sitting down to yank off her snow-covered boots.

"Where were you?" Joanna demanded. "We were worried about you. Plus we wanted you to be here at midnight, which is in ten minutes."

"I went for a walk," Meg said. "I feel so much better now. I'm just starved. What smells so good? Onions?"

"We had omelets. Do you want me to make you one?" Amy volunteered.

"That's a hell of a walk, five hours in the freezing cold dark on New Year's Eve. Where did you walk to?" Teddy asked. "Bridge-port?"

"I wasn't walking for five hours. I needed to think," Meg said. "Ames, I would love an omelet, would you mind? So I went to the Franks' apartment in JE. I knew they would be away, but I thought I could just think quietly for a while. Then I walked all the way up Whitney Avenue to the reservoir in Hamden and back. It's a beautiful night. The little waterfall at the Eli Whitney Museum is frozen."

"Didn't you hear the phone ringing in their apartment?" Amy demanded from the kitchen, where she was slamming cupboard doors and clattering pans. "That was us."

"No, sweetie, the bell is turned off, it just goes straight to voice mail. Did you—"

"Don't worry, we didn't leave a message, if that's what you were thinking," Teddy said.

"I know I've been so secretive," Meg began. "I really want to talk to you all. I've been thinking. It's been really hard for me. You probably have no idea—"

"But we know more than you think. Like we know about your rendezvous at the bakery on State Street," Joanna blurted. "Teddy saw you."

"You know?" Meg asked, clearly startled. She looked around at the three somber faces. "You know, and you're not furious at me?"

"Why would we be furious?" Joanna said. "I mean, I think you're making a stupid mistake, but it's your life. I guess. But no, I'm not exactly furious. Did you think we would stage an intervention or something?"

"I'm just kind of disappointed," Amy said primly, emerging from the kitchen with a whisk and a bowl of beaten eggs.

"Teddy?" Meg looked at him with puzzled and guilty eyes. She sat down heavily next to him on the sagging sofa. "You don't think it's a horrible betrayal of Amy and Joanna? Why are you all being so nice? Did the Health Plan call and say I have a brain tumor?"

"What does it really have to do with Amy and Joanna?" Teddy said. "It's totally your own life to fuck up. I mean, I suppose in

some sense it is a betrayal of the famous Green family values or
something, but it's much more of a betrayal of Mark Frank's family, isn't it? With the kooky wife and the disturbed kids and everything." Teddy gazed at her solemnly. Joanna and Amy stood still
in fascination at Teddy's candor, waiting for her response. The
smell of burning butter made Amy dive back into the kitchen for
a moment to turn the heat down, returning to the discussion without starting the omelet.

  "What?" Meg looked utterly stricken. "I have no idea what
you're saying, Teddy. What do you mean? How could my meeting
with Lou a few times at Marjolaine be a betrayal of Mark Frank's
children! That just makes no sense at all!"

  "Your meetings with *Lou?!*" Joanna and Amy chorused together.

*Reader's note: This is very one-sided. It's unfair that you haven't told the
story from Meg's point of view for so many pages. MG*

  *Author's note: At this point in the story it seemed a better narrative
strategy to limit the points of view for a tighter and less panoramic focus.
Some of the tension arises from the very lack of access to Meg's point of view,
after all.*

  *Reader's note: So no matter what you claim and no matter how clev-
erly you claim it about how a novel is constructed and how it should owe
no debt to reality, this novel is really more about your experience than it is
about the experience of the other two sisters. AG*

  *Author's note: The novel does spend more time in Joanna's point of
view. It is an inevitable emphasis. It's about artistic choices, not family
politics.*

  Reader's note: It's all about you, in other words. MG

  Author's note: In a certain sense, that could be said of every novelist.

  *Reader's note: In a very certain sense, we're saying it of this novel-
ist. AG*

THIRTEEN

Darkness and Light in January

Unhappiness coated everything. Two days had passed without any communication between Meg and her sisters. Only Teddy, though he was in his own state of half-sweet, half-bitter melancholy, was able to speak casually with Meg. Meg avoided Joanna and Amy completely by spending most of her time, when she was in the apartment at all, in her room, with brief bathroom interludes.

Joanna had made herself go to work, her last long Starbucks shift before school began again and her afternoon shifts would return to the usual three hours. She was happy to get away from the poisonous atmosphere in the apartment, and they needed the money, but it had been tempting to stay in bed under her old red patchwork quilt, because she had woken up with a bad headache and a stabbing sore throat that made swallowing an agony.

Amy seemed to be nursing her fury, and there was nothing to do for it. She crashed around the apartment, ready for a fight with anyone about anything. She even rebuffed Teddy's generous offer of letting her rearrange all the furniture in his room, which she had been keen to do.

"We could have been great, we *were* great, and now we're nothing," she cried, when Joanna tried to talk with her. "Why did she have to ruin everything? Why does everything good in this family have to be destroyed?"

She had hoped that after a while she would shake off her headache and sore throat, but two hours into her shift, Joanna felt truly sick. She was sweaty at one moment and had chills the next. She kept sipping from a mug of tea, which was temporarily soothing, though each swallow hurt as if there were a burr stuck in the back of her throat. As the busy afternoon progressed, everyone in New Haven seemed to be in a simultaneous mood for complicated cappuccino orders. Twice, an impatient customer grabbed the wrong order and left, causing a domino effect of confusion and irritation. The second one had known what he was doing, Joanna was certain. She hated all of these people who seemed to have something intensely invested in indulging themselves so precisely. Why the hell couldn't they just drink ordinary coffee and get over themselves?

Then came a sudden influx of teenaged girls who reeked of cigarette smoke and gossiped about shoplifting strategies for the Chapel Square Mall. Joanna was still working the bar, because she was faster than anyone else. She thought she would go mad as each of the six girls ordered a tall, decaf, skim latte (which the staff called a "why bother"), each one slightly different in its requirements for caramel this and extra foam that. By the time she had served them all, she was trembling and had a sheen of cold sweat on her face.

"Jeeth, you look like shit," the assistant manager, who spoke with a slight lisp because of his various lip and tongue piercings, said. "You thtill wathted from New Year's or thomething?"

When Joanna confessed to feeling sick, he backed away from her shaking his head, saying, "Man, you look really bad. You better go home before you thcare the cuthtomers."

By the time she was opening the door to the apartment, Joanna felt like crying. She hated being sick under ordinary circumstances, but being sick right now was just more than she could bear. She flung herself down on the sofa in the empty apartment, still in her coat. There was a note on the table from Teddy, saying that he had taken Amy to a movie. What a sweet boy. She put the kettle on to make some tea and felt her forehead with the back of her wrist. At home, Janet always diagnosed fevers with her lips, lightly kissing her daughters on the forehead, which in itself was always soothing. Joanna felt sorry for herself. She didn't know what to do.

They didn't have a doctor in New Haven, and she felt too sick to take a train to New York, if she could even get an appointment with Dr. Rosenthal. All of this would take too much time and energy just to figure out. Her mother always made appointments for them. And if Joanna used the health insurance card in her wallet, then a statement would automatically be mailed to Janet and Lou, a notification of sorts that she had been sick. How did she feel about that? She had no idea. The whole thing was exhausting and impossible. Her throat stabbed. She made herself a cup of mint tea and immediately burned her lips sipping it.

Did they even own a thermometer? She rummaged in the bathroom medicine chest but found nothing, not even aspirin. Meg always had aspirin, and Joanna recalled seeing it on her dresser, so she went to look in Meg's room, which was unusually messy. Drawers were half open with clothes spilling out. She spied the aspirin bottle. Beside it, on a plastic lanyard, was Meg's Yale ID card, which she ordinarily wore around her neck during the semester because she needed it so frequently when doing research in the libraries.

Joanna looked at the photograph, and saw in it many of her own features, the way she did occasionally in photographs of either of her sisters, though the resemblance was never so obvious in real life. She studied Meg's face and recalled the remark about the brain tumor. Maybe there really *was* something seriously wrong with Meg. Had she eaten a peppermint from the notorious basket of hard candies on the counter at the copy shop, the one rumored to hold the occasional hit of LSD? Or perhaps she had a tragic secret disease for which she was being secretly treated and they would all be sorry when it was revealed. It dawned on Joanna that with Meg's ID she could get medical treatment at the Yale Health Service. She knew where it was, having walked by the building once, up on the corner of Hillhouse Avenue.

Oddly enough, she had been there with Lou, when she had spent a day with him visiting Meg because Warren had been closed owing to a Jewish holiday. Lou had asked Meg to direct them to that part of the campus for a walk, while she had a class, because he had read about the computer science professor who had, just a few years before, opened a parcel sent by the Unabomber. The professor had saved his own life by managing to get down five flights of stairs in Watson Hall and across two campus blocks, wounded and bleeding, to the Health Service. He would have died waiting for an ambulance.

Lou had wanted to retrace the steps of this brave man whose work he also admired. He and Joanna had done so, holding hands and swinging them slightly, with no need for any talking, that fall afternoon of Meg's freshman year.

The walk across campus in the icy January air made Joanna feel better, although there was a slight tinge of unreality to everything around her. She was clammy with sweat under her clothes by the time she got to the entrance. Joanna read the directory and decided that she should go to the Primary Care department, which she located by following signs. She supposed she should have been prepared with some vague explanation for her lack of appointment, but the nurse at the desk got one look at her and sent her down to Urgent Care, where she could be seen right away.

Misrepresenting yourself seems fascinatingly easy in New Haven, whether at school or here, Joanna thought, as the Yale ID

at the end of the lanyard around her neck was scanned through a
card reader without question by a distracted woman who seemed
impatient to return to the Nora Roberts paperback she was reading. Joanna panicked when asked at the next desk if she had visited the Health Center in the past three months, not knowing the
correct answer, but before she could respond, the woman had
pulled up Meg's records and answered her own question.

"Oh, I see you were just in before the break, got it. Okay, have
a seat, Margaret, and someone will see you in a moment."

The nurse practitioner who saw her took one look at her throat
with a light and a tongue depressor and tsked "Poor baby!" before
swabbing a culture for a quick strep test, which made Joanna gag.
Joanna was self-conscious knowing that she probably had terrible
sore-throat breath, plus all that tea didn't help. The nurse popped
an alcohol-tasting thermometer into Joanna's mouth, looked into
her ears, and took a pulse while waiting for the digital beep,
which sounded just as she was writing down Joanna's pulse on
Meg's medical chart.

"Ooh, hundred and two, you must feel pretty lousy, Margaret,"
she said sympathetically, feeling Joanna's neck and jaw, which
made Joanna cry out.

"Tender and somewhat swollen lymphs, too. Let me go finish
up one other patient and then the rapid strep culture should be
done. If it's positive, we won't have to send this to the lab and we
can start you on Amoxicillin right away. I'll bet you a nickel that's
strep."

Left alone in the room under the glaring overhead fluorescent
lights, Joanna felt too sick to read any of the crumpled magazines
in a rack by the examining table. She lay on the examining table
with her eyes closed. When the door opened and the nurse returned a few minutes later, she had been dozing.

"Strep it is!" She picked up Meg's chart and began to write on
it. "Okay then, Margaret, here's a scrip for your Amoxicillin, you
know where to go down the hall for the pharmacy. If you take one

right away, you can take another before you go to sleep tonight. Warm salt-water gargles will help, too, and you'll start to feel better by tonight, I promise you. But limit your activities until your fever has been gone for twenty-four hours, okay?" She finished up her notations and scanned the top of the page.

"I see you were here not so long ago, on the nineteenth, and you were treated by Dr. Tirone, who gave you Preven. How did that work out for you? Did you get that bad headache? Most women we treat with Preven say it's almost a migraine. It's too bad—it's really the only common problem with this drug. But it can be treated. Did you take something for it?"

"What?" Joanna said dully.

"The headache, Margaret. Did the ECPs give you a headache or nausea? The first round don't usually do it, but the second two pills can give you a really wicked headbanger. Lots of people vomit, too, it's nothing to worry about, but I know it can be rough."

"ECPs?" Joanna said.

"Oh, sorry, you know, emergency contraceptive pills, the pills we gave you. People call it the morning-after pill even though it isn't always 'the morning after,' just so long as you're within seventy-two hours, which I see here, you were, yes, more like forty-eight, good."

"Uh, no, it wasn't too bad," Joanna said, trying to stay on track with this startling conversation. "I, um, took aspirin for my headache."

"Any unusual bleeding or spotting?"

"Um—"

"Well, you're going to return for a follow-up, let's see, next week, with Sandy the nurse practitioner in GYN, for birth control pills, right? So you can discuss any concerns you have with her then. And did you make that call to Student Peer Health Educators? That's important, Margaret, after what happened. You signed the agreement that you would schedule a meeting with a

Peer Counselor." The nurse looked at Joanna, who looked down at her shoes, at a loss for the correct words.

"I do understand that with the holidays it's been especially difficult for you, Margaret," she said sympathetically. "So just promise me you'll do it as soon as you feel better. We want you to take care of yourself. That's the plan, right? We don't want you to have to repeat the Preven, do we, Margaret?"

"Um, no," Joanna agreed. "We don't want that."

Joanna had no recollection of her walk home, except for the iridescent haloes around the streetlights which kept forming before her fevered eyes. It was very cold but it was a still evening and every step she took seemed to echo strangely. The usual sour food smell in the lobby of their building made her gag. She just wanted to get into bed and close her eyes. She could hear music as she trudged up the stairs, first the inevitable Joni Mitchell jamboree on the second floor, and then, from their apartment, an unfamiliar woodwind solo of some kind which stopped and repeated, which made Joanna realize, as she put her key in the lock and went inside, that it was Amy practicing the flute, a sound she hadn't heard in months. So that was something good.

"Hey, kiddo!"

Joanna looked up, startled by the unexpected voice, as she was hanging her coat on a hook in the hallway beside two unfamiliar coats. It was the photographer they had met that day in New York, Harriet. And there was a man beside her; there were two attractive people sitting on the sofa while Amy played the flute for them. Joanna was flabbergasted and had a passing thought that her fever had now actually put her into a hallucinatory state.

"Look who I found on Chapel Street!" Amy said, her eyes shining. She waved her flute in their direction. "Teddy and I had just seen the scariest Hitchcock movie at York Square, about this guy with a broken leg who watches all his neighbors—"

"*Rear Window,*" Harriet prompted, "my absolute favorite. Amy and I have been discussing how many tastes we share in music and movies."

"And then Teddy said he needed to go to the bookstore, so I was coming home on my own, and there they were, leaving the Yale Art Gallery! We had hot chocolate at Atticus. We looked for you at Starbucks, but they said you had left early because you weren't feeling well," Amy continued with her giddy summary of the afternoon. "But you weren't here when we came in. Where were you?"

"This is my husband, Benedict," Harriet said, getting up to greet her. "Benedict, I'd like you to meet Joanna."

"Wow," Joanna said as they all shook hands a little awkwardly, appreciating the kindness in his face. There was something comfortable about him. Benedict hardly spoke yet he didn't seem shy, just like someone who didn't have to talk unless he had something to say. He looked exactly right with Harriet—somehow, they went together perfectly. "It's great to see you, and great to meet you, it's a terrific surprise, really, but I am *so* sick. I don't mean to be a wet blanket, but I have a horrible strep throat and I feel totally crappy." She rummaged the antibiotics from her bag and held up the pill vial as evidence.

"Where'd you go to a doctor?" Amy wondered.

"Yale Student Health," Joanna said, throwing herself down on the sofa.

"How did that work?" Amy asked skeptically. "You can't just walk in there, can you?"

Joanna flipped up Meg's Yale ID, which was still on the lanyard around her neck. "I'm Margaret Green, as far as they know," she said wearily.

"Wow," Amy said. "You're a criminal genius."

"Why don't you get into bed and we'll bring you something hot to drink," Harriet suggested. She came over to Joanna and knelt down, and then she leaned over her until her lips were just touching Joanna's forehead. "You have a fever. Poor you! What can we do for you? Tea? You probably don't have a hot water bottle."

"No college student owns a hot water bottle," said Benedict. "You'd worry about the kind of life any hot water bottle–owning undergraduate could possibly be leading."

"Okay then, how about some tea with honey," Harriet offered. "Do you guys have honey?"

"We do," Amy said, "unless Joanna ate it all. She just sits there eating honey with a spoon sometimes. It's gross."

"Thus speaketh the eater of a Nutella and bacon sandwich," croaked Joanna.

"So tea with honey, then," Harriet said. "Why don't you go get into bed and we'll bring it to you there?"

"That would be wonderful," Joanna whispered.

A little while later Teddy came in, whistling his adaptation of the Green family tune. Ever since they had told him about it, and Joanna had taught it to him, he had gotten into the habit of whistling a variation of the little tune in F sharp, a Lou invention (a conceptual herald of his electronic Cliqk gadget) that they had always used in crowded places to connect with one another.

"Hello? Where is everybody?" he called out.

"In here," Amy replied from her place on the floor in the room she and Joanna shared. "In with a sickly patient plus a wonderful surprise!"

Introductions were made all around, Joanna's pathetic state was explained, and it was quickly organized, minus the usual fractious debate—Amy being a Pad Thai fascist—about which Thai restaurant in the neighborhood (there were at least five) was best, that Harriet and Benedict would go out for Thai food to bring back for everyone, including some lemongrass soup for Joanna.

While Amy bustled about in her newfound state of cheer, cleaning up kitchen mess and unwashed dishes and setting the table so it would be ready for their meal, Teddy sat on the foot of Joanna's bed for a quick little summit conference.

"So where is she?" he asked. "Have you seen her all day? What time is it, anyway?"

"It's dark o'clock," Joanna said. "And I have no idea where she is, but, Teddy, the most awful thing!" Quickly Joanna explained what she had inadvertently learned from the nurse practitioner about Meg and the morning-after pills.

"Should I set a place for Meg?" Amy shouted from the kitchen.

"Sure, yes," Teddy shouted back. "Let's just hope she comes home in time."

"Oh, Joanna, I feel like such an asshole," Teddy said mournfully. "I am a total shithead for telling Meg that he had called."

Joanna closed her eyes and nodded.

"Yes, I'm an asshole, or yes, I'm a shithead?"

She shook her head.

"Neither?" Teddy asked hopefully.

She nodded, eyes still closed, and reached out one of her hands from under the covers. He took it in his and squeezed it gratefully.

"It's horrible enough that here I was picturing someone in my mind's eye as her postmodern English guy and he turns out to be your father, but then to think that there really was a whole big-deal crisis going on between her and the real Mark Frank." Teddy thought for a moment. "I can't believe what a mean thing I've done to poor Meg. I shouldn't be allowed out in public."

"Teddy, I just don't know what I think right now," Joanna croaked in her sore-throat whisper, opening her eyes. "I know I should be furious at her for sneaking behind our backs and meeting with Lou. I mean, who knows what else went on, what else she did. Maybe they've secretly been paying for stuff all along, and I guess this means she's probably been talking with Janet too. I guess we'll find out, sooner or later, but I'm starting to think it doesn't make any difference anyway. And I just feel bad for Meg, I'm not mad at her. She's been through so much on her own. We turned to her, without even asking. Amy and I made her take responsibility for us without ever stopping to think for a second if she wanted it, but she didn't feel she could turn to us for her problems."

"Shh," Teddy said. "Don't strain your voice. And anyway, it's not the same. But what do you mean, it doesn't make any difference?"

"I can't explain it. It's just that Amy and I had to know *everything*, you know what I mean? We had to be certain about all the *facts*. But the facts aren't the same thing as feelings. I was thinking about Lou, and about Janet, and about the whole Phil Hart thing, when I was walking to Hillhouse, and somehow, my rage, which was always there, it wasn't just a smaller glow, like a fire going out, but it was gone."

"What was gone?" Teddy asked gently.

"My rage. My anger. I just told you. I mean, it's still there, in a certain way, you know, in principle, but the feelings are gone. I just don't have the, you know, the passion for it anymore. I am just so *tired* of this. It doesn't seem so unforgivable. I just want everything to be back the way it was before. Not you, Teddy, you're the best thing that's come out of this, but I just felt today that we've been in a kind of crazy nightmare, you know? And I felt like I was waking up from it."

"Because you know Meg has been in touch all along? Or because of something else?"

"Now you're making me talk and my throat hurts," Joanna protested in a whisper. "With Meg, I feel bad for her more than anything else. And I just think that we've been really hard on Janet and Lou, and somehow we ran away with our self-righteousness."

"What are you guys talking about?" Amy came into the room, wiping the spaghetti pot with a dish towel. "I heard some of what you said and I don't know why you're letting Meg off the hook so easily. How can we forget that she betrayed us?"

"So, Ames, you're ready to shift your anger from your parents to your sister now," Teddy inquired. "Is that how this works, just so long as somebody is the villain? Someone is to blame for wronging you?"

"You're twisting everything around, Teddy," Amy said crossly, giving him a shove so he would make room for her at the foot of the bed. She plopped down beside him. "I have a right to be upset that Meg lied to us, in effect, by pretending that were living independently while she was secretly in touch with them."

"But you *were* living independently," Teddy pointed out. "You are. You didn't know she was in touch with him. Maybe it was just something *she* needed. Did you ever think of that? You needed her to share your anger, but maybe that wasn't fair to Meg. You had no contact, just as you planned. You have absolutely succeeded at making a go of this. Look at you. Look at all of this! It's been totally real. You've succeeded! The question now is where do you go from here. You and Joanna need to work that out, don't you think?"

"Well, what about her thing with the married professor? What about that? What if it's really an affair?" Amy asked him angrily, jumping to her feet and stamping across the room. "And anyway, you're jealous that we have parents and you don't, I know that's mean but it's true. It doesn't make you so wise." Amy stood there glaring at Teddy, her chest heaving. She was still holding the dish towel and the pot, which she had polished in her fervor. "You're so full of observations but you can't just live on books, and you've got to stop acting like we're characters in novels to be deconstructed whenever you feel like it. What's wrong is wrong!"

"Nothing is so black-and-white, Ames," Joanna protested hoarsely.

"It just blows dead bears that everyone in this family turns out to be such a traitor," Amy said. "And that I cry so easily," she added, snuffling and wiping her face with the dish towel.

"Charming," Joanna whispered.

There were footsteps in the hallway and then multiple voices as Harriet and Benedict returned, along with Meg.

"We just keep finding Green sisters like Easter eggs on the streets here," Benedict said.

"Dinner's on the table in two minutes," Harriet said. "Are you able to come join us, Joanna?"

While they ate, and while Joanna managed a bowl of the promised soothing brothy substance, about which she was tactfully silent concerning the presence of loathsome bits of coriander leaf—she believed the flavor to be identical to that of old aluminum doors and mildewed canvas awnings—they took turns of conversation with Harriet or Benedict, so the absence of connection between each of the Green sisters was somewhat camouflaged until the end of the meal, when there was a lull in the chatter and everyone looked around at everyone else.

"Twenty past?" Benedict predicted. "Yup," he confirmed, checking his watch.

"What?" Amy demanded. "How did you know the time? Had you just looked?"

"When there's a lull in conversation with a group of people, it's always twenty past or twenty of," Benedict said. "It's a known fact."

"Among the insane," Harriet added.

There was another awkward silence.

"So how about them Mets," Amy threw out, and got a laugh.

"Totally cromulent," added Teddy after another silence.

"There's that word again!" exclaimed Benedict.

"Okay, I have a confession," Harriet finally said after another self-conscious lull. "It's not the total coincidence it seemed to be that you ran into us on the street, Amy."

"*What?*" Amy demanded.

"Actually, we came up to New Haven specifically to see you. When we got to your apartment, nobody was home. Then we went to Starbucks looking for you, Joanna, but you weren't there."

"What?" Joanna whispered.

"What?" Amy demanded.

"I don't like where this is going," Meg said quietly.

"So we went to the Art Gallery," Harriet continued, "and after, we were going to try the apartment again. But that's when we ran into you, Amy. We were going to tell you that we were looking for you, but you didn't give us a chance and after a while it was kind of too late."

"So that's why the Starbucks manager looked at me like I was nuts when I insisted on going in there and asking for Jo-Jo, because I was with you, and he had already told you she was out sick?"

Harriet and Benedict nodded.

"So I don't get it," Amy said. Then she saw Meg's face. "But Meg gets it, I see," Amy said with bitterness. "We're the little babies being handled again, is that the way this works? Make them feel grownup and independent while manipulating them behind their backs?"

"Not exactly," Meg started. "See—"

"I'd rather hear it from Harriet if you don't mind," Amy interrupted.

"Okay," Harriet said. "Here's the thing. After I met you that day, I looked you up in the phone book, and a few days later I called the number for Green children at the address which wasn't too far from the gallery, which I thought it was a good guess. I wanted to ask you if I could photograph you, the three of you together, I mean."

"Oh no, you spoke with *them*?" Amy was aghast. Joanna felt so dizzy that she couldn't tell if it was the strep reaching her ears or the unreality of what was being said.

"Well, I did—wait, don't interrupt me, Amy, hear me out—I

asked for any of you and ended up in a long conversation with Janet."

"Uh-huh," Amy said. "How charming."

"And then we met for lunch," Harriet confessed.

"Oh for God's sake," Amy exclaimed, throwing down her chopsticks and starting to get up from the table. "This is just insane."

"Ames, don't, please stay and listen," Teddy coaxed. "There is nobody at this table who really has the complete story of whatever is going on."

"I understand why this is so upsetting, believe me," Harriet said. "But you have to understand that I had no idea of your situation when I tried to call you on Seventy-fifth Street. Anyway, that was a while ago. I had been thinking of calling you here in New Haven one of these days anyway, maybe coming up to see you, really, but then yesterday Janet and Lou called me."

"Why did they call you?" Joanna whispered. "Amy's right. This is nuts."

"Because Meg must have called them," Amy shouted. "Why am I the only person who sees where this is going? Meg knows what this is about!"

"I did call them," Meg said quietly. "May I speak, please, or am I only to be spoken about from now on?"

"Go on," Amy said begrudgingly.

"I called them because I just really needed to talk with them. Maybe you don't need them to be your parents anymore, either one of you," Meg said, looking first at Joanna and then at Amy. "But I still need them."

"But aren't you angry at Janet for what she did to us?" Amy said desperately, snuffling back tears.

"Yes, I am," Meg said simply. "I'm really angry. But I understand it, a little bit, and she didn't really do it to us. She did it to herself, and to Lou. This is about them, not us. Maybe it isn't our business as much as we thought it was. I don't know what good can be achieved by punishing her this way, and punishing Lou, too. I feel as though we've all taken rat poison and we've been waiting for the rats to die, and it doesn't work. Don't you think they've been punished enough?"

"I don't know," Amy said belligerently. "What's enough? She did an immoral thing. He didn't stand up to her. Why should there be no consequences for what she did? We're the ones who didn't do anything wrong."

"Virtue itself turns vice, being misapplied," Teddy said absently.

"What the hell is that?" Amy turned on him with irritation. "Another one of Avery's cute sayings?"

"No, dummy, it's one of Shakespeare's cute sayings," Meg scolded, and Benedict laughed briefly.

"I'm sorry," he apologized, "but you're all very amusing even when you're having an intense angry conversation and you're not trying to be amusing."

"I'm glad we amuse you," Amy muttered.

"Really, I do apologize. I shall endeavor to cease being amused," Benedict said with mock solemnity, a merry look in his eye.

"So are you and Benedict on a mission?" Joanna whispered to Harriet.

"Sort of," she admitted. "But I guess we've blown our cover, you know? We were just going to see how you were doing and then let them know. They were very worried about Meg, mostly, but they wanted a reality check for all of you."

"Why were they worried about Meg?" Amy asked. "They should have been worried about their estranged children! They were in touch with Meg."

"Exactly," Harriet said, looking at her steadily. "Don't look away from me, Amy. Look at me, please. Okay. Are you listening?"

Amy nodded. Joanna's hand crept across the table and took hers. Meg took Amy's other hand. Teddy let out a deep sigh as if he had been holding his breath for a very long time. Benedict stopped pretending that he was trying to look solemn and really did have a serious look on his face now.

"They knew she was very unhappy and dealing with some big life things and they were worried about her," Harriet said gently. "They love her. They love all three of you. Both of them love all three of you very much and that has never had anything at all to do with any mistakes either of them has made. They're your parents. You're their children. They love you. Can you accept that? Can you just accept that?"

FINAL READERS' NOTES
ON THE MANUSCRIPT

Reader's note: It is of course a real cheat to the reader that you began the book with a reference to this being the story of "the year" we left our parents, when in fact we only stayed away from them for four months. AG

Author's note: It isn't improper to refer to an event as having been a "year" even if it didn't take place in an entire year. In any case, I didn't want to alert the reader at the start of the book as to the limited duration of the New Haven interlude. One of the limitations of a novel—of any story printed on paper—is that the reader can see for himself just where he is in proportion to the remaining pages of a story. If you are three pages from the end of a novel, you know it; if you are ten minutes away from the end of a movie, you don't know it. If the reader has been misled into believing that the time the three Green sisters spent away from their parents was an entire calendar year, or for that matter a school year, then no harm has been done. If anything, the deception has added to the reader's surprise when the New Haven days come to an end so abruptly. After all, Meg, Joanna, and Amy have every intention of remaining in New Haven through the school year, at the very least.

Reader's note: That seems like another pretentious literary cop-out. Why aren't you describing the rest of the year, when Joanna and Amy go back to New York, and Meg ends her involvement with Mark Frank and lives with Teddy and the terrible new roommate through the spring semes-

ter, and then gets romantically involved with Teddy? And what about Amy taking painting lessons with Benedict? Or that trip to Paris with Avery for the literary award ceremony? At the end of chapter 11 you said you left it out, but I still don't see why. Why are those events left out? It seems you only want to show Amy's immature side. AG

Reader's note: Amy is right. There are so many things missing from this novel. How can you just end it there, that night? Why didn't you include the fire in JE that began in Mark Frank's apartment? That was only two weeks later. And don't you think readers want to know what happens to these characters? You could write some scene in the present that would explain where you go to college, or where Amy goes, or where Meg goes to work in New York after graduation from Yale. You don't explain anything about how they go back to their New York life. And why not mention that one of the "Jennifers" died at the World Trade Center on September 11? And why wasn't there some way to include a reference in passing to the death of the real "Professor Baldwin"? Yet you bother to mention the future AIDS death of a minor wedding guest. Where's the logic here? MG

Author's note: All these events took place after the moment that ends the novel. The real Professor Baldwin's death was very sad, but it has nothing to do with the story. These are all matters of artistic judgment. There is no "logic," per se. As I was forced to say earlier, the book's about what the book's about. It's not about what it's not about. And were I going to include an act of destruction, rather than a gratuitous reference to September 11, or to that mysterious fire in JE, surely the time Amy deleted my writing journal from the hard drive of our computer would be far more useful for the purposes of this narrative, considering when it took place and what that loss signified to me. I decided to omit that incident from the story because I had a concern that it could make readers unsympathetic to Amy. And it would have slowed down the narrative momentum at just the wrong time. Also, to be completely candid, I was uncertain that I could render that particular scene based on such a painful event in my life with any artistic objectivity.

Reader's note: A statement like that is meant to suggest, of course, that you have rendered every other scene in the novel with perfect artistic objectivity. MG

Reader's note: It was a mistake and I apologized for it about a million times. Don't you ever regret anything you have done? Do you feel that you've never acted irresponsibly for even a moment? If you can't think of anything, I can make some suggestions. AG

Author's note: Faulkner said the writer's only responsibility is to his art.

Reader's note: Faulkner also said, "If a writer has to rob his mother, he will not hesitate; the 'Ode on a Grecian Urn' is worth any number of old ladies." MG

Author's note: I cannot disagree with that sentiment, though I don't think any old ladies have been harmed in the making of this novel.

Reader's note: The real Mark Frank was investigated in connection with the Kolbert murder—surely that is material worth using for a novel. That whole story could be an entire novel in itself. In fact, you really should have written a novel about that instead of this one. People like to read fictional solutions for true crimes. AG

Author's note: It is true that the murder of Susie Kolbert, an undergraduate for whose senior thesis the real Mark Frank had been a second reader, took place in the same academic year as the events of this story. It has never been solved. The real Mark Frank has never been named as a suspect, though he was questioned several times by the police. It would have been cruel and tasteless to appropriate this terrible crime simply to add one more interesting element to my novel. It had nothing to do with the story I had in mind to tell.

Reader's note: Do you expect anyone to believe that you would hesitate to appropriate anything at all for your novel if it suited you? Perhaps you just couldn't see a way to use the Kolbert murder in your story. MG

Author's note: It's always a question of proportion and the best way to tell the story. Some of the material mentioned above was actually appropriated for scenes which were in fact written but were then ultimately cut from the final draft of the manuscript after consultation with my editor.

Reader's note: So you did consider using those things, and the only rea-

son you didn't has nothing at all to do with what would be cruel or taste-less. Why not admit that? MG

   Author's note: Asked and answered.

   Reader's note: Not really. MG

   Author's note: Look, the material isn't in the final draft. A writer has to feel free to write about anything she wants to write about as she writes her way through a novel. At a later point, the writer applies a different sort of critical judgment about the material.

   Reader's note: But what sort of critical judgment do you expect readers to fall for when you keep wanting to have everything both ways? First you claim to be motivated by ethical standards; next you wrap yourself in the banner of artistic freedom. Which is it? Are you sure you didn't omit men-tion of the murder simply because you discovered that Robert Stone was writing a novel about it? MG

   Author's note: I can just imagine your moral outrage if I had included elements of the murder in the narrative. Talk about wanting to have it both ways!

   Reader's note: Why don't Janet and Lou ever appear again? Is that fair? Why don't you want to give some closure to the whole episode which started the story, the real Phil Hart graduate student involvement? You never really explain what that was about in the first place. Why don't you have something dire happen to him, like a fatal accident, as a device for getting him out of the way? Why don't you show the father's point of view about this, at least? You don't focus enough on any of the men in this story. They're much less real than the women. The only male character whose point of view you represent is Teddy, but you don't really give him enough time. AG

   Author's note: It's a novel, not a democracy. It's definitely not fair, in a certain sense, to those characters whose voices are mute or whose points of view are underrepresented, but fairness is not a problem for a novel. I didn't want to put any more focus on the Phil Hart character. He isn't really in the story beyond the discovery of those e-mail messages and what they signified. As to Janet and Lou—the Green parents are simply not present, although it is their actions which drive the story forward. There are many literary precedents for excluding the parents.

Reader's note: For example? AG

Author's note: David Copperfield. The Chronicles of Narnia.

Reader's note: You can't do better than that? AG

Author's note: Lord of the Flies, *then.* A Death in the Family. Franny and Zooey. A High Wind in Jamaica. The Member of the Wedding.

Reader's note: So you feel your silly little self-indulgent novel follows the literary tradition of those great novels? What you've done is infuriating enough, but your glib and condescending explanations are the worst of it. Don't you agree that there's something fundamentally dishonest about the way you have packaged this whole story, when you think about it? You've bent everything into crazy shapes to fit your agenda. What makes you think this is a worthwhile enterprise at all? All you have done is write a lot of incidents and characters and called it a novel, but you've taken everything from our lives! And then you've distorted it all! So it's neither the truth of our story nor really what I would call a novel at all. In the end, it's a manifesto of the way you wish everything had been or the way you insist on thinking everything was. Why do you think there's any literary merit in that? Or any honor at all? MG

Author's note: John Irving has written about the risks of being tyrannized by the authenticity of what you remember. Of course, the sad fact is that it's not really authenticity at all—you both share a fantasy of the authenticity of what you remember.

Reader's note: How many writers are you going to hide behind? What we remember is a fantasy, while what you remember is material for your artistic brilliance, is that how it's supposed to work? How dishonest is that? AG

Author's note: Henry James wrote, "What is character, but determination of incident? What is incident, but the illustration of character?" I don't have to justify the thinking of this novel to either of you. Who are you to call me dishonest? You are, in the end, only characters in my novel.

Reader's note: If we're fictional, then you are too. AG

Author's note: That's not for you to say. You are a character. I am the author. I made you up. I made up your reader's notes as well. That's why there were no reader's notes in the previous chapter. I thought they would be inappropriate at that point in the narrative. You are not real. You only have a voice because I decided to give you a voice.

Reader's note: But it's our story! AG

Reader's note: Isn't it a bit late to call us fictional characters? We didn't comment in that last chapter because we decided to wait until this chapter. Isn't your trying to pull the plug this way a sign of your own insecurity, a so-called decision made in a panic at the very end of the manuscript when you can't think of a better solution? MG

Author's note: I have written a novel and for it I have created fictional characters, some of whom closely resemble actual people, as has been very clearly explained. In certain instances I have changed certain names and other identifying characteristics and made up fictional elements that are not inharmonious with the actual details or events that inspired the narrative. Some of the characters are inside the narrative and some of them— the two of you—also exist at its margin.

Reader's note: If we're fictional characters, then why do we have a binding legal agreement with you? MG

Author's note: The binding legal agreement, is, of course, also a fiction.

Reader's note: I don't know which is worse, having the events of my life cannibalized by my sister for her insanity, or being told that I don't exist at all. MG

Reader's note: Does it bother you that readers will find out that you're a lunatic who argues with your own fictional characters? AG

Author's note: I look forward to the experience.

FOURTEEN

The Three Sisters

❦

Joanna was content, sitting in the armchair they always called "the lady chair" with a book and an apple from the basket on the floor. She was even wearing a dress, for the occasion, because she wanted to please Harriet. Meg sprawled in a reverie on the old green sofa, one foot on the floor and one foot on the cushion beside her, trying to be ladylike and comfortable simultaneously in an old red shirtwaist dress of Janet's that made her feel like a thrifty housewife from a *Life* magazine advertisement for Frigidaires. Amy sat awkwardly on the floor at their feet wearing a strange getup of her own devising, little shorts and a shirt which made her look, her kind sisters said, not just like a ten-year-old but like a ten-year-old golem. The sound of her crunching as she devoured an apple made Joanna call her Mr. Ed.

"You crunch too! There's no way to eat an apple silently," Amy protested.

The late summer heat lay heavily in the un-air-conditioned room, and everyone was drowsy. Resisting the urge to lie down and curl up on the rug beside Amy, Harriet looked through the viewfinder and asked Joanna to cock her right leg flat over her other knee, which Joanna did without looking up, giving Harriet the complementary angles she needed.

"Amy, are you comfortable teetering in that pretzel position?" Harriet asked. "Put your right hand behind you for balance. Good. Isn't that better? Now, can you turn your head and look over your shoulder just a little more? Good."

She made a small adjustment to the shutter setting and looked at her composition for another long moment. She loved the way the verticals united the three figures although each was isolated in her private space.

"Can Benedict come over for dinner?" Amy asked. Amy had developed a severe and forthright crush on him. She admired everything about him and was very funny about it.

"We had dinner with you night before last," Harriet reminded her. "Your parents might not want to see us again so soon, the way we devour everything Janet cooks. I am sure she was planning on leftovers the other night, but we must have eaten five chickens."

"That's okay," Amy said. "Lou doesn't really like meals of leftovers anyway. I heard him say so. We had sushi last night, so it was perfect that you guys ate all our food."

"Benedict is like Teddy," Meg added. "He can be quite grownup in his manners for someone who actually eats like a pig."

"So I was right! Anyway, we're going to a movie. Stop talking. The three sisters at home." Harriet snapped off a dozen exposures, the shutter clicking like a series of tumblers opening an internal lock. "The three sisters on Seventy-fifth Street. Everyone look out in front of you without changing the angle of your heads. Just kind of gaze into space, okay, try not to focus on anything. Good, good, good." She took more exposures in a long racheting burst. "Anyway, Teddy is coming for the weekend, right? You don't want a crowd, do you?"

"We love a crowd," Joanna said without looking up from her book. She was on the last page of *Gatsby* again.

"The three sisters in a room. The three sisters reading and eating apples and thinking and being. The three sisters exist. When do Janet and Lou get back from their walk? No, nobody answer.

That's perfect, hold it. Who was the one with the apples, Snow White?"

"That was the first movie I ever saw and for a long time I thought it was called Black Snow," Amy said. "Do you like these shoes? I got them in Paris."

"You've told us that about thirty times," Meg said gently. "Yes, the shoes are very nice. Where did you get them? Paris?"

"Snow White and the Three Stooges," muttered Harriet, moving a few inches back and then forward again. "The three sisters at home. I said that, didn't I? Three tall women. Olga, Masha, and Irina contemplate the universe. The three sisters sit around and get photographed on a summer afternoon," Harriet rattled on, aware that her babbling was eliciting precisely the half-tuned gazes she had envisioned.

"The three sisters meet the three bears. The three sisters need a title for this photograph. The three sisters meet three men in a boat."

"'So we beat on, boats against the current, borne back ceaselessly into the past,'" Joanna intoned, closing her book with a satisfied sigh.

"What does that mean again?" Amy asked, but then didn't wait for an answer before launching into a cascade of rhyming words, "Boat, doat, foat, gloat—"

"Emote," Meg contributed.

"Stoat," suggested Joanna. "Goat. Bloat."

"Don't you think it means we remember everything that happens and even when we're in the present, the past is still happening to us?" Harriet said from behind her camera. "You could probably get a far more brilliant analysis from your mother."

"I'll ask her later," Joanna said. "Or we can ask Teddy. He wrote a whole paper on the last chapter, I think."

"I think it means that utopia is a myth," Meg said. "And you have to go back to go forward."

"Myth, pith, width—" Amy began.

"Okay, just a few more," Harriet focused again. "The three little sisters and how they grew. The Green sisters. The three Green sisters. Joanna, don't jiggle your leg, we're almost done. The sisters Green. Sisters three. Help me out here, you guys!" Harriet made a few final exposures, her shutter clicking more slowly and deliberately now.

"Just the three sisters," Joanna said.

Katharine Weber is the author of the novels *Objects in Mirror Are Closer Than They Appear* and *The Music Lesson.* She teaches fiction writing at Yale University and lives in Connecticut. She is married to the cultural historian Nicholas Fox Weber, and they have two daughters.